By R

You can find my blog at:
https://imadeitup.wordpress.com/blog/

*Dedicated to Roberta C. Ballou-Franks (1961-2019),
a light in the darkness.*

Copyright 2020 by Randall Krpoun
All Right Reserved
ISBN: 9798616306470

<u>Chapter One</u>

Burk was going on about freedom. Again. Me, I've never been free, but I think if I was to be made free the first thing I would do would be to pick up that brick over there and use it to smash in Burk's skull.

Not that I hate Burk; I don't really hate anyone, but his talk gets on my nerves. It isn't proper talk, Burk's chatter, but an endless drone on uninteresting things punctuated by sudden questions so that if you manage to ignore him you are suddenly made to look stupid. I *am* stupid, as Master Horne assures me on a regular basis, but I do not like to be made to *feel* stupid by other slaves. That is not proper.

It was mid-morning on a miserable spring day whose low-hanging clouds looked pregnant with rain, and the air still had some winter's teeth in it. Everything was muddy and clammy, and I was inclined to bash in Burk's head just for those reasons.

Unaware how thin a thread his life was hanging by, Burk rattled on as if he had to get everything in his head spoken aloud before noon. We were leaning against a hitching rail at the East Gate, waiting without much hope for an escort job, or rather, I was sort of leaning, sort of perched on the rail with my ankles crossed and my thumbs hooked into my belt, and Burk was standing tall, feet spread, fists on hips, as if posing for a statue of a Noble Slave Prepared To Seize Freedom By The Scrotum.

Not that Burk was tall: I topped him by a good measure. More still if I applied the brick with force and skill, both of which I possess in abundance.

I was slouching because I was a slave waiting for work; Burk was standing because he had Standards. Standards are like Whore's Pox, I believe: as soon as you got it, you had an urge to give it to somebody else.

I really wished he would shut up. Our position at the hitching rail put us within easy earshot of the windows of one of the classrooms of the Tepton Academy for Boys, and I liked to listen to them recite their lessons. Both Burk and I spoke far better than most slaves, as good or better than most free men, because Master Horne had hired an old tutor to instruct our age-block in the proper manner of speaking in good company, including good manners.

Listening to the classes' reciting kept my lessons fresh, and reminded me of our whole age block chanting proper words and sentence structure as we ran and drilled. Our better-quality speech helped with escort jobs, and on more than one occasion it had made competitors think us weak; Master Horne always said no advantage was too small to pass up, that you can win a match on small things. Now even in my head I talked the way Elder Fasi taught us.

There was a question. "What?"

"I said, why should we continue to obey? We are a noble mixture of Human and Ukar blood resulting in warriors that are bigger, stronger, faster, and tougher; we are highly trained pit fighters with many kills to our credit. This city should recognize us as *leaders*!"

"We are bigger and all that. We are also slaves."

"But why do we not cast down our shackles and rebel?"

"Because first, we're not wearing shackles, second we are outnumbered by many-many to one, and third because Master Horne would go spare."

Burk held his head as if it pained him. "Then why do we not simply walk out this gate and be free?"

"Because the guards...well, they *should* be watching. In any case, we walk out the gates, and then what? I've never been outside the city, not really. Who feeds you?"

"Feed yourself."

Brick, skull; skull, brick. It was a happy thought.

He waited, but I wasn't going to answer a stupid question; it wasn't like we hadn't had this exchange many-many times. *Many* many-many times. The Tipton Academy for Boys held its classes on sums and counting elsewhere in the building, so for me the numbers beyond my fingers remain an unexplored realm.

Some travelers were coming in, and I straightened up and tried to look alert and trustworthy, because a job would get me away from Burk, or at least he would shut up if they hired both of us. Despite his Standards, I was first choice by dint of being taller, broader and less-Ukar-looking.

They were a mixed bunch, travel-worn and badly battered, which boded well for our prospects. There was a man in the lead, a warrior, limping and looking sick or wounded. A female Nisker led two pack mules in train, and a female Dellian in a dazzling white fur cloak was sitting sideways on the lead mule's pack saddle, apparently trying to avoid the dung, mud, and puddles that dominated the gate area.

She flipped back her hood, revealing a very pretty, fine-boned face and thick silver hair worn in a combed-back crest atop her head and shaved to a close burr on the sides. A diamond sparkled in the stud in her left nostril, and blue fire flashed from the gems mounted in silver that hung from her long, pointed ears.

Figuring she was in charge I stepped up, hands clasped across my belly so as to look respectful. "Need an escort, my lady? The streets are not always safe."

The mule and the gear on the pack saddle lifted her to eye level with me, although she gave the distinct impression she was looking down at me. Her eyes were golden, the part that is normally colored anyhow, but they were colder than steel in winter. She looked me up and down, granted Burk a glance, then looked at me again. The mule had stopped when I had spoken.

"I don't doubt the streets are not safe, but can you change that?" Her voice was nice; I was surprised.

"Gladiator, my Lady. Sixty death-matches, give or take." Master Horne told me to say sixty. I can't count much, but it was a lot of matches, that was certain. "Many more to first blood. We do a proper job of escorting and have never lost a hire; we are of Master Horne's Ebon Blade barracks."

She gave me the up and down again. Maybe she didn't like my kind; that wasn't unusual. I had never spoken to a Dellian before because there weren't many in the city, and none were slaves. I knew they had a province mostly to themselves somewhere, were a little physically different from Men, and that Men liked them. They liked Men, too.

"Very well. What is the rate?"

I held up the glass. "One shilling each time the sand runs out, one shilling if we draw blood, one shilling noon meal, two shillings evening meal, one shilling night watch. Each."

"Both of you, then. The shorter leads the mules."

Burk took the lead rope without comment, but I could see his hide was burning. I flipped the lever to start the sand and then pulled on my fighting gloves. As a slave, I wasn't supposed to display a weapon unless working.

"Hey, big 'un. Hold on," the Nisker nimbly hopped onto the hitching rail and scraped her boots clean with the brick I had had planned for Burk; her hood fell back, revealing a bright, merry face under a unruly mop of red hair held back by a folded scarf of green and brown. "Give us a lift, then" Niskers were just like Men, only short, less than four feet tall.

It took a moment to figure what she meant; then I carefully grasped her around the waist and set her on my shoulders astraddle my neck. "If I have to fight, you'll fall."

"I'll be off, but I'll land well." She drummed her palms on the top of my bare skull as I caught up with the lead mule. "I'm Hatcher. Who're you?"

"Grog."

"Grog's a drink, rum and water. Who named you that?"

"I don't know." Burk was finally quiet and now I had another voice. I kept my eyes moving, but it wasn't a nice day, and there were fewer people about the streets then was usual.

"Why don't you know?"

That one I knew. "I was a baby when I came to the slave barracks. They named me."

"Good thing they didn't name you Really Bad Ale instead, I suppose." She drummed some more. "You don't speak like a slave."

I explained about the tutor.

"So you fight in the pits?"

"Yes."

"And do escorts?"

"The pits are only open a few days each month, and I only get a few fights because I am of the High Rate. So I practice, train lesser-ranked pit fighters, and earn extra money for my master by escorting people safely through the city."

"How much does a High Rate win?"

"The purse on my last fight was a hundred Marks, but the betting went many-many times higher."

She whistled. "How much did you get?"

"I got a very good supper."

"Ah."

The battered warrior led us to the Golden Cockerel; as we walked Hatcher asked many questions about the city, most of which I did not know. The inn's courtyard was cobbles that were freshly swept, so the Dellian hopped down from the mule to stand on her own feet.

"We shall see to our rooms and then I wish to undertake an errand or two; you, Grog, shall escort me, the other can go." She flipped a shilling to Burk. "Hatcher, see to the mules." She flipped me two shillings. "For the time. Wait here."

I found a patch of wall in the sun and leaned on it; Burk kicked at a cobble and then left, improving my day. After a while a servant came out with her nose in the air and gave me a tankard of good ale and three large sausage rolls wrapped in a clean rag. A while later she came out to collect the rag and the tankard, and to give me a sneer. The bulb emptied; I turned it over and moved a bead on the base to the other side of the wire.

Without Burk to ramble on, waiting was not unpleasant. You learn about waiting in a slave barracks, or at least you learn or you get sold off to someplace where you worked very hard. I could out-wait a brick, if Burk wasn't talking. I don't mind talk, proper talk, to pass the time. Proper talk is telling about matches, or about food, or girls, or about who hates who in the barracks and why. Not freedom this and freedom that and the injustice of slavery and Standards and the superiority of the Ukar blood. I have been a slave all my life, and while I may be stupid, I don't need Burk to tell me about being a slave. And while he rants about injustice a great deal, I am still not clear on what injustice actually *is*. As to Ukar blood, I've shed a lot of it, both mine and others', and it flows as quickly as anyone else's; in my opinion that's about all you can say on that subject.

Hatcher and the Dellian came out the side door donning their cloaks when the bulb was almost empty. The Dellian flipped me two more shillings. "Noon meal and time. Now the Temple district."

The staff had a sedan chair and two slave Men waiting out front for the Dellian, while Hatcher rode on my shoulders. Other than worrying about her falling off if I had to fight, it wasn't a problem: Niskers are Men, just from a different part of the land; they looked like all the other Men except they were short: Hatcher was not quite four feet tall, and mostly slender except in the bust. Master Horne said I was just three fingers shy of seven feet, and very broad even for a half-Human, half Ukar, so she wasn't any sort of burden. I had seen Men carrying children the way she was riding me.

The sedan chair slaves and I waited while the Dellian, whom Hatcher said was Provine Sael, Provine being a title, and Hatcher went inside a temple.

The sedan Men wanted to dice, but I had no money, so they diced against each other. I used the time to ponder the noon meal shilling. It was against the rules not to eat on a job because hunger was bad for training. But I had eaten. Tips were to be turned in with other funds, but this was not a tip. Would it be proper to keep the shilling for myself? What would I do with it? Other slaves had money, but I never had encountered an opportunity to get money. Was this an opportunity? It was a matter to study carefully.

After the temple we went to three big houses, each in turn, and I waited with the sedan Men at all three, twice in courtyards, once in the street. In the second house, in the courtyard, a fat serving woman brought us mugs of ale and talked with the sedan men. She ignored me, which was fine because I was still busy pondering the shilling issue.

"Now we need to go to the Desert Abyss," Provine Sael announced after she emerged from the third house. We had waited in the street, and the visit had been short. She looked peeved, in a genteel sort of way.

"That is in the Brocks," I gestured towards the west. "A very bad part of town. The Abyss is safe, the owner brooks no trouble, but the Brocks are dangerous."

"Which is why I hired you." She climbed into the sedan chair and rapped on the roof. The carriers eased it up and set off.

"Bad neighborhood, eh?" Hatcher drummed on my head. This was a nice part of the city, with cobbled streets kept clean, so I guess she just didn't want to walk. "You've got a neck like a tree stump, you know that?"

There was no answer for that, so I kept silent.

The sedan chair slaves grounded their chair at the entrance to the Brocks and explained they weren't allowed to enter. Provine Sael climbed out and paid them, and tossed me another shilling. "Do you know the way to the Desert Abyss?"

"Yes, my Lady, but the Brocks are not a good place…"

"Which is why I hired you," she finished for me. "Call me 'Provine', not 'my lady'." She shrugged the fur cloak back and settled the lay of a sheathed short sword with a hilt that had blue gems set into its silver-inlaid pommel. "Hatcher, you need to walk."

Hatcher flipped off my shoulders and landed like a cat. She had two of the heavy fighting knives her people carried, each blade angled forward a bit for chopping. Good weapons, but she was still little more than half my height. Provine Sael was almost as tall as a female Man, but slight of build and too elegant to be taken seriously. This could not possibly end well.

The Brocks were a very old part of the city, old and forgotten in many ways. The buildings sagged and leaned, and the streets were narrow, twisting, and nothing but mud. There were many gaps between buildings as no one built anything in the Brocks when buildings burned or were torn down. If you wanted to buy or sell things that were not legal, or were unpleasant, or enjoyed a rougher sort of entertainment you visited the Brocks. If you were dirt poor and desperate you lived there. It was also home to the slave market, which I dislike. Being a member of the Ebon Blades, a proper barracks of the old school, was a good thing, even as a slave, but I do not like the blocks.

There were eyes on us from the very first step, and I kept mine moving, too. I expected Provine Sael to mince about worrying about her fancy boots, but she slogged along at a brisk rate. I had my cudgel in hand, twirling it occasionally as if a yard of black oak with iron bands was a stalk of grass. It and the others' blades kept a lot of people we passed honest. The mud actually helped: no one was going to try to snatch an earring or that white cloak and try to flee in this footing. Which was good because I'm not built or trained to run fast.

It was still daylight, which helped, as the Brocks were

more a night-time place, but there were still people moving around doing whatever free people had to do. Many down here knew of me, knew what I was capable of, and that would help, too. To others I was just a haffer, a tusker, half Human-half Ukar brute, but that counted for something, too.

I am big, not just tall but broad, with more bone and muscle than a Man of the same height. I am as big as a pure Ukar, without the tusks (I have none at all, which is unusual) or the out-thrust under-jaw. My skin is not as course and pebbly as a Ukar's, although tougher than a Man's and sort of olive-gray; I have no hair, but my ears lay flat against my head (unlike Burk, whose ears stand at pure Ukar right angles), and while they are a bit pointed they aren't spiky like an Ukar's. My face is like a Man's in the way a statue hacked out of rock looks like a Man: blunt, simple, and not showing much of what goes on behind my eyes. Being stupid, as Master Horne points out regularly, there isn't much actually going on behind my eyes, but people can't tell that just by looking, I think.

As I suspected, trouble found us, or rather, was waiting, but it wasn't what I had expected. We had cut across a couple empty lots where the ground was less muddy, and were just a short way from the Abyss when a half-dozen men moved from across the street to confront us. Five were Brocks toughs, mean-looking bastards in worn clothing, while the sixth was a nondescript fellow in good clothing with a dark scarf covering the lower half of his face. He hung back slightly as the bravos moved forward.

I stepped out in front of my charges, venturing a quick look to the flanks and rear to see if there were surprises afoot, but there weren't.

"All right, tusker, time to go about your business," a dark-skinned bravo with a puckered scar across his forehead announced.

"On my business." I stretched my arms to my sides first, then overhead, up on my toes, both to loosen up and to emphasize my build and height. Master Horne says you can win on small things, and instilling a bit of fear was one such edge.

"Escort job, right?" He grinned, showing missing teeth. "A slave about his master's business." He held up a six-shilling piece. "Here's for your time. Tell your master he made a wise investment.'

It works that way, sometimes, because an owner would not be happy if his slave got cut up in a street brawl. Behind me I heard blades leaving their scabbards.

I shrugged. "Sorry." I really was: the odds were not in my favor, but I wasn't going back to Master Horne and tell him I had given up an escort without a fight. He ran a proper barracks of the old school, and losing customers was not how our reputation had been built or could be maintained. When you engage the Ebon Blade, you get quality work, that is the rule.

He flipped the coin to me but I let it bounce off my chest. He frowned and did a double take: coin, slave. Slave, coin. "You confused, brute?"

"No." I was not confused, but I certainly wished I had a blade and maybe a shield. Or Burk. There was a decent chance I could die here.

"Pick up the coin and leg it, tusker. This isn't your fight."

I shrugged again. "I got no fights. I'm a slave." I twirled the stick. "What I have is *commands*. Command says guard, I guard." Inspiration hit me. "Maybe you aren't paid enough: I got sixty death matches behind me."

"I seen him," a scrawny type on the left end of the line spoke up. "Pit-fighter, he is. He's not lying."

"Double." The better-dressed man in the back didn't speak loudly, but everyone heard him.

"Defend us," Provine Sael said quietly; as a slave, I could not start a fight.

I am big, but I am quick for my size, and my reach is a couple inches' longer than a Man of equal height. Back in my youth I fought as a pugilist before I got my last growth, and that gave me an appreciation for reach and footwork that many fighters don't have, especially toughs who lack formal training.

Too many see a stick as just something you swing, but I'm not one of them. A full extension lunge put the iron cap atop my cudgel into the leader's solar plexus with enough force to knock him back a step, curling into a fetal position as he fell and the air *whooshed* out of him.

A lot of fighters train to attack, think, attack, think. Master Horne always taught me that a fight is one single action drawn out until only you were still standing. Never quit, never pause, just *fight*. A warrior flows like a stream, he always says. I am stupid, but I can learn if you give me time.

Even as the shock of my cudgel hitting the leader registered I was moving forward and to my left, catching the top of the club with my left hand and giving the next thug a two-armed strike horizontally across the forehead as he was drawing his dirk, a sort of pushing blow because I needed him to fall back. Two on one are fatal odds if they both act; the way you deal with a group is to work it so you take them one at a time. I wasn't optimistic with this bunch, though: I figured they knew the same thing.

There was a soundless flash behind me, like a fireworks except at shoulder height, but it wasn't my concern because the third, and last to my left, thug had his blade out and was swinging. I parried with the cudgel in my left hand and lost it in the process, but it got me inside his reach where I drove the back of my right fist up into his jaw, snapping his head back and sweeping him off his feet in a spray of blood and tooth fragments. My fighting gloves were heavy leather with half of each finger-length removed so I had contact with my weapons; iron studs a half inch across dotted the backs to give a slapping or swinging blow more force.

Spinning, I ducked under a wild swing from a bravo who was pawing at his eyes and slammed two good jabs into his belly, finishing with a backhand blow to the temple as he doubled over, dropping him neatly into the mud.

The fifth was down, screaming and clutching a hamstrung leg until Hatcher darted in and nearly severed his head with a brutal chop.

The leader was still down and trying to get air into his lungs, the second thug was out cold or dead, the third was crawling away, the fourth was lying on his back and smearing mud around his face with both hands, and the fifth was dead. The well-dressed man was nowhere in sight. I recovered my cudgel and the six-shilling piece, and awaited orders.

Hatcher was wiping her blades clean on the dead man's shirt and sheathing them; Provine Sael was standing where I had last seen her, thoughtfully rubbing one of the tiny horn nubs on her forehead. Seeing me looking at her she dropped her hand and started walking. "We must be going. Hatcher, leave him be. Grog, well done."

That startled me: *well done*? I felt hot and nervous, like my skin just shrank. Who thanks a slave? I wasn't sure it was proper.

Hatcher hurried to catch up, tossing the dead man's purse aside. "They didn't get paid in advance, that's for sure. You move fast for a big'un. Sixty death matches, eh?"

"Probably."

"You don't know?"

"I don't count much. I know up to ten," I offered, feeling stupid.

"Sixty is a number, this many tens," Hatcher held up six fingers.

"Huh." I thought about that. "Yeah, that's about right. Maybe a few more."

The little Nisker shook her head. "And he seemed like such a *nice* fellow."

"Who?"

She grinned at me, it threatened her ears. "Never mind. I'm glad we met you, Grog."

Twice: that was something to remember. This was the best day ever.

Master Horne had taken me to the Abyss several times in the past, as a bodyguard; I killed a brute there, not a real paid fight but rather a meeting that went wrong. He had been nearly as big as I was, but slower, not as well trained. The owner of the Abyss had been angry, but the other parties at the table had started the trouble, and so they had to pay money to make things right.

Outside it looked like a worn-out warehouse, but inside it was fairly nice as taverns go; once Master Horne had commented that a tenth of the city's money flowed through the place, although I never saw anything special in it, except that there weren't many drunks, and a lot more serious talking than in most places. And always several bodyguards standing and watching.

The outside bouncer opened the door for Provine Sael and she glided past as if he was invisible; I knew him, a Man who had fought in the pits, he had been late in his career when I entered, so we never faced each other. He wasn't wearing a collar now, I noticed as we exchanged nods, so he had won or purchased his freedom.

Inside it was smoke and smells and dim lighting, a lot quieter than most places, and a lot of people in deep conversations. A serving woman, a fat red-faced hulk, stepped up to greet Provine Sael and accept a coin. *Ooohing* over Provine Sael's cloak she reached towards the fur, but I caught her wrist before she could touch. She flushed at this, but held her tongue: she knew you never put your hands on an escorted person.

Provine Sael looked around, then headed towards the back wall where a row of tables were separated by partitions; there were even curtains for more privacy. Hatcher muttered something and followed; I trailed at the proper distance.

The Dellian choose a table where a scruffy man lounged with a bar girl on his lap and a carafe of wine on the table. As Provine Sael approached he kissed the girl and sent her off with a slap on the rear; standing, he grinned. "You must be desperate."

He was average height for a Man, slender, and had no more hair on his scalp than I did, although he had a goatee and mustache. He was wearing loose clothes like the

Academy students preferred although he was a good ten years older than they usually are. Other than a dirk I couldn't see any weapons.

Provine Sael nodded to him and sat at the table; Hatcher followed and pulled the drapes closed; I found a spot at a nearby post and proceeded to wait. I had two compliments to ponder, which was something nice. They were proper praise, not like when Master Horne finally admitted I had managed to learn something, or had won a match. It was something new.

It wasn't a long conversation; Provine Sael emerged looking displeased and strode briskly to the door, Hatcher trotting alongside.

Outside the Dellian rubbed one of her nubs; she had a little horn peeking out of the smooth expanse of her forehead over each eye, neatly centered between eyebrow and hairline. I think the small size meant she was young, but I wasn't sure.

Hatcher spat into the mud. "Now what? We can't get a blade for love nor money."

That made no sense: there were any number of weapon smiths available, but they weren't asking me.

"Nothing has changed." Provine Sael's chin was set. "This *happens*. We work with the tools we have."

"You can make rock soup, too." Hatcher retied the folded scarf that did its best to keep the unruly mop of hair out of her face. Sweat, as well, I supposed. "But you can starve doing it."

"Lead us out." I realized that was addressed to me, and pointed the way. When we passed where we had faced the bravos the four injured men were gone, and the corpse was naked.

"Fun bunch around here," Hatcher commented as we passed. "Would we have been raped before they killed us?"

"Probably," I nodded. "Pretty certain, in fact."

"Great."

Provine Sael stopped so suddenly I almost bumped into

her, and she turned to look at the corpse lying in the mud. She stood there for a long moment, then abruptly spun on her heel and continued on.

When we reached safer environs I was dispatched to find a sedan chair while they took tea at a handy shop where the owner fawned over the well-dressed Provine Sael. They were done and waiting by the time I returned. "Take us to your barracks," Provine Sael instructed me as she climbed into the chair. Hatcher rode on my shoulders again, and off we went.

"This is the way to go," the Nisker observed as we made our way across town. "I'm sick of walking. We were twelve days walking to get here, and my stride's the shortest in the group. Am I heavy?"

"No."

"Tell me about yourself."

"I'm a slave." Stock answer.

"All right, but what was it like growing up?"

I shrugged, and she giggled. "I grew up. When I was old enough, I did chores. Then after a bit I trained. Then I fought as a pugilist, and then as a full pit-fighter. So far, I've come through every match. Master Horne bought me when I was a baby."

She was drumming again; it was like standing in the rain. "Do you have friends in the barracks?"

"Not really. There were a bunch of us as kids, they call it an age-block, all within two years of each other. Except for Burk and me, the rest of our age-block died in the pits. Some age blocks have some who fail training and get sold, but we didn't have any fail."

"All of them? How many where there?"

"Uh...ten and nine plus me and Burk."

She was quiet for half a block. "How many die in the pits in, say, a year?"

"Slaves? I don't know. A lot. There are around ten fighting-barracks, and some private houses that train fighters. Plus groups who travel around, and there's captured creatures, wild beasts, that sort of thing."

"How many slaves are in your barracks?"

"I don't know. A bunch of age blocks in training, and a few entering the matches, but the number changes regularly, and I don't count much."

"Un-huh. What weapons are you good with?"

"Hands, feet, club, war hammer, mace, short axes, most blades."

She picked up the beat. "What do you plan to do?"

"When?"

"Whenever."

That required thought. "Well, I plan to get some supper…"

She hooted and rocked, thumping her heels against my chest. "No! I mean…what are your plans for the future."

"I'm a slave."

"Don't you want to be free?"

She had paid me a compliment, so I thought about it carefully. "I won't. Sooner or later I'll get killed in the pit or hurt too bad to fight again. Then I'll work around the barracks until I die. Most likely I'll get killed."

"Have you ever thought about running away?"

"Not really. I've never really been outside the city, and I stand out. There's a couple free brutes here, but very few. The rest of us, and there's not a lot, are slaves. Besides, all I know is the pit. Master Horne sees to it that I get fed. Master Horne says being free includes the right to starve, and I should be grateful I can earn my keep."

She popped my right ear with a snapped finger. "But what if you got free anyway?"

Relentless. "I don't know. Escorts, I guess, or the pit; I can't read or count, so I would have problems."

"Maybe not."

It was getting dark when the barracks came into view; they were actual barracks, military quarters surrounding a parade field. Sometime in the past a consortium of slavers bought them from the city and modified them to their needs; I knew this because back before I moved up in Rates I had spent a lot of time helping keep them in repair.

About a dozen different masters own the building, and other parts were leased out to masters with smaller groups of slaves.

A block short of the gate Provine Sael stopped her chair and got out, moving out of earshot of the carriers. She looked at Hatcher above me, and I felt a small shift: Hatcher had nodded or shook her head. The slender Dellian cocked her head and looked me up and down. "Grog, how would you feel if you had to fight a full-blooded Ukar?"

"Again?"

"You've fought them?"

"Captured ones in the pits, yes."

"What about a wild one? Would it bother you?"

"No. They hate us more than Men do."

She muttered to herself and made a small gesture with her left hand. "Grog, if your master took you out into the wilds, and an opportunity arose that allowed you to run away and be free, would you take it?"

I thought about it carefully. "No."

"Why?"

I shrugged. "Where would I go?"

"Anywhere."

Shrugging seemed the best option. "I'm a slave."

"What if your master set you free?"

"I guess I would find a job." That sounded stupid even to me. Trouble is, I don't know much about anything.

"What if your master taught you about being free *before* they set you free?" Hatcher asked from above me, knocking on my skull like it was a door.

That set me back. "Yeah...that would be good."

Provine Sael muttered and repeated the gesture. "Are you loyal to your master, whomever they may be?"

"Yes."

"I am...undertaking an important task, and a dangerous one," she said slowly. "I am putting together a group to accomplish this task. As you saw earlier, there are those who do not wish this task completed. What I need now is loyal and competent bladesmen."

"There's lots of fighting men in the city."

"How many are as good as you are, or better?"

That gave me pause; I rested my hands on Hatcher's booted feet and thought about it. "There's some pit-fighters, some Temple guards, a few bodyguards, a couple hunters…I can't count."

"Not one man in ten, would you say?"

"No." It was the truth, not pride. Men in the city seldom saw violence except street brawls and ambushes; there were some veterans in the garrison and Temple guard, but other than those the blooded warriors were all gladiators. And I was ranked High Rate, a member of the fighting elite.

She nodded. "I am going to buy you from your master, Grog. You will help me and my group in our task, and while we do this Hatcher will teach you what you need to know to live in the free world. When the task is complete, which may take as much as a year, I will set you free. Do you understand?"

It took a moment. "Yes, Provine."

"Will you be loyal to me after I purchase you?" she made the same little gesture.

"Yes, Provine."

"Good" She turned and strode up the street.

"I was half right," Hatcher observed from above.

"About what?"

"We couldn't find anyone out of love. Money, it turns out, wins through in the end."

Chapter Two

Master Horne and Provine Sael had tea in his office while I turned the money in to the clerk and my cudgel to the armory warden. When I returned they were waiting in the courtyard.

"Get your things, Grog, you've a new mistress."

I was rooted to the spot: Master Horne had always been my master, and this barracks was my home. He was a squat Man, much weathered and gone bald over the years I had served him, sour of disposition but stingy with the whip, and I had no complaints. He and Burk were all that remained of those who I had known in my youth.

"Go on, now. Serve Provine Sael as you've served me. And tell Burk he's going, too, so make sure you get his mind in the right place." Master Horne fixed me with a beady eye. "Mind your manners, brute. You hail from a proper barracks of the old school: uphold our good name."

"Ye...yes, master." I was choking up, but I managed to get the words out.

He flapped a dismissive hand. "Off with you, then." Turning, he limped back into his office. I turned and slowly made my way across the parade field, feeling very unsettled and hollow. Life under Master Horne had not been easy, but it was my *life*; he had fed us regularly, and was constant in his expectations and rules. My future was suddenly uncertain and fearful, and it felt like I had a cold ball of greasy ice in my belly. It was worse than my first time in the pit.

I did not have much to gather: my cleaning things, some clothes, a small bag of rocks from places I had been. Then I gathered Burk, got his mind right, and returned to Provine Sael.

"Take off those collars and leave them," she instructed and strode off to her sedan chair without a backward look. This was going to cause trouble with Burk, but I unbolted the leather collar around my neck and placed it on the bench outside Master Horne's office. Unlike most slaves we of the Ebon Blade did not wear iron collars, as Master Horne did not like them for some reason.

"Take point," I told Burk, who moved out in front of the chair; it was getting dark, and trouble could come from any alley. I still had my gloves, but otherwise we were weaponless.

Hatcher wasn't any more interested in walking than before, but at least she wasn't drumming. "What did Horne mean by getting Burk's mind right?"

He was Master Horne, but it wasn't my place to point that out. "Make sure he understood to be on his best behavior."

"And how did you do that?"

"I hit him until I was sure he understood."

"I can see you are going to fit in well with this band, Grog," Hatcher chuckled. "Tomorrow we'll be shopping. What's your favorite color?"

That took me aback: colors were colors. "I don't know."

"You don't know? How can you not *know*? Mine is green, usually forest green, although some dyers call it summer green. It brings out my eyes and compliments my hair. Red never suits me, but black can work if..."

We stayed at the Golden Cockerel, not in the slave quarters, but in a small guest room on the same floor as the rest of the group. It was a bad idea, and I had to get Burk's mind in the right place first thing in the morning. Normally I would not mind hitting Burk until he said he understood, but I had other things on my mind.

We took our breakfast onto the back courtyard steps to avoid further complications and issues, and then waited outside near the back door for instructions. I was feeling unsettled and hollow-chested at the prospect of a new owner and new tasks; the pit I understood, and I missed the barracks already.

"Outside the city, armed, and without collars!" Burk muttered, proving how distracted I was: obviously, the last beating had not taken.

"Shut up."

"We could..."

"You could get your head caved in," I over-rode him,

stepping close and glaring down on him. "We serve as instructed. Master Horne said we have to uphold the honor of our barracks. We are of the Ebon Blades, a respected establishment of the old school with a long and glorious history."

Burk started to sneer and caught himself. "But we could be free in a few days."

"We do this right, we're free in a year, and really free, not running scared."

"I wouldn't be running scared," Burk muttered.

"Yes, you would. Because I would be hunting you."

Hatcher on my shoulders, we went shopping. It was amazing: when Master Horne bought us things, it was quick and the only question was 'how much'. Hatcher considered colors and style, and strength of material; she asked the artisans a hundred questions. What surprised me was that they had ready answers and seemed to expect this.

The clothing had to be made for me, and altered for Burk, but they said it would be ready by mid-afternoon; they were nice clothes, stout cord trousers, boots of good leather, loose cotton shirts, and rain-proofed traveler's cloaks. We both got soft caps to protect us from the sun.

Travel gear was easier: packs on wood frames, waterskins, blankets and ground sheets, eating ware, work knives, candles, pouches, tinderboxes, stout cord, and many other items you apparently needed on the trail. We bought the packs first and Hatcher showed us how to store each purchase.

Weapons we didn't need help on, just a budget. Training for the pit meant we had no skills in ranged combat, but for melee we knew our business and more. Armor was scale shirts and kettle hats; Burk took an un-rimmed round shield as well. I chose a beaked war hammer, a long fighting dirk, and a dopplehander that was five feet six inches from point to pommel, just shy of five pounds of fine steel with foot-wide guards and triangular flanges six inches down from the hilt. Burk got a dirk, short sword, and morning star. Hatcher bought us crossbows and accessories, saying she would teach us on the trail.

It took us much of the day because Hatcher liked to haggle, and we had to buy a mule, pack saddle, rations, and a bunch of other gear; by the time we were done we had to retrace our steps and gather up all the clothes and the armor.

The pack didn't impede Hatcher riding, but at least her prattle kept Burk sullen and quiet. "Why are there those triangle bits on your blade?"

"Those are called ricassos, amongst other things. The blade between them and the crossguard doesn't have an edge, so I can 'choke up' on the blade and use it if someone gets inside the normal reach. The flanges are to prevent an enemy's blade from sliding down the blade and hitting my hand when I'm doing that."

"Its fugging *huge*."

"I'm big. It's a skilled piece, well-balanced so a good swordsman can use it as quick as an old-style longsword."

"And you're good?"

"So far, the best I've met. Who was the wounded man who came in the gates with you?"

"That's Chabney Torl, he goes by Torl by preference. He wasn't wounded so much as sick, we got ambushed on the way here and he fell into a pond full of ice, caught a bad ague before we could get him dried out. Provine Sael had used up her abilities trying to save the others, and so he has to wear it off. He'll be fine by the time we leave."

"Provine Sael can heal people?"

"Yes, she's a sort of churchwoman amongst her people, that's what 'Provine' means. When those thugs jumped us in the Brocks she made a flash of light which blinded two of them. Just temporary, of course, but it was enough. Mostly she can heal wounds and stuff like that, but she's young and can't do a lot all at once. She knows regular healing too, and a lot of other things. Very educated. And her clothes, what I wouldn't give for that cloak. And the *jewelry*, she has…"

When she paused for breath I got a question in. "What about the others you mentioned?"

"Huh? Oh. One died and the other two quit. They were fighting men, Merian mercenaries. That's why we need you two. Torl can fight, so can I, but we're specialists, as is Hunter Sonelon. We need good fighting men to round out the group."

"What is your specialty?"

"Me? Ah, I'm, well, I am an expert in containers, access points, that sort of thing. Torl is a scout, and a very good one, and Hunter is a spell-weaver."

"Who is Hunter?"

"You saw Hunter, we met him at the Abyss. We came here to get a spell-weaver and some better fighting men, the mercenaries weren't up to the job. Trouble is that nobody wants to get involved. Nobody with skills, that is. You can hire thugs all day long, but that's pointless."

"Why are people trying to stop Provine Sael?"

"Because...well, she'll have to lay it out for you, it's not my place. But what we are trying to do is a good thing, and there's people who don't want it to happen, and a couple who wouldn't mind it happening but not by Provine Sael. The latter are not sending thugs, but they're sending word, and that's why we're having trouble raising a group."

"Uh-huh." I really didn't see it, but I'm stupid. "Have you known Provine Sael long?"

"A few years; I did some work with her before, moderate stuff. S'why she keeps me close, she trusts my judgment. Torl has worked with her before, Hunter she knows but not well."

"When do we leave?"

"Soon. As you will have noticed, certain people are aware that we are here."

After our evening meal, eaten on the back steps, Hatcher found us and said we were leaving in the morning, and gave each of us two shillings' worth of pennies for ale. Burk and I worked out with our new weapons to get their weight and feel, and sparred a bit. We took turns hauling water for baths, as Master Horne was rigorous about clean bodies and clean clothing.

Burk went to bed; wearing my new clothes, I went down into the common room for a mug of ale. I had been in inns before; sometimes Master Horne put us up in an inn near the pits when our barracks was posted in a lot of fights, but it was strange to have money and even stranger to be able to decide to go to the common room. Normally we were locked into the slave quarters.

There were women who liked to rent gladiators fresh from a fight, I was told, but Master Horne wasn't standing for any of that sort of behavior; he sent girls in for us when he felt we had done well.

I reached the door to the common room, but the sound of the voices and laughter stopped me in my tracks, and after a moment I headed back upstairs. I was still a tusker, still a slave; new clothes and no collar wouldn't change that. Best to keep my own mind in the right place, too.

The staff woke us early with a basket of breakfast and a bucket of hot water; Master Horne was intolerant of slackness, and Burk and I were in the courtyard washed, dressed, fed, and ready to go before anyone else. While we waited I worked saddle soap into my new boots; I had kept my old ones despite their being nearly worn out because I knew I wasn't going to walk an entire day in new boots. Burk did the same, and buffed his to a bright gloss in keeping with his Standards.

While we were finishing up a man came out of the stables leading three loaded pack mules; in the light of the courtyard's lantern I recognized the mule Hatcher had purchased yesterday and stood up, boot in hand. "Where are you taking those mules?"

The man led them over. "Somewhere north, I'm told. You must be the muscle." He stuck out his hand. "Akel Bedmaer, pack-master and cook."

I shook his hand, which was strong but not very callused. "I'm Grog, this is Burk, we're slaves."

He nodded sagely. "So I was told. Still, we all have our places in life." He was of average height, with solid shoulders and an average build; he was mostly bald, with a thick beard cut to a point and piercing blue eyes. He was simply dressed, with a short sword at his belt and a small target shield and spear thrust under the ropes of the lead mule's pack.

Torl emerged from the inn looking a lot healthier than when I had first seen him; he was slender, weathered, and tough-looking, with grey eyes and dark blond hair pulled back into a queue. He wore the same fighting leathers I had seen on him at the gate although they were clean now, and was armed with a longbow and broadsword. He glanced at the three of us, grunted, and set his pack by ours. "Torl, scout." He didn't offer to shake hands.

"Grog, Burk." I gave Akel a hand carrying the packs to the second mule, where he expertly lashed them into place. Burk stood and stared at the sky, back to his statue pose.

Provine Sael and Hatcher came out shortly thereafter; apparently the staff had taken their belongings out to Akel before breakfast. "I suppose Hunter being on time was too much to hope for," Provine Sael observed dryly. It was not long, however, before a handcart pushed by a slave preceded Hunter into the courtyard. The handcart contained a pack and a small wooden chest which were added to the mules by Akel while a tipsy-looking Hunter conferred with Provine Sael. He looked as he had at the Abyss, except that he wore fighting leathers and had added a short sword.

Provine Sael had a sedan chair to carry her mud-free to the gate, Hatcher rode me with a folded blanket to protect her rear from the armor, and everyone else walked, Akel leading the mules, who seemed to be inclined to cooperate. Outside the East Gate, one of the few times I have ever actually seen the outside of the city walls, we paused so that Provine Sael could dismount and pay the porters, and then we followed the high road heading north-northeast. The Dellian gave Hatcher a cool glance but made no comment, and Hatcher stayed where she was.

My stomach churned and my chest felt empty at leaving the city. Fellhome, I dredged up from memory, it was called Fellhome, although since I never left I had never really thought of it as having a name before. Now it was a place, not my home. That felt odd, and not in a good way.

Marching was nothing new to me, though: Master Horne used marching with weighted packs as a regular part of our conditioning, either around the courtyard or along the military road that circled the inside of the city walls, thirty to fifty miles in a given march. With just my arms, armor, and Hatcher my load was half what it had been on those marches. We took a break every hour; during the first break I traded my new boots for my old, putting them back on for an hour after the noon meal. I would increase this by an hour each day until I wore them full time; they would be broken in properly in such a fashion.

Hatcher dozed above me; the road was good hard-surface gravel so I could maintain an even pace. Her leaning on my head meant I had to remain 'eyes front', but by walking a weaving path I could take in the sights. I had seen the countryside from the barracks tower and from a couple matches held on the fairgrounds outside the city, but this was something else entirely. The pace was easy compared to what I was used to and the sights made the trip entertaining. People, peasants I supposed, were doing things in fields, some of them with teams of horses or oxen; we saw herds of sheep and cows and off in the distance, and on secondary roads there were little clusters of houses where I guessed the peasants lived.

The road followed the river, and there were ducks and other birds on or around the water, and once I saw a deer. Even Burk forgot his Standards and openly stared at everything. It was still cool, but there was some sun breaking through and after the first mile it was nice walking.

There was a little traffic on the road; we passed a couple peasants driving a small flock of sheep, and a half-dozen loaded wagons heading the same direction we were, escorted by four hung-over mercenaries. On the river a barge with a canvas-covered cargo passed us heading towards the city. It was a very memorable day.

Hatcher would walk a quarter mile after each break to stretch her legs, and then ride on my shoulders and doze; I saw her problem: due to her height she had to move at nearly a trot to keep up. After the third break she started me and Burk on counting out loud each time my left boot hit the road, and by the next break I knew all the numbers up to fifty. Then came counting whatever we saw something that was more than ten.

The hourly breaks were short, just long enough to attend to calls of nature, drink some water, and give your legs a little rest. The mid-day break was longer; Akel passed out hardtack, soft greasy jerky, and raw potatoes, which explained why my equipment had included a cruet of vinegar and a container of salt.

The group walked according to their nature; Provine Sael led, with Torl alongside, so I kept about twenty feet behind. Akel led the mules in single file on a long lead, and Burk brought up the rear; Hunter staggered and complained and was now up by Provine Sael arguing for a slower pace, then back hanging onto a pack saddle, and then up around my location peevishly demanding that Hatcher shut up because his head was about to explode. He threw up twice in the first hour but didn't seem any better for it.

When we weren't counting things Hatcher waxed vocal on many subjects, a great number of which had to do with either clothes, shoes, or the colors of either. Jewelry made a frequent appearance as well. I had no idea there was so much involved with such ordinary things, but years of Burk had taught me to push a voice into the background, and unlike Burk, Hatcher asked no questions and required no more interaction than an occasional grunt.

Torl vanished into the countryside as the shadows were growing long, and re-appeared as Provine Sael was choosing a campsite. He tossed a length of cord with four dead rabbits hanging from it at me. "Get 'em ready." It was the first thing he had said to me since this morning; I looked at the rabbits, and then back at him.

Hatcher slapped my leg. "Grab your knife and Burk and come with me, big 'un. Here's a lesson that will do you more service than counting."

By the second rabbit I had the hang of it, as did Burk; blood and cutting bothered us not at all, so it was just a matter of what to do and why. We were scraping the skins when Akel came up with a leather bucket that was sloshing more than it should. "We're in luck, a few fat river treckle. Bone and chop those conies for the stew, there's good lads."

We both knew how to chop meat for stew from our days helping in the kitchens; cleaning the fish took a bit more effort than the rabbits, but we managed it. Hatcher sat on a log above us on the river bank and talked us through the various procedures.

The evening meal was bread, baked potatoes, and a stew of potatoes, rabbit, fish, and dried beef, a fine repast by my standards. Provine Sael had baked fish and some green salad, and Hunter ate some bread and drank a bottle of wine.

Hatcher produced a battered metal flask and liberally sprinkled a greasy black liquid over all her food.

"Bekker sauce?" Akel asked.

"The best, brewed it myself," she offered the flask to the muleskinner, who smiled and shook his head. Catching my look, she explained. "It's a mix of red wine, beef broth, and fermented stock, a Nisker delicacy."

"A delicacy they put on every cooked meal," Akel smiled. "You don't want the details of how they make the 'fermented stock'."

"That's just nonsense," Hatcher corked the flask and tucked it away. "Sausage-making sounds disgusting, too."

The meal over, everyone turned in; no guards were posted, but I didn't ask why. Hatcher showed us how to pick a sleeping position and dig a little hole for one's hip; afterwards, I lay on my ground sheet with my water-skin for a pillow and looked up at the stars that peeked through the tattered clouds. I was a good twenty miles from the city, and tomorrow we would keep walking. It was hard to get my mind around it.

I hoped Master Horne was keeping well.

Morning was cold and damp, two facts Hunter cursed as if they were the products of poor planning, which was not proper conduct in my opinion, but my opinion did not matter so I kept my own council. Breakfast was hardtack, fried salt pork, and a soup made from dried onions and beef jerky; Akel made sure everyone had a pint of vinegar for their waterskins, except for Hunter, who used brandy, and more than a pint.

Hunter was in less agony and tended to walk with Akel talking of many strange things on the second day; otherwise the group remained as before.

Traffic on the road was sparse, but we passed a patrol of a dozen mounted road wardens, and saw several barges and one patrol boat on the river. Twice we passed caravans of wagons, both heading the direction we were going but moving half our speed. With Hunter recovered Torl set the pace for twenty-five miles a day, not hard on a good road. He hunted in the evenings and Akel caught fish on some rest breaks, extending our rations.

Like my boots I was breaking in to the sights and sounds on the road, and while I was still enthralled by everything, I didn't get distracted as much; while the high road was fairly safe, I reminded myself that this amounted to an escort job. As before Hatcher dozed for the first hour or two, and thereafter helped me and Burk with numbers, both counting and learning the symbols that each number had. She had a small slate and chalk for the symbols. When she felt the lessons were done for the day she chattered on any number of subjects; there seemed to be no limit to the topics that rattled around her skull. It was preferable to Burk, who only had one line of thought, but I could have used some quiet.

Burk was just as in awe of the situation as I was, and there was no more talk about running because the world looked a lot different outside the city; unsettled, he reverted to the Noble Ukar, being stiff and formal to everyone. It was annoying to me, but it was better than the alternative so I let it ride. It was apparent that keeping Burk in a proper frame of mind was going to be my duty, and in fact we were largely unsupervised; the others treated us like they treated each other.

Every break I practiced getting my weapons into play, something that had never been a large part of my training before: in the pit you entered with weapon in hand, but out here, trouble could come fast and without warning. I wore my scale shirt every day to get used to the weight and to break in the leather so it would move smoothly; it was stiff at the moment, but saddle soap, sweat, and wear would change that soon enough.

A broad leather belt with three buckles worn over the armor helped take some of the weight off my shoulders and distribute it more evenly; I hung my war hammer from a leather loop on the left hip, and the long dirk on the right, with a large belt pouch worn on the right hip as well, but hung low enough that it didn't foul the hilt of the dirk. I tucked the sheathed work knife into the top of my right boot, and hung my kettle hat from a cunning little hook behind my hammer.

My great sword I carried slung over my left shoulder on a sling attached to the scabbard because it was too long for anything else; sometimes I carried it slung under my left arm, nearly horizontal and level with my belt.

This got complicated during the mid-day stop when Hatcher dug the crossbows out and announced we were going to learn to use them; this meant carrying a case of spare bolts. Eventually the hard leather bolt case went on the left side of my belt just behind the hammer, and I hung my kettle hat on it. There was also a graffle, a foot-long rod ending in a metal hook that attached to the front of your belt. You set the crossbow's string in the graffle's hook, put your foot in the stirrup at the front of the crossbow, and stepped down while straightening up, cocking the crossbow. It turned out I was strong enough to just set the string and lean into the crossbow to cock it, so Akel cut the hook off the graffle and riveted it directly to my belt, and removed the iron stirrup from the crossbow, which made it a bit lighter and handier.

During the breaks Hatcher showed us how to take the crossbows apart, clean them, and put them back together, and that evening we shot at a tree, which didn't suffer as much as we had hoped. I was impressed with the weapon, however: when I aimed correctly, it punched a short bolt deep into the heartwood.

"You don't talk much." Hatcher observed in the afternoon of the third day.

It would not be proper to point out that there had not been many gaps in the conversation since we left the city. "No."

"Burk talk much?"

"Oh, yes. Around other slaves."

"Yeah, I keep forgetting that; slaves aren't usually heavily armed. So, homesick at all?"

"A little. If I learn my letters do you think I could get word back to the city?"

"Fellhome? Sure." It had been my whole world for so long that it was hard to remember that it was just a place to others. "Who do you want to send a letter to?"

"Master Horne, to let him know we are well and conducting ourselves in a proper manner."

She was quiet for a bit. "When we reach a place that can do it, I'll write what you want and you can send it. Are all slaves as loyal as you?"

I shrugged. "Master Horne raised me."

"He sent you into the pits to kill or die."

"That was my place. Provine Sael will send me into a fight someday, won't she?"

"Yes," Hatcher answered slowly. "He's sort of your family, your Master Horne?"

"I suppose. I never had any family. There used to be more brutes in the barracks, but they're dead now."

"Huh." Hatcher was quiet for a while. I kept the pace and watched the countryside, as it was a nice day.

After the evening meal Provine Sael clapped her hands to get our attention. "Tomorrow we're leaving the high road, so a sentry will be posted at night camps; Torl will make the assignments. We'll be on country roads for four days, and then strike out across country."

The others accepted this without comment, and the night proceeded as usual. Hatcher had taught me and Burk a game of skill and chance involving a board marked with indentations and colored pebbles, and beat us at it every night. As we moved our pebbles in turn a question occurred to me. "Where are we going?"

"You mean next? Some ruins. Provine Sael is looking for some carvings."

I considered this. "Why did people leave carvings in the ruins?"

She chuckled. "When they weren't ruins, people carved things on the walls, as decoration."

"I see. Why does Provine Sael want to look at them?"

"Because if the carvings are intact, she will be able to learn some things."

"Oh."

"Of course, this will make the third set of wreckage we've looked at," Hatcher eliminated two of my pebbles. "We got some stuff off one of the other two."

"They carved the same stuff onto a lot of buildings?"

Hatcher sighed. "No, but it was an important poem in some ways, written in an old language, one people don't use anymore. In the years since the poem was written, the words have changed quite a bit, by language and from other poets making things more...*nice*. You read the poem in a book today, it's different from how it was originally written. A lot different."

"What's so important about this poem?" I took out one of Hatcher's pieces.

"That was a good move. It was a tribute to a man, a dead man, and it described a lot of details of his life. Because of the passage of time and the changes later copies of the poem are not accurate."

"Why was the poem only carved in places that became ruins?"

"They were carved when the poem was new, over three hundred years ago."

"And nobody would help you go look at these carvings?"

"Actually, they hedged their bets: they gave money. That way they get credit if we succeed, and aren't out much if we fail."

Hedging bets was something I understood; there was a lot of gambling at the pits.

"So if she reads the carvings…," I frowned.

"If the carvings are what she hopes, it fills the gaps in her knowledge," Hatcher explained. "Maybe ties together the bits she actually has. Which takes us to the next step. We're still in the early stages."

"That's why Provine Sael said it could take a year."

"Yup. You in a hurry?"

"No. I've got a lot to learn."

Chapter Three

We turned off the high road less than an hour from our night camp, and things immediately changed. Hatcher got five hand axes out of her gear and hung them on the ornate girdle she wore, which was already hung with several (matching pattern) pouches of odd sizes. The axes were of an unusual design, with a long head flowing back to a handle that was slightly curved. Hatcher caught me looking.

"Throwing axes; I'll show you how to use them once you get the crossbow down pat."

Hunter donned a harness of plain leather that had many pouches, each hardly bigger than a coin, and had capped leather tubes on the belt portion. Torl slung a round shield over his shoulder, and strung his bow. Provine Sael produced a short staff from her gear; it was about as tall as Hatcher, made of what looked like ivory banded with silver, set with blue gems that matched her earrings, and was very ornately carved. Akel took his spear and shield off the mule.

Burk and I were already fully ready so we stood and watched.

Thereafter Hatcher did not doze; the road we used was just a rutted path, but it was still easy walking and the twenty-five miles really didn't take any longer to cover each day. Each rest break we had to fire two bolts at a target, and at each noon break Hatcher would teach Burk and I a simple task, like how to set up a fire pit, starting a fire with flint and steel, or how to use some cord, cut branches, and a cloak to provide a rain cover for your bedroll. At night besides cleaning whatever game Torl brought in, we would help Akel prepare the meal, as neither of us had ever really cooked, although we knew a little from kitchen duty back in the barracks when we were young.

The lessons in numbers continued, and besides symbols we were required to chant a table of numbers. It seemed that my head might explode from all the numbers Hatcher was packing into it, but I discovered that numbers had a pattern, like the threads in cloth, and things started making more sense. I was learning faster than Burk, but not by much.

There was almost no traffic on the path; we saw peasants at work in the fields, and once we passed a shabby peddler leading a mule. In mid-afternoon we passed through one of the little villages such as we had seen at regular intervals from the high road. It was small, about twenty thatched cottages and half that number sheds (I had to count them), with rutted dirt streets and a single tile-roofed building that served as tavern and store, Hatcher said from the sign. Hunter wanted to stop there but Provine Sael refused.

There were some old men sitting on benches in front of the store who stared at us, and a group of small children followed us through the village, calling excitedly and throwing stones at Burk and me.

"Little *bastards*," Hatcher rubbed her arm where a rock had clipped her.

"I'll put you down before the next one."

"No, I mean throwing rocks at all. You're not hurting anyone."

I shrugged. "I'm a brute. Free or slave doesn't change that." I said it loud enough for Burk to hear. "Master Horne always says to expect strangers to think the worst of us."

The next break I collared Burk as we were pulling bolts out of a tree. "See what I mean? Running gets us nowhere."

"One village isn't the whole world," he tried to sound like he believed it, but he was shaken and it showed.

"Did they throw rocks at Provine Sael? She has *horns*. No, they *oohed* over her. We're half-Ukar, and that means we're hated. We stick to our mistress and learn. We do what is proper and reflect credit upon our barracks. Maybe we get freedom, but first we learn."

He didn't reply, but I knew it had registered. I hoped we got someplace where Hatcher could write a letter for me soon; I wanted to tell Master Horne that we were serving well and that I had Burk's mind in the right place.

"Does it bother you?" Hatcher asked later in the afternoon.

"What?" I had been watching a hawk; I knew it was a hawk because I had asked Hatcher about one the first day.

"People not liking you because you're half-Ukar."

"No, it's natural. Provine Sael is different, but she is pretty, and that's all right. It's being different and ugly that makes it hard to like us. Most people are all right once they see we don't mean trouble. A brute has to prove his worth each day, Master Horne says."

"Horne's got a saying for everything, huh?"

"He is smart," I observed guardedly; I liked Hatcher and I didn't want her saying anything bad about Master Horne.

"He trained you well," she observed, and the moment passed.

Guard duty was divided between me, Burk, Torl, and Akel; three shifts a night, so every fourth night you slept uninterrupted. It wasn't hard duty, although having midwatch was sort of disruptive. We kept the time by an hourglass, and the only challenge was to stay awake.

Our first night camp Torl brought in a goat he said was wild, and Hatcher made a lot of jokes about that. Torl had to show Burk and I how to dress it, as Hatcher only did small animals. It wasn't hard.

"Yeah, we're here now," Hatcher muttered as we approached another village.

"Where?"

Hatcher drummed lightly on my head. "Look at the village."

I did. "Looks like the last one, maybe four more cottages…"

"In my profession, if you want to keep your fingers, Grog, you have to look at things differently. Size them up, didn't you do that in the pit?"

"Yeah."

"This village has a ditch and a stake belt, and the cottages have shutters with firing slits in them."

I saw the X shaped slots she was referring to, and thought about it. "They have troubles?"

"The area has troubles," the Nisker said grimly. "Bandits, Tulgs, all sorts of troubles are possible. Always watch the locals, Grog. Like you would watch them in a bad neighborhood."

That I understood.

Trouble found us the next day. The countryside had been changing: the trees were not just neat rows between fields that Hatcher said were to keep the wind from ripping up the ground, but in big tangled untidy clumps; I had heard the term 'forest' before, but now I was seeing some. The road got more and more faint, and the clumps of forest got bigger and closer together until the fields were just gaps in the forest.

Torl kept an arrow in his bow, held in place against the string by the pressure of a single finger, and Akel wore his shield on his arm all the time and his spear in hand. The trees pressed close to the road so we walked through dappled shadows, and the gloom further in the forest on either side spoke unpleasantly of ambushes and sniping archers. I knew about such things because you hear about them from veterans talking in taverns and grog shops while on escorts.

Rounding a bend we found ourselves confronting a low barricade of rocks and tree trunks that narrowed the passage down to just wide enough for a loaded mule to pass. There were a half-dozen men at this barricade, and there were about the same number coming through the trees to either side. Hatcher vanished from my shoulders in a neat flip as I slid my sword free and dropped the scabbard.

Burk and I eased towards Provine Sael as a man stepped forward through the gap in the barricade with his sword sheathed at his hip; he wore rusty mail that was holed in a couple places and a conical helm with an officer's brass trim. The men at the barricade wore boiled leather armor such as I had seen the garrison at home wear, but battered and in poor shape; two had bows, three had banged up shields (no two alike) and spears, and the last had a halberd. Those to either side included women, and were armed with spears and clubs, with little or no armor. They all looked unkempt and hungry.

"Good day, my lady," the armored man sketched a bow. "A moment, if you would be so kind."

Hunter muttered something, slipping a roll of paper from one of the cases on his belt, but Provine Sael ignored him. "Stand aside: we are but peaceful travelers with many miles yet to cross." She was as calm as if ordering tea at a shop.

He grinned, revealing gaps. "Your peaceful intent is quite clear, but I'm afraid there is a toll, my lady."

The talk gave me the opportunity to get my kettle hat on. "Hunter and Hatcher, left flank, Burk, right, Grog, the barricade," Torl muttered.

"I'm not inclined to pay tolls," the Dellian observed. "But I'll ask: how much?"

"One mule and pack; you may choose which."

Her chin came up. "I think not."

"I'm afraid it's not an option, my lady."

"There's always an option. And in this case, I would suggest you consider how this will end."

The man raised his hands in a gesture of helplessness. "We are but poor and hungry folk asking for no more than what you can spare."

"You are blind if you think your band will fare well against mine."

The man flushed. "We have surprised bolder foes."

"I think not. The man beside me can drop a bird in flight, and my two swordsmen have each killed more men than your band contains. We are not peasants to be bullied and robbed. Stand aside or we will extend no quarter."

On the first day on the road Hatcher had warned Burk and I that if Provine Sael mentioned quarter, surrender, or prisoners while in a confrontation it meant that we were about to attack, so it wasn't a surprise when Torl sent a shaft into the eye socket of a bandit archer; I launched into a charge even as the sound of the releasing bow string registered.

The leader was fast, far faster than I was: he had his blade out and up in a classic guard as I closed the gap between us. It was a good guard position, the angle just so, and it would have presented me with a challenge if I had been swinging overhand. His problem was that I was swinging from a middle-low guard, so my blade swept in well below his and severed his left leg just above the knee before embedding itself in his right thigh.

That is the problem with a classic guard: it only works if you faced a foe who also trained in the classic style or wasn't trained at all. I wasn't trained in any particular style, because following a style made you predictable; I was trained to win.

Expertly relaxing my arms, I let the hilt bang into my chest as I twisted the blade free without losing much of my momentum; the problem with a cleaving strike is the instinct to maintain a forceful grip, which makes it harder to free your blade and slows you down. The trick, as Master Horne had pounded into us, was to relax your arms and lever the blade free with your movement. It was a tricky technique and had taken a lot of goat carcasses before I mastered the timing of it.

The leader was screaming but I ignored him, focusing on footing, getting my now-free blade back up to an inside right guard with the pommel nearly touching my right armpit, the blade horizontal in front of me.

The other archer was down with an arrow in his throat, and the halberdier was moving into the gap, handling his weapon like he knew his business. Polearms are tricky because they have a long reach and terrible leverage; my scale shirt or kettle hat would not save me from a solid hit. The danger in using them is that a good halberdier can get used to having the reach in the fight, whereas I am very tall, with arms a bit longer than a man of equal height, and my sword was a long one. Master Horne had always reminded us that too many think with the edge, and to always remember that a sword has a point.

Stepping into the lunge, I put the point straight at his face. He was good, and he almost parried the thrust; as it was, he clipped my blade, notching the shaft of his weapon and saving his life, if not his face: my point opened his cheek from his chin back to his left ear, which was nearly severed. I saw teeth through the rent in his face before the blood flowed.

He staggered back, managing not to drop his weapon, but pawing at the wound rather than fighting or defending; I caught my blade behind the ricassos and ran the point up under his breastbone before he could figure out what happened to his face, levering him with a blade-flexing shove to the side to clear the gap in the barricade.

Catching movement out of the corner of my eye, I twisted, elbows lifted high, and a spear point screeched across my armor, raising a bruise but failing to get enough purchase to penetrate. My return swing was clumsy and the spearman deflected it with his shield, although the linden boards split at the impact.

Parrying his second thrust with my crossguard, I bulled through the gap in the barricade and stepped into a proper swing which he blocked as well, although I cut away the top third of his shield. Both smart and quick, he took to his heels before I could bring my blade back into position.

Mindful of my footing I pivoted, but the other spearmen had fled at some earlier point. Broadening my search, I realized the fight was over: on the left flank were four bodies, three whose clothes were smoldering; on the right Burk was standing over three corpses, looking around just as I was. The bandit leader had stopped screaming at some point; he was mumbling curses as he gripped his leg just above the stump to stop the bleeding, or at least he did until Hatcher walked up and gave him a chop to the neck that separated his head from his shoulders. The halberdier was completely dead.

"Grog, are you injured?" Provine Sael was as unruffled as always.

I ran my hand across my side; the scales were grooved but unbroken. "Just a bruise."

"Good. Well done, all of you." She was free with compliments, and I tried not to grin. I was upholding the honor of the Ebon Blades, of that there was no doubt.

Torl lithely vaulted the barricade as I was wiping my blade clean on a dead archer's scarf and looked to his arrows, but only one was recoverable.

Burk was scrubbing the head of his morning star with dirt when I walked back to get my scabbard. "Three, I see," I nodded towards the bodies, settling the blade into its sheath.

"Amateurs," he shrugged indifferently. He glanced about, but we were alone for the moment. "These people know what they are doing; we could learn a lot from them."

I nodded sagely.

Hatcher checked the bodies, then handed Provine Sael a fistful of coins and gave Akel the leader's sword and helm plus a couple knives to add to the mules. I boosted her into place as the mules threaded their way through the gap in the barricade, tossing their heads at the smell of blood.

"Who were these people?"

"Deserters," she replied. "Runaway slaves, that sort of thing. Some scum, some with bad luck in hard times."

"Why is it hard times?" I followed the mules through the gap. Times were just times for me; Master Horne had seen to it we ate every day, but I had overheard the term many times.

"War and disorder, mostly." Hatcher drummed a few strokes, but my wool cap made it ineffective. "The Dusmen attacked the Empire-you know we're part of the Empire, right? They came with whole armies of Ukar and swarms of Tulgs about thirty years ago. Took a decade to pound 'em back, and there's some bits of the Empire they still hold. That's where you got your blood: the Ukar raped a lot when they were advancing. By the time the Empire got things settled down with the Dusman there was an uprising at the capitol, a grab for the throne. Took a couple years to get that sorted out, and it ends up with a Queen-Regent on the throne who nobody likes or trusts. So this lord or that gets ideas above his station, and the Legions have to deal with disloyalty, traitors, Ukar raids, Tulg forays, and the Dusmen still holding part of the Empire. You end up with bandits in the forests, too many sacked towns, too many abandoned farms."

"Huh." That sounded stupid, but then, I am stupid, so it might just be me. I knew there had been a big war and a lot of little ones, and I knew that the Empire was shaky, but that had just been...*things*. I mean, it had always been like that. I never considered how things were before I was around to hear about them.

"It might get better, though: the Emperor has come of age and married, and things have calmed down a bit. Trouble is, the Dusmen look like they're getting ready for another try."

I knew the Dusmen were bad news: the pit-master in Fellhome had gotten one as a captive a couple years ago and there was a lot of excitement about fighting it. It had killed a High Rate and crippled another before it died, fighting in solo fights. I hadn't been a High Rate back then, so I didn't get to see it fight, but I knew the reputations of those it fought, and both were the cream of the crop.

"Anyway, maybe we'll do some good," Hatcher mused above me. "That's what we're doing, really: trying to make the times a little better."

"By figuring out a dead language?"

"By translating a poem written in the old language, which should lead us to a place where we can find something important. And that's secret, by the way, so tell no one."

I wouldn't; that would not be proper. But even if it had been proper, I really had no idea of what we were doing.

I found myself walking by Akel after the next rest stop and Hatcher was stretching her legs up ahead, teasing Torl about something.

"Bloody business, that barricade," the pack-master observed quietly. "Shame, really."

"Was it?" I hadn't thought much about it.

"It is. Look at this," he swept an arm towards the trees. "Land aplenty for the clearing, and instead it houses bandits and hopeless vagabonds who will face armed men for the hope of hardtack. It's a waste."

I didn't know what to say, so I said nothing.

He grinned at that. "I imagine killing isn't something you lose sleep over, eh, lad? Much like a butcher fears no blood."

"I'm a slave."

"Aye, and more than that. I saw you fight: there's real craft in the way you handled that blade. A dullard doesn't fight like that."

I shrugged.

"Thing to remember, m'boy, is that killing is far too easy; take care that it doesn't become the only thing you know. Don't make what you do in life amount to a trail of corpses."

"I'm learning my numbers." I felt stupid the instant I said it, but Akel just nodded and clapped me on the shoulder.

"That's the spirit! A man who can't see to improve himself isn't much good to those around him. Take the time to look at the path you've walked, and you'll get to a better place in the end."

Hatcher had stopped in the road, the folded blanket over her shoulder. "Lecture him on ethics some other time, Akel. I'm done walking for a while."

Later, while we were gathering firewood out of earshot of the camp I stopped Burk. "You hear what Akel said to me earlier?"

"Yeah. He said something like that to me, too."

"What does it mean?"

Burk wasn't one to admit ignorance. "I think he means we should do things other than just kill people. Useful things."

That made a certain amount of sense. "Like gather firewood?"

He scratched his nose. "Maybe. I think more like *good* things, sort of…helping people. Maybe if they can't do it for themselves."

"Huh." I kicked a log to dislodge most of the bugs. "It would have to be something simple because I don't know much that isn't fighting."

"Me, either. Maybe we ought to ask somebody. You know, for details."

"I'll see if I can bring it up to Hatcher."

We passed through a village before making camp, and I noticed a watch tower standing in its center in addition to the ditch and stake belt. The next day we passed through what had been a village before someone burned down all the buildings; a large patch of turned earth in the center of town showed where someone had buried the inhabitants.

"Tulgs," Torl held up a short length of what looked like a broken staff. "About a month ago, give or take."

"The border used to be a hundred miles from here," Hunter shook his head.

"The border used to be guarded," the scout shrugged. "Now it's a line on a map. The Legions are under-strength and over-busy."

"We should have re-provisioned in the last burg," Hunter groused, shocking me. That was not proper: Provine Sael was within easy earshot. She ignored the comment and Hunter equally.

"Ganter's Fist will still be standing," Torl grunted. "If it isn't, then we might as well turn back. If the Tulg can kill that bastard we don't have a chance."

"How does Torl know it was Tulgs from a broken staff?" I asked Hatcher when we were on the road again, passing untended fields on either side.

"It was a javelin shaft, and he could tell you the clan that made it, too, from the markings. Torl can track, scout, hunt, and anything else you need done in the wilds, besides being an archer of the first water," Hatcher explained. "He spends most of his time on the frontier hunting Tulg and Ukar scouts."

Later, during one of Hatcher's infrequent silences I thought about the fight. Killing those men hadn't been an issue for me; they were a long time from my first, and it wasn't my business in any case. Akel's comment about your path was interesting but I couldn't see how it really applied: I was a slave, and it wasn't my road that I was walking. Master Horne had raised me for the pit, and Provine Sael had chosen me because she needed people killed. Which people and why I still wasn't clear on, but that was just details.

Times were hard, now, that was something I had heard a lot, but times were always the same if you were a slave: you did what you were told and stayed out of everyone's way. That ruined village we had passed through had seen a different kind of hard times, and so had some of those people who had attacked us.

It occurred to me that the Brocks back home had been a place where times were always hard for the people who lived there. Those men that had jumped us on the way to the Abyss were doing it for money, and not so as to get rich. That was part of being free, apparently: looking for money to live on.

It was a new thought for me, and not a good one; I looked at the clumps of trees and the untidy bushes on either side of the road and wondered what would happen if I was free and had to find my own supper.

The evening of the same day as the ruined village saw us approaching another village, Ganter's Fist, a lot larger than the others, and completely encircled by a log palisade, plus the ditch and stakes; it had three watch towers, and armed men stood guard at the gate.

"There's the Fist," Hatcher said. "I'll walk the rest of the way."

"Close up," Torl said, just loud enough to reach our group. "Stay alert, and stay calm. The Fist is no place for too much pride or too much humility."

I wasn't sure exactly what his words meant, but I understood the message: it was like the Abyss, where you minded your business carefully, but brooked no nonsense. I thumped my fists into my palms to seat my gloves: I knew this sort of place.

Three spearmen in good leather armor were at the gate, young men but hard-eyed and scarred, their shields on their arms. A fourth warrior came from inside the Fist as we reached the timber bridge across the ditch, an older man in ring mail with a bearded axe at his belt and a javelin held casually in his right hand.

The man pointed with the javelin. "I know you: Torl, isn't it? You scouted here for a season a few winters ago."

"Indeed, Watchmaster Zebin. How fares the Fist?"

Zebin smiled sourly. "We hold. Some months it is a bloodier business than others. You've brought us a mixed bunch."

"We've business in the timber," Torl grinned, the first time I had seen him change expression, but it didn't reach his eyes. "A transaction in steel."

"That can be profitable." Zebin was looking at me now. "Ganter himself will want to greet you. You know the way to the hall."

"Ganter? When did he become so social? We just want beds and provisions."

"Ganter has his whims, same as any other man. Have no fear, you can rest and re-provision to your heart's content, and hire some extra blades if that suits you as well."

"You've bodies to spare?" Torl frowned. "When was the Fist ever over-full?"

"Since lately. Three more villages were lost during the snows, and the survivors made their way here."

Once inside and out of earshot, Torl shook his head. "Something is wrong. More than just hard times."

There were hard times visible in the Fist, for while the street was cobbled and the buildings were well-built, every alley and cranny had improvised shelters housing ragged, hungry-looking people. Beggars crouched at every street corner, and skinny girls with scared eyes loitered, too.

Ganter's hall was in the center of the Fist on the north side of the open merchant's grounds, a long wide rectangular building built of square-cut timbers with a tall thatched roof that leaked smoke, making it appear that it was steaming. It had a big chimney at each of the narrow ends, and double doors at the center of the side facing the plaza, with guards standing watch outside.

"Akel, stay with the mules," Provine Sael instructed the pack-master, keeping her voice down.

"Zebin said we should pay our respects," Torl advised the senior of the guards at the door, who looked us over and then gestured for the doors to be opened.

"Go on," he jerked his head. "It won't take long." Like any slave who wants to avoid trouble, I listen closely to people in authority, and I did not like what I heard in his tone. He knew what Watchmaster Zebin knew, and I had no idea what that was. But I was getting a feeling about what it might be: Zebin had looked at Burk and me in a way that was familiar: a weighing up. I had seen owners of fighting slaves do that countless times in the pits.

The hall was one large room with exposed rafters and a long fire trench running down the center, stopping fifteen feet short of each fireplace. It was dark, illuminated only by the flames in the fireplaces, the red glow of the mounded coals in the fire trench, and a few oil lamps on the walls. People sat at trestle tables lining the long walls except to our right, where a table sat on a platform raised a foot above the floor, angled across the corner.

The floor was dirt, and the open area in front of the platform was heavily sanded. I exchanged a glance with Burk, and he nodded slightly.

The people at the side tables were mostly fighting men or prosperous-looking craftsmen, with a lot of young women scattered amongst them, while the raised table had two older soldiers, a skinny man in a fur-trimmed robe, and a big man gone to fat, bald but for greasy strands of gray hair that reached his shoulders.

Provine Sael lead us to a point on the sanded floor in front of the table. "I am Provine Sael, here to rent quarters and purchase supplies. Your master of the gate suggested we pay our respects to the ruler of the Fist."

The fat man slouched in a big chair padded with furs draped across the seat and back, thoughtfully studying Provine Sael with eyes that were keen and alert while he sipped something pale green from a stein of glass panels set into a gold frame. This was not a stupid man, and not a friendly one, either.

"I am Ganter the Bear-killer, Master of this hold," he announced, resting his tankard on one large thigh. He had a strong voice, one that sounded like he was used to giving orders and being obeyed. "What business brings you this far north?"

"We are on a pilgrimage to a ruined monastery to the northeast."

"Very well." He took a deliberate drink of the green liquid. "I see you have a couple Ukar with you, fighting Ukar."

"Ukar-blooded, yes, good and loyal servants." I hadn't been called a servant before.

Ganter smiled like a skull. "We are a simple burg here, but we enjoy a show now and again. I'm minded to pit my champion against one of your servants."

Provine Sael bridled but Torl touched her elbow. "We are just looking for shelter and provisions, Lord," he kept his voice neutral. "We couldn't afford to lose a fighting man to your champion."

"If your *servant* loses, I'll loan you a half-dozen warriors as an escort," Ganter shrugged. "Asking a guest to entertain isn't uncommon or unseemly."

Torl nodded slowly. "All right. What terms?"

"On the sand, no armor, short blades. The big one first, then the shorter one if my champion prevails."

The scout nodded. "All right."

Provine Sael looked like she was going to explode, but she held her tongue. Hatcher didn't. "Since we're all having an evening's entertainment, let's bring on the fun; twenty Marks on my boy," she rattled a pouch of leather dyed blue. "I'll give you straight odds, sight unseen."

Ganter chuckled at that. "All right, twenty it is." He waved a hand that lacked the two last fingers, and I heard the rattle of someone walking in manacle chains behind me. Turning, I watched as they led Ganter's champion to the sand.

He was the biggest pure-blood Ukar I had ever seen.

Chapter Four

He was easily a half-head taller than me, broad but rangy, not as heavily muscled as I was, a medium-heavyweight. He wore a pair of stinking breeches and a full set of chains, and six armed men accompanied him, keeping a close watch. Like all pure Ukar he only had three fingers per hand, but all three were topped with a sharp boney ridge, and two long bony spurs grew along the bottoms of his forearms, and I didn't have to look to see that they were filed sharp. They wouldn't have to give him weapons to face me.

His face was not very human: two big turtle eyes, slits for a nose, a massive underslung jaw with brass-tipped tusks thrusting up almost level with the bottom of his eyes, and two spiny fans of ears standing out at right angles to his hairless skull, looking like the back fins on a pike. His skin was gray and coarse, marked with a web of clan tattoos, victory brands, and battle scars. He stank like a cesspool and looked like death on two legs.

I stepped back and conferred with Burk as I unstrapped my belt. "Taller, longer reach," I muttered.

"Lean, looks quick," Burk nodded, helping me take off my scale shirt. "Question is, work in close, or try to maneuver him?"

"Two blades, you think?"

"A buckler would be better," Burk scratched his chin. "Use your kettle hat, maybe."

I left my undershirt on, untucked to increase the chance of snagging, and kept my gloves. Burk added the straps from his kettle hat to mine to strengthen the improvised grip while I stretched and loosened up.

"I am sorry about this, Grog," Provine Sael kept her voice very low as I finished touching my toes.

"Mistress?" It startled me: no one apologizes to a slave.

"The fight: I'm sorry you have to fight that…*thing*."

I shrugged. "It's what I do. I'm a pit fighter, a High Rate from the Ebon Blades, a proper barracks of the old school."

Hatcher slapped my leg. "I'll cut you in on my winnings, Grog. Kill him quick."

The hat was not a great buckler, but it was better than nothing. I got it adjusted to my grip as best I could, got my dirk settled in my fist just so, and looked up at Ganter. He beckoned me forward. "What's your name, tusker?"

"Grog." I barked it as Master Horne taught us, deep from the belly. A short name you could belt out, that was what he always said was best, something you could snarl.

The big man started a bit, then grinned. "You think you can walk off the sand alive?"

The crowds win no fights, Master Horne always said, but they do kill fighters. He meant that those who worried about the crowd could get fatally distracted. I looked Ganter square in the eye and grinned.

It wasn't the answer he expected.

Four men had crossbows aimed at the Ukar while two others unbolted his manacles. It ignored them, watching me. When the men stepped off the sand it rolled its shoulders and rotated its neck, then leisurely stretched out and clawed at the air.

I ignored it because the finger-ridges were on the backs of its hands, so it wasn't going to claw. The Ukar I had faced in the pit had used weapons, but Master Horne had one of the clerks read us a lot of stuff on how Ukar fought. I was looking at its legs: the breeches might be used to cover a scar that marked an injured limb.

Burk drummed the heels of his hands across the top of my shoulders to loosen up the muscles. "Left eye," he muttered.

He was sharp: was that a film on the Ukar's eye? Could be.

"Ready?" Ganter called, and I stepped towards the center of the sandy area. The watchers were making noise but it droned into just background noise, like the wind blowing. The only things in the world were my feet, hands, and the target. Only one leaves the pit: that is the rule.

And sometimes no one does.

Ganter must have signaled to start, but I wasn't paying attention; some try for the first attack, but Master Horne always said to ignore the starting horn and make the first move count; if your start was sure, your finish was more likely.

The Ukar was fast, a lot faster than the ones I had fought before; it led with a right forearm sweep, trying to slash high, at my neck. I ducked, knowing that the slash was for show and that the left coming in low was the real move. I met that strike with my left, the kettle hat ringing from the impact and two straps parting from the shock, stepping in to meet the blow and continuing in one motion for a cut at its thigh.

It twisted, lithe and quick, but I felt the dirk's edge slicing, a glancing cut but first blood. Deflecting a right slash with the increasingly loose hat, I extended the motion into a roundhouse that slammed the kettle hat into its face, snapping the Ukar's head back and ripping the hat from my grip.

I ignored the loss as I tried to open its belly, but the Ukar managed to get out of most of the cut, although the blade did meet hide. I kept the momentum going, boring inside its reach, my left arm up and angled to block, going for fast chopping slashes aimed at mid torso.

The Ukar gave ground quickly; they usually are more aggressive and arrogant fighters, but this one was too smart. A horn bellowed as he reached the hearth, and reflexively I stepped back, raising my dirk; the Ukar lifted both arms.

Keeping my eyes on him, I backed to the center of the sand, kicking my kettle hat off onto the floor to safeguard my footing. I couldn't tell how deep I had cut him on the thigh as his breeches were too dark in this light to see the amount of blood, but he had several good long cuts on his torso that were bleeding freely. I had a cut on my lower left forearm and a shallow slash across my ribs; I didn't remember getting either, and didn't care. Neither was a problem.

The horn blew again, and for a long heartbeat we stood, watching each other; it was learning. I didn't bother with its eyes: I watched the belly because breathing will signal a move, and that kept its hands and legs in clear view.

It knew that to parry I would have to accept a wound, and that decided its move: it went with the same slashing forearm strike it had gone with last time. The problem with the obvious is that it is, in fact, obvious.

The Ukar was learning, though; it kept its left arm, blade side out, curved in front of its belly, ready to block low. It was learning, but I already *knew*. I blocked left, catching part of the blade on the cuff of my glove and ignoring the pain and blood for what the glove did not protect, moving to deflect the force of his attack while I stepped into a low extended thrust. The clerk's reading had emphasized that because of their natural armament Ukar fight with the edge and the swing or slash; seldom do they grasp the utility of the point.

If you turn a slash with sufficient force it usually misses, but a thrust is a much different proposition. The Ukar parried my thrust, but knocking it a few inches to the side just slowed it. I felt the point punch through hide, hit heavy bone, and then glide off into softer flesh, to the right, away from the sack of organs I was aiming for, but you fight with what you get, and I threw my lunge into a full-arm heaving twist on the dirk's hilt. I felt the tang fighting to rip free and the blade flex against the tough muscle; I wouldn't have been surprised if it had snapped.

But the steel was good, the forging was clean, and the edges keen: the blade rotated, equal parts of cutting and ripping as it came free of the Ukar.

It might have screamed, but I wasn't paying attention to anything but my footing and getting the blade back into play. The wound wasn't going to be fatal, and the fight was not over.

It was bad, though: the Ukar's left hip had been laid open; it looked like a respectable wound for an axe. The Ukar hopped backwards, trying to get its footing and balance and I bored in, catching a slash across the ribs that felt like a line of burning ice pressed against my skin.

I ignored the pain and caught his right arm in an underlock: his forearm braced in my armpit, my left arm under and inside his, the top of my forearm jammed into the inside of his right biceps, immobilizing his arm. Pounding the thick brass oval of the dirk's pommel into its forehead once, twice, parry a clumsy left-arm slash with the blade, strike again. Pommel, forehead; forehead, pommel. One turtle eye burst, and the sloping forehead dented in from the force of the blows. I ignored the convulsions, the flailing, clawing left hand, the horn's bellow.

Only one leaves the pit: that is the rule.

Burk slapping the center of my spine brought me back to the larger world: I realized I was supporting nearly all the Ukar's weight and that its deformed head was twitching like a fish flopping after being poured out of Akel's bucket.

Unhooking my arm, I let it fall and stepped back to the center of the sand, trying to draw enough air into my overheated lungs to kill the burning in my muscles. No matter how hard you train there is never enough air in a fight.

Ganter was scowling at me and his men looked uncomfortably alert; Burk was standing next to me, my sword leaning casually against his left shoulder, thumbs hooked in his belt near to, but not quite touching, the handle of his star. I knew the others were ranged to either side, but I stayed focused on the ruler of the Fist.

"We thank you for this...*entertainment*," Provine Sael announced grimly. "With your leave, we shall depart."

Unexpectedly, the big man grinned. It was a sour grin, but a grin nonetheless. He gestured to the man in the robe, who tossed a pouch to Hatcher. "You live, and you learn." He glanced at the still convulsing body of the Ukar, and then at me. "I'll triple whatever the lady is paying you."

I shrugged. "I can't." For some reason, it seemed very unwise to mention that I was a slave.

He nodded. "I should have known that if she could hire Torl, she could hire good blades. You've fought in the pits?"

I nodded. He was old and fat and mean-looking, but he was smart, too; I could see that. Best to keep my mouth shut.

He gave a dry little chuckle. "You gave us a fight to remember." He gestured at a serving girl standing nearby. "Take Provine Sael and her party to the green hostel. At least the Fist will get back some of my money ere she departs."

Despite the overcrowding there were rooms available for guests with money, and we were soon established in a long room with a big plank table and a cheerfully-blazing fireplace. Doors off this room connected us to three bunkrooms and a bath, so it was like having our own little tavern to ourselves.

Once the girl left us Provine Sael poured hot water into a bowl and unpacked a leather satchel onto the table. "Grog, take off your shirt."

I had been Healed often; if I hadn't the pit would have left me a mass of scar tissue and lacking the use of my left arm, perhaps the limb itself. I got my shirt off with Burk's help without re-opening most of my cuts. Sitting on a bench at the table, I waited while Provine Sael plied a wax stick and oils, murmuring softly as she caused each wound in turn to Heal seamlessly and swiftly. When she had finished she sent me off to wash up and get a clean shirt while Burk and Akel hauled our gear up from the mules.

Servants brought us a steaming brown beef roast, two roasted chickens, a tub of pork stew, two big serving bowls of potatoes swimming in butter, and a half-dozen crusty loaves. A half-keg of ale was trundled in on a little barrow, already tapped.

Burk and I were hanging back, but Torl waved us to the table. "Don't stand on ceremony."

Hatcher slid a greasy drawstring pouch across the table to me. "Your cut: five Marks."

"That wasn't his first time," Hunter observed from down the table. "You might have cut the rest of us in on the action."

"We are not in the business of pit fighting in any regard," Provine Sael snapped. "I would have refused the fight if there had been any way around it."

"You could have mentioned your pet was pit-trained," the mage shrugged as he ladled stew onto his plate. "They were offering odds against him; I would have put down serious money if I knew he had a real chance. As it is, we're going to get crap for odds now."

"There isn't going to be *any* odds and no more of these obscene spectacles," Provine Sael slapped the table. "This time was unavoidable. Hatcher should not have bet at all; the entire business is a disgrace in every particular."

"Would you buy a race horse and then use it to pull a plow? These rustics don't understand what a ranked pit fighter can do, and it looks like we've got two good ones. We can do your errands *and* clean up along the way."

If intensity was force Provine Sael's glare would have stripped the flesh from Hunter's skull. "Grog and Burk are thinking beings, not *animals*. They will fight for our cause, the same as any hired sword, but I will not expect nor allow them to take part in barbaric travesties of entertainment. We will *not* discuss this again."

Hatcher cheerfully broke the tense silence that followed Provine Sael's hard words. "You missed quite a fight, Akel: Ganter had a pet Ukar, a big bastard. Grog took him apart, made it look easy, and Ganter just about swallowed his own lips. Apparently he thought he had a lock on close-in fighting."

The packmaster nodded slowly. "The guards told me what was afoot after you went in. The local champion has killed a half-dozen men and two half-breeds since last summer. Ganter has used it to track runaway girls as well."

"Ganter didn't used to be such a bastard," Torl observed, passing out slices of beef. "He was always hard, you don't hold as much land as he has against the odds he faces by being otherwise, but this is something new."

"The guards said since his wife died, he turned mean."

"Hard times will do that."

Burk and I were careful to let the others serve themselves first, but there was plenty. We were the last to stop eating. The others treated it like an ordinary meal, but it was something memorable by my standards. We were cleaning up the remains of the feast; Hunter had finished eating first and left without a word, obviously angry. Akel unpacked some tools and leather and set about repairing our kettle hats, Torl sat cross-legged in front of the fire doing something with arrows and tools and a small pot of some thick liquid. Hatcher dug out whetstones and oil and touched up the edges on her knives while Provine Sael paced, deep in thought.

I was using the last bit of bread to extract the last of the butter from the potato bowl and Burk was cracking chicken bones when the Dellian sat at the end of the table with a richly carved wooden case from which she extracted parchment and various items.

"You two ever have a full meal before?" Hatcher asked as we stacked the serving plates.

"It was *good*," Burk muttered, half-embarrassed. I nodded empathically.

She chuckled. "You two are something. You're soaking up the numbers like that meal. Another week and I'll start you on letters. I thought teaching sums would be harder."

"The Tepton Academy for Boys," Burk said, and fell silent when Hatcher looked questioningly. That was not proper: a slave only volunteers expertise, never conversation.

But he was in it, so I joined him. "We waited for jobs by the Academy, and heard lessons. They didn't make much sense then, but now…it comes…like when you come on something close in the fog."

"In focus," Hatcher nodded absently, marking on a slate. She held it up. "Out loud: Aye is for…"

"Acorn," we chorused automatically, having heard it many times.

"Yup. Aye is a symbol, you build words out of the symbols same as you build a house out of bricks. This is the symbol." Catching Torl looking, she grinned. "They know the words, just not the image. This is going to be easier than I thought."

Later, in my bunk I thought about things. Hunter had wanted to field us in pit fights, which was our proper use, but Provine Sael had gotten angry, and she had said it wasn't…no, she said it was a disgrace. But people *liked* pit fights, and there were always packed crowds for the death matches.

What Hunter had said was proper, but Provine Sael had apologized to me, a slave, because I had to fight; Hunter's words were true, but Provine Sael had spoken better about us…it was very confusing. I was a tusker slave trained for the pit, so why would Provine Sael object? But she was very smart and had real Standards, so maybe…it made no sense. Hatcher hadn't seemed too upset by the fight, but she hadn't thought I would lose, either.

Killing an Ukar certainly wasn't a bad thing: they were the enemy. That part I was completely clear on.

Provine Sael sent Akel and Hatcher to buy supplies, with me as an escort. They bought cheese sealed in wax, flatbread because they had no hardtack, flour, potatoes, smoked sausage, and similar foodstuffs that would travel well, plus some odds and ends.

"Why were Provine Sael and Hunter angry at each other last night?" I ventured when Akel was ahead of us. Hatcher was walking for a change.

"They're not fond of each other," Hatcher shrugged. "Provine Sael does not like Hunter's drinking. But the thing is that she hates slavery and especially pit fighting, free or slave."

I turned that over in my mind. "Why? The pit-fighting, I mean."

"Says it barbaric. Lots of people feel that way; me, I don't like the fights, although last night I enjoyed you showing up Ganter. I knew you could take that thing."

"What is 'barbaric'?"

"Horrible, primitive, something bad that people should have outgrown."

"Huh."

"She doesn't think *you* are barbaric, though."

"Good." I thought on it for a bit. "Why doesn't she like slavery?"

"A lot of us think it is wrong to treat people as property. There aren't enough hands to go around as it is, so we shouldn't be beating the spirit out of a whole section of society." She caught my look and laughed. "Hunter wasn't wrong on one point, Grog: you may be a slave, but you are an *expensive* slave. You haven't seen quarry or mining operations that use unskilled slaves."

I didn't know what to say, so I just shrugged.

Later Burk and I sparred in the hostel's yard and lifted buckets of water to maintain our strength.

"I hope we leave tomorrow," I commented as I shifted a bucket to my left hand. "I don't like the looks of things. I wouldn't want to be a slave here."

"I wouldn't want to be free here," Burk nodded, shocking me so badly I nearly dropped the bucket.

"Things are not proper here," I observed carefully.

"Master Horne knew what he was about: no pointless fights." Burk chinned himself on a beam projecting from the eaves. "A fat purse and a good crowd, that was his way. That fight you had was a disgrace. Twenty Marks wagered on a High Rate? It's a crime, I tell you. No healer in attendance, no crier to recite your barracks and record, nothing."

"It's a different world out here," I nodded. "We need to learn more about how things work. Obviously there is some pretty poor planning going on outside the city. No real organization at all, at least out here."

"Skills are not enough, not the ones we have," Burk dropped to the ground. "We need more knowledge to be free. The letters and numbers, for a start, and how to talk to these people. It's a good thing we're clever."

Burk's mind was certainly in the right place. Master Horne would be pleased.

We left the Fist first thing the day after buying provisions; Hunter complained about taking a longer rest, but Provine Sael paid him no mind, and I could see why: the sooner we were gone, the better. The ruler of the Fist had not liked losing his pet, and if he found out Burk and I were slaves we would never leave.

We went north on what quickly became the worst road yet once we were out of view of the Fist, a very overgrown pair of fading ruts that plunged into the forest like a dagger-thrust. A mile or so after the track entered the forest Torl led us off the path seemingly at random and we moved through the trees.

It was profoundly unsettling because the trees had no sense of organization, and while there were not a lot of bushes, those that were grew any which way. Old branches and whole trees were left lying about where they fell, and the entire impression was one of clutter and confusion. Within moments I was completely lost.

And Torl started to talk to us, which was almost as unsettling. At the mid-day break and at night he would point out types of trees, and tell us how to watch in the woods, how to hide, how to move without making as much noise.

Equally unsettling was that Hatcher did not talk; she still rode, but in silence now, a throwing axe held casually. She was out of her element, I believe; she knew more than Burk and I, but she was clearly not an expert. Hunter didn't like the forest at all, but Provine Sael treated it no differently than she did anything else. It was hard to tell if she knew a lot about forests because she always acted as if she was where she was supposed to be.

Burk and I were carrying our crossbows, and fired four bolts at mid-day and eight at night; we were comfortable with their operation, but our accuracy still needed a little work.

The woods were wearing on me: everything was so untidy and irregular; there wasn't any sort of order anywhere. Things just were scattered around, no planning whatsoever. And I was growing very tired inside; there were too many new things happening, not just every day, but every hour. It was exciting at first, but now it was making me feel grey inside, low and dull.

Back home the barracks were the barracks, the same as they always were, a bit more repaired as time passed, but slowly and you could watch it happen. Your duties changed, but gradually; training was hard but the same sort of hard throughout.

I wanted to wake up in the barracks, stand outside the Academy and listen to the lessons while I waited for another escort job, which would be different but also the same. I wanted Master Horne to tell me I was stupid. I wanted Burk to blather about freedom and our noble blood. I wanted to be a guard and a High Rate and do what I was told.

Instead I was out here in these disorganized trees and untidy bushes, someplace different every morning, and they kept expecting me to think and learn. I had to learn numbers and crossbows and moving in the wild and skinning things and so many more details that my skull felt like it was going to explode. I was tired, more tired than sleeping could fix.

For the first time since my earliest days in the pits I *wanted* a fight, a good fight, close in and brutal. I wanted to get in and do what I knew best, like with the Ukar back in the Fist.

The second morning in the forest I was helping Akel load the mules. "You look like a man on his way to a funeral," the pack-master observed casually. "Something on your mind?"

I shrugged.

"Things are a bit different out here, eh?"

"A lot."

"That's life, sometimes. Things get comfortable for a while, even if they aren't perfect."

"Sometimes they keep changing."

"Yes, that can be a problem, too. Some thrive on new vistas each morning, new places, new people, new challenges. Others like a nice quiet routine."

I nodded.

"Thing is, in troubled times it sometimes develops that you have to pick your place. Someone has to go about making sure things happen properly, that people are protected, goods move about, the law is applied fairly. Sooner or later it falls on some poor bugger to go out and see that it all gets done. That's sort of what we're about here, as I understand it: trying to make things a bit better. Makes up for a bit of hard living, helping others does. Ought to count against your sins, by my way of figuring."

It was something to think on.

Later, during a break, I approached Hatcher. "Are we doing good for others? This group, I mean."

She nodded. "If we are successful, definitely. Even if we fail, we're certainly trying." She looked closely at me. "Why?"

I shrugged. "I dunno. Just thinking."

"Careful how much thinking you do in the woods, it can get you into a bad place," she warned. "Best talk it over if it gets too intense. Is that fight at the Fist bothering you?"

"No. It wasn't a big fight, I've had a lot worse." I hesitated: a slave keeps his feelings close because our job was to serve, not speak. But Hatcher was friendly, and she liked to talk. "Things keep changing."

"Ah." She thought for a moment. "You don't understand where things are going, right? We're dragging you all over the place, and you're not sure why. I get it." She stood. "Come with me."

She led me to where Provine Sael stood examining the trunk of a tree, motioning Burk to close up as well. The Dellian gave us a cool look as we approached.

"Time to get the muscle read in," Hatcher announced cheerfully.

"Really." Provine Sael did not appear impressed by the idea.

"Yeah, *really*. We're dragging them all over, getting them into fights and general hard living, all without explaining *why*."

"A certain amount of secrecy is advisable in our undertaking."

"Sure, don't show them your notes. But don't treat them like a couple expendable slaves."

The Dellian visibly flinched. She opened her mouth, a flush on her cheeks, then closed it with a click of her teeth. After a moment she spoke. "I understand your concerns. The Empire is weak, has been weakened, by events of the last thirty years. There is a need for…rallying points. Symbols to help shore up the authority of the central government. I am tracking one such symbol, which was lost centuries ago. I know the name of the area where it likely ended up, but that name is a very old name, and no longer appears on any map. I know that a certain ballad has information in it that will let me put a modern name to the old name, but the ballad has been translated many times and the language changed so much that I need to see it in its original form. So we are traveling to places where the original ballad was engraved. If I can gather enough pieces of the ballad in its original form, I can puzzle out what I need to know, and we can recover the symbol."

"Your part in this is to provide security. When we are done, you will be free, and should have sufficient skills to survive on your own." She gestured back towards the mules. "After the fight in the Fist I wrote out your letters of manumission so if anything happens to me, you will still be free. Is that acceptable?"

We both nodded, and quickly withdrew.

"What was that thing about symbols?" Burk muttered as we walked.

I had been thinking about it. "Its music, two round plates they bang together. Apparently people like them."

"Huh." He was quiet for a while. "Why is the central government on a shore?"

"Probably the capitol is next to a lake. A city needs water."

"Yeah. So we get these music things, and someone plays them on the shore next to the capitol, and people rally?"

"Apparently. I think rally means 'to gather'."

We walked in silence for a while. "Seems awfully complicated," Burk finally observed.

"That was my thought, but I haven't been around much."

"Still, it is nice to know what is going on."

Chapter Five

By the third day the effect of the forest was easing off a bit; I was starting to get used to the lack of organization and the random clutter, although I was still eager to get back to civilized lands again, even just a road and farmer's fields. Someplace nice.

There was a heavy fog when we broke camp, and the clouds pressed close onto the tops of the trees, but Torl didn't seem to be affected, and led us off without hesitation.

The fog thinned so you could see maybe sixty paces (my counting lessons included gauging distances, as Hatcher said you needed to apply numbers to truly understand them), but it started raining to keep things complicated. Not a heavy rain, just occasional brief showers, but I quickly learned that among all the other bad things about a forest was the fact that rain gets spread out over a longer time under the trees because they do not drain properly and drip long after the rain stops. Trees are very useless things, in my opinion.

Hatcher wore her rain cloak which sheltered the upper half of me so I did not bother with mine, mostly to avoid the hindrance in a fight. Nothing so miserable and ugly as a forest could possibly be traversed without violence; you could tell from the way it looked that a forest was the sort of place horrible things lived.

By mid-morning we came across a long gap in the trees and began following it, and I realized it was a road, but one so badly overgrown that all that remained was the cleared line through the trees and the faint hint of ruts under the grass.

We took our mid-day break in the lee of a timber watch tower that had collapsed or been pulled down, lying alongside the road like a framework for an unfinished building. Wrecked or not, it was still nice, some straight lines and sense of order amongst this worthless wasteland of trees.

I was sitting on a waist-high beam chewing a mouthful of flatbread, cheese, and smoked sausage and watching a little frog swim in a puddle of water when Torl suddenly hushed Hatcher. We all stopped what we were doing and looked at the scout, who had his head cocked to the side, frowning.

He suddenly straightened. "People coming from the south." Three strides and he was gone, vanished into the trees, Hunter on his heels.

"Grog, Burk, have your crossbows to hand. Everyone act naturally," Provine Sael positioned her short staff across her lap and resumed eating the greens she had arranged on a small plate. Hatcher stuck two of her axes into a support beam, close to hand but out of sight of the road, and resumed her conversation with Akel. I cocked and loaded my crossbow and set it across my pack, not really out of sight, but not real obvious, and put on my kettle hat.

We heard them long before we saw them, the sound of boots on grass and the clinking of metal and wood bumping each other. Then shapes came swimming up out of the damp gray mist, looking strange and inhuman, just moving shadows that slowly became damp and mud-spattered travelers.

First were two tuskers in fighting leathers and armed with glaives, scarred and wild-looking, walking well apart, looking for trouble with the air of people who found it regularly enough. They slowed at the sight of us and one whistled. The next to appear was a red-haired man, older than me, in blackened ring mail with a sword and dirk at his belt, and a shield on his back. A couple more men, battered fighting types followed, and then two lines of people in peasant clothing walking bent under a double load of packs and fatigue. They were women and teens of both genders, healthy but exhausted and sick with fear.

It took a minute for the significance of the ropes running from one leather collar to the next: slaves, two files of ten each.

Slavers, heading north. Out of the Empire; I knew enough to realize that meant these slaves were bound for non-Human tribes, Tulgs most likely.

At a gesture from Hatcher I moved into the center of the track, crossbow in one hand, sheathed sword in the other, Burk beside me. I was glad to step up, Fellhold had a slave market, but this was different: these people had just been *made* slaves, and not legally, you could see it in their faces. This was not proper.

The red-haired man in the ring mail favored us with an appraising glance before hailing Provine Sael. "Well met, my lady. We mean no harm, and with your leave will continue on our way." His teeth showed in a smile from within a wet beard.

"Grog, Burk, kill them." Her voice was as flat and hard as the blade of a sword.

I shot the near tusker in the chest and dropped my crossbow, but Burk had hit him, too; the scabbard swept off the blade as I brought my sword into position, the further tusker coming at me fast. I choked up on the ricasso and deflected his ripping thrust, continuing the movement as I stepped in to punch the blade up through the bottom of his jaw, the roof of his mouth, and on into the brain pan.

The brute's convulsions and bone structure wedged the blade; releasing it, I swept my hammer free of my belt and charged forward, the dirk coming into position in my left hand as I faced off with the leader. Burk was fighting one of the other men but I paid him no mind; the leader had his broadsword in hand and his shield in place, one of Hatcher's axes stuck in its battered front.

Turning his thrust with my dirk I aimed a solid swing at his balding pate but just dented the iron-bound rim of his shield. He was faster than me, but I had reach and height; my hammer was a tad quicker but he had a shield; in terms of armor we were equal. I had fought more often, but he was a veteran as well, and much more familiar with his weapons and war harness. We moved, feinted, and shifted across twenty feet of trail exchanging blows and parries, dealing out damage to shields and armor without drawing blood.

He was good for someone without pit training; I had fought a lot worse. I was going to have to hammer his shield apart, I figured; I could tell he would not be as comfortable fighting without one. Eliminate the shield, and the fight would be mine. His shield was well-made, but a war hammer is an armor-cracker delivering terrific shock, and I could feel the slats wobbling more and more with each hit. The iron rim helped it stay together, but it couldn't last forever.

The slaver was trying to get steel into one of my legs to cripple me; reduce my mobility and my dirk wouldn't be enough to keep him off me, but I was having none of that. My longer reach was key in keeping that blade away, and I knew I could win this.

Except that Burk stepped up behind the man and casually stove in his skull with a short, sharp swing.

The other slavers, including two rear guards, were already dead, I saw as I staggered back, breathing hard and sweating harder. Torl's arrows stood out from a couple bodies, and Hatcher had gotten an axe into at least one.

"If you danced any longer we would have started another song," Hatcher called, grinning.

"He was good," I shrugged. "But I would have gotten him eventually."

"This is excellent," Hunter shook his head disgustedly. "Twenty peasants slowing us down." He glanced at Provine Sael. "Unless we…"

"We'll escort them south," she cut him off, calmly finishing her greens. "After we accomplish our task. They can live with a minor delay, and we are not overly pressed for time at this juncture. The place from which they were taken is only two days' travel, and not far out of our way."

He shook his head. "Wonderful."

I stayed out of it, moving down the line unfastening collars. The younger ones flinched away when I approached, scared of my size and the blood splattered on my armor; I had gotten most of it with handfuls of grass, but you have to take scale armor off and really work it to get all the blood after a good bleeder, and there wasn't time for that.

It felt strange freeing slaves, although they weren't legally slaves, I suppose. I was a legally a slave, but right now I was sort of freer than they were. It was interesting to think about.

Hatcher and Akel went through the packs and the belongings of the dead guards. "Plenty of rations, and a lot of metal," she announced, weighing a foot-long, inch-thick iron bar in one hand before pegging it into the forest. "Iron, copper, some steel."

"For weapons I don't doubt," Provine Sael shook her head. "A good day's work stopping them. Dump the metal and anything else we don't need. Torl, make sure that Tulg patrols don't find the metal. Akel, make sure no one is overloaded, and that they have bedrolls and enough clothing. Hatcher, divide the dead men's money amongst the captives." She held up a hand to forestall Hunter. "I don't care how much they were carrying."

"This is turning out to be a pretty thin trip,' Hunter snarled, ignoring the hand.

"I dunno about you, I made an easy fifteen Marks the other day," Hatcher shrugged.

The lean man flushed. "You didn't mention he was a pit fighter; I would have cleaned up if someone had read me in. That was a bull Ukar fighting close in so I figured our mutt didn't have much of a chance."

"He has a *name*," Hatcher glared at Hunter.

"Use your winnings to tattoo it on his chest."

"Both of you be quiet," Provine Sael interjected. "Enough about money. Hunter, you're being paid and I told you in advance that there would be little or no loot."

The slender man grunted angrily and shook his head. "And yet we keep finding it."

"We have an agreement."

Hunter nodded sourly. "A finite one."

I helped drag the dead into the bushes and move the discarded metal and trade goods while the captives huddled in a group and watched us with frightened eyes. I would have thought that being freed would make them happy, but they didn't look much different than they had before the fight started. Of course, they hadn't been slaves long.

When we resumed travel the former captives did in fact slow us down. Hunter pointedly ignored them, but Akel moved amongst them with a word here and a helping hand there and seemed to perk them up a bit. By the first rest break quite a few were looking less worried.

"Maybe that was what he meant," Burk muttered as we returned from wetting down the bushes.

"Who meant what?" I asked.

"Akel, when he said we should help people. Like he's doing with the captives."

I thought about that. "Good point. 'Course he's not bloody and carrying a lot of weapons. I think we wouldn't do so well."

"Yeah, I know, but it's an…," he sought the word. "Example! An example of what he meant."

"Something to think on," I nodded.

The added people made camp a much different proposition. On the one hand they performed the chores that normally fell to me and Burk, but on the other, there was a great deal more noise and confusion. Despite his complaints earlier I noticed Hunter chatting earnestly with a couple of the captives, both girls.

Hatcher took advantage of the free time to put us through our paces with the crossbow, practicing firing on the move, standing, kneeling, and prone. As the light faded she pronounced us trained; all that remained was practice and experience.

The food was better than usual because apparently some of the women were better cooks than any in our group, which Hatcher said wasn't a great distinction. Burk and I sat near Torl; Hatcher for a change was off with Provine Sael, deep in conversation, so we ate in silence, which was nice.

"How did these...people get taken?" Burk ventured to ask Torl as we were cleaning our plates.

"Spring planting, it takes everyone to get the seed into the ground. These backwards northerners still strip-farm." Seeing Burk's expression, Torl explained. "The village owns the fields, each field is divided into strips a few feet wide, and each family farms specific strips, the number of strips based on various factors such as the size of the family. In the spring the men repair drainage, haul fertilizer, and plow all the fields. The women and young people follow on, planting their strips. So you end up with a group such as you have here working in a field with just a couple men nearby. Slave-takers know this, and swoop in and grab groups moving between fields."

"Why is this backward, other than the risk of slavers?" I asked.

"It wears out the land," Torl spat. "Elsewhere in the Empire a farmer divides his land into three sections, each section in turn has a season with a grain crop, a season with a low-plant crop, and a season fallow, each in turn so he has two-thirds planted at all times. It keeps the soil healthy, you see. But here, farming in strips, no family can afford to let land lay fallow, and the soil grows weak. As villages grow and the soil gets tired, you have to keep expanding the number of fields, which means that you get groups like these," he jerked a thumb at the captives, "Trudging around further and further from home, easy pickings for a few slave-takers."

"Why don't they change the fields, then? Go to the rotation thing?"

"Dirt grubbers get very upset when you start changing who owns what land. That's why you have these villages hanging on so far north: men will go a long way and face a good deal of hardship for land they can call their own. Even if it's just twenty-foot-wide strips of a common field."

Because of the larger group, standing watch meant walking the perimeter of the camp instead of just staying awake. The ex-captives were huddled together in groups, families I supposed. I wondered what that was like: a family. I supposed an age block was sort of like a family, although I think most families don't die off so quick. Burk was sort of like a brother would be, except I don't think you are supposed to think about killing a sibling. Then again, I guess that most people don't think about killing as much as I do.

I hoped Master Horne was doing well. I know he would be glad to hear that I had taken out a bull Ukar in an even match; that certainly reflected well upon the barracks. It made me feel good to think on that.

In the morning instead of heading straight out Torl took some of the captives to cut saplings while Akel heated a block of pitch in a pot and Hatcher supervised a couple women in cutting a roll of burlap into long strips.

It turned out that this was for torches: they wrapped strips of burlap around a length of green sapling, coating the burlap with hot pitch in between wrappings. With all the extra hands it wasn't long before we had a couple dozen made. Once the pitch had cooled and hardened we bundled them up and set off.

"Ever worked underground?" Hatcher asked once we were underway, lightly drumming on my head.

"No."

"The thing to remember is that it's tight work, not much room to fight. The main point is to stick close with the group, keep your torch moving, and don't touch anything unless I've looked at it first."

"If it's a ruin, that means no one lives there, so why would we have to fight?"

"It's shelter, so we could run into Tulgs, renegades, or just people who don't want to be bothered. Plus Tulgs like to put traps in ruins because they know Humans are nosey and will poke around in odd corners. Could be we find nothing more than rats, spiders, and roth pigs, but its best to be ready."

"What's a roth pig?"

"A kind of a pig, small, like maybe forty, fifty pounds full grown, with short straight tusks; they're mean as a snake and stink to high heaven. They like roots and mosses that you get underground, so if you've got mines or underground areas that are unoccupied, they tend to find their way in. And then predators show up to hunt the roth pigs, sure as night follows day. It's a real pain to deal with the little bastards because they tend to run in packs. It's a mess skinning one so eating them is out unless you're pretty desperate. And they crap everywhere. Personally, I hope there's Tulgs or renegades at the ruins because they're easier to deal with than roth pigs. I *hate* roth pigs."

I wasn't sure what to expect; in my mind I was thinking of something like an old uninhabited building like you occasionally saw back in the city, but when we stopped in early afternoon there wasn't anything at all, just an area with smaller trees scattered a bit more widely than usual and a lot of mounds.

"We're here," Hatcher announced, somersaulting to the ground.

"Looks like forest," I observed, handing her the blanket she used for padding.

A closer look showed that the mounds were actually piles of cut stone blocks and roof tiles that had had grass grow up over them; if you raked away the thin layer of sod you could see more stones and bits of blackened beams as well. Apparently the buildings had burned, or at least the wood supports had burned, and grass covered the piles.

Provine Sael, Hatcher, and Hunter prowled the mounds, deep in discussion. They settled on one mound that didn't look any different than any of the others and put Burk and me to work on the south side.

Scraping away the thin sod, we set to work pulling out rocks and pitching them aside. I was surprised to see the outlines of a collapsed doorframe exposed fairly quickly, and within an hour we had uncovered the upper edges of a stone foundation set deep into the ground. Less than an hour after that Burk pried loose a particularly tightly wedged block and exposed the edge of a stout trap door.

Once we had uncovered the trapdoor Burk and I were sent off to wash up and have a snack while the three discussed things. By the time we returned the door had been pried open and Akel was laying out supplies.

"Take ten torches, a coil of rope, your water skin, and what weapons you think you'll be able to use," Hatcher instructed us. "We're heading in."

I left my sword and crossbow with Akel, who was staying on top with Torl, the mules, and the captives.

The trapdoor had covered a round shaft of old brickwork that dropped straight into darkness; Hatcher tied a rope around her waist and scampered down the row of hollowed places that served as a ladder. I paid out the line and stood ready to take up her full weight, but the rope slid out smoothly for sixty feet before stopping. Two hard tugs signaled that she was at the bottom, and after waiting for a fifty count I drew back the now-unburdened rope.

Hunter went next, then Provine Sael, Burk, and finally me. It took a moment to adjust to using the hollow spaces to climb with, but they were easily big enough for my booted feet, and I made the descent without much trouble or delay.

The shaft led to an empty room walled in the same brown brick as the tunnel, an oval chamber about thirty feet across. The shaft had a rusty iron grate closing it off at the chamber's ceiling, but it was open when I reached it. A heavy door in the north side of the room was open despite the presence of a stout-looking lock, and Burk was alone in the chamber, torch in hand. Light and shadows visible through the doorway indicated that the others were moving on.

"Hatcher opened the locks with little tools," Burk explained as he held his torch so I could light mine. "They're up ahead."

"I don't see any ballad," I observed, settling my grip on my war hammer.

"Maybe it has its own room," Burk shrugged. He had his short sword in hand, a good choice in my opinion. I had considered using my dirk, but had gone with the hammer in case there were roth pigs to be faced.

The corridor sloped down, and not far into it the brown bricks covering the floor stopped and three dressed-stone steps led down to seamless stone flooring. As we continued down the corridor the bricks in the wall ended, revealing a two-foot-thick foundation of dressed stone, and then on further there was blank stone underneath the foundation.

"Bedrock," Burk observed, scuffing a heel against the stone.

The air was faintly damp and stale-smelling under the sharp burning-resin odor of the torches, and I noticed that the smoke was rising and moving sluggishly back the way we came, so apparently there was some air flow through here. The big door had a row of holes drilled through its upper portion, perhaps to help the air move.

The others were waiting in a chamber that was not much more than a widening of the corridor; a rusted iron gate had secured it, but now stood open. Three identical gates were set at what I thought were the other points of the compass, and Hatcher was carefully using a thin metal probe on the lock of the one I guessed went north, a long delicate tool or probe held ready in her teeth and a number of others visible under the opened flap of one of the pouches on her belt. Hunter was holding two torches to give her light.

"Remain alert," Provine Sael advised us quietly. "There are other openings to this complex."

The foundation line was at mid-chest to me, I noticed as we waited.

"There," Hatcher removed the tool from her mouth and stepped back, stowing her equipment. Taking a torch from Hunter, she twisted the lever that opened the gate and moved through, keeping her torch low, watching the floor.

Burk signaled that he would take the rear, so I moved up behind Hatcher, who was advancing at a slow pace, Provine Sael and Hunter behind me.

Hatcher moved slowly but purposefully, a battered flat-topped, short-billed leather cap protecting her hair from sparks or drops of hot pitch from the torches. She was watching for traps, I supposed from what she had mentioned earlier. To either side the line of bricks climbed steadily upwards until only the foundation was visible, and twenty feet further the foundation vanished. Support arches of cut and mortared stone appeared every twenty feet or so, scattered unevenly.

Looking at the walls (and watching uneasily for big cracks), I nearly stepped on Hatcher when she stopped abruptly.

"Easy," she murmured and crouched, feeling the air before her.

Watching her, I suddenly realized that there was a black line bisecting her fingers. Not a black line, but a thread running horizontally across the passage about a foot off the ground. Hatcher followed it to one of the arches and studied the stone carefully. "Here, hold this close to the wall," she passed me her torch and opened a case on her belt.

The black line vanished into the wall, or at least it appeared to until the little Nisker applied a steel rod and carefully scraped away plaster covering a shallow niche in the stone.

After several minutes' work she sat back and stowed her tools.

"What was it?" Provine Sael asked quietly.

"Bottle of spirits of anther on a line of braided spider silk," Hatcher advised, coiling the trip line.

"Tulg?"

"Most likely."

"How old?"

"Can't really say. It was intended for long service, you can smell the moth-bane on the line to keep spiders from anchoring to it. Likely it's just harassment work."

This was an entirely different side of the Nisker: gone was the happy chatterer, replaced by a calm, slow, careful trap-scout.

We moved onwards, passing several doors and two intersections with other corridors. At each of the latter Provine Sael, Hunter, and Hatcher would consult before choosing a direction. Hunter was different down here as well, I noticed: calm, alert, serious.

As we moved further in things were less orderly: dirt had been tracked into the hall, the soot clinging to the ceiling was not dried and flaking, markings were chalked or scratched onto the walls.

"What was this place? It's mostly just tunnel," I asked as we lit new torches.

"The ruins we entered were a military outpost, a guard point," Hatcher rubbed her forehead with the heel of her hand, leaving a smudge of dirt. "This tunnel was used to connect several such guard points to the main fort. That way guards could move between posts and the fort in the dead of winter, that sort of thing. They added storerooms, sally routes…when labor's cheap it's easy to expand underground areas. We're looking for the tomb of a hero who was buried here."

"At least there's no roth pigs," I pointed out.

"Yeah, but I wouldn't be surprised if we run into Undead. Necromancers like to practice in old places like this, and they're like the Tulg: they like to leave surprises for the curious."

I didn't like it down here: the dry air, dust, and stink of the torches combined to give me a headache, and the flickering shadows from the torches and the uneven surfaces of the walls made everything look like a trap. The fact that Hatcher found and disarmed three more traps and we found the stinking remains of a roth pig that had tripped a fourth did nothing to improve the place for me.

Hatcher said the place had been abandoned for centuries, at least abandoned by the Empire; other groups had used the tunnels and expanded them to suit their purposes. I could see that the quality and style of workmanship in the side-tunnels we passed were vastly different from the one we were following.

"So why did the Empire abandon a big fort?" I asked during a rest break.

"The main position was stormed and razed," Hatcher ripped a strip of jerky free with her teeth and chewed with difficulty. "Damn, this stuff is tough. And bland. Anyhow, the fort got razed, so they built somewhere else because of cost or military necessity or a better view, whatever, and other'n smugglers, Tulg, people looking to do stuff they shouldn't do a long way from anyone else, it didn't see any use."

"Sounds like a lot of use, actually."

"It is, really. They ought to have a sign out there, *'welcome to tunnel-side, population a hundred and sixty. Please don't feed the fuggin' roth pigs'*, that sort of thing. Only that's stretched out over a couple centuries, so figure maybe a quarter of the time someone's here."

"And the tomb was left here."

"Well, not the guy buried in it; they moved his body to the capitol before the fort fell. But they left the tomb itself, obviously, and that's what we're here to see. See, he was part of Old Umbargen's Red Guard, his original personal retinue." Seeing my blank look, she explained: "Umbargen was the guy who turned the Empire...well, he united a bunch of squabbling little countries and city-states and what-not into the Empire. He's a legend now, folk-story stuff, great and noble and wise. Truth be told, he was tough and mean and smart, and in the right place at the right time with enough balls to pull the whole thing off. And lucky as blazes."

"Anyhow, near the end of the period where he was just a warlord with a bunch of loyal mean bastards, a scholar fell in with him, or maybe he hired him. Anyway, this scholar, Hamer, saw part of it, and got the rest of the story of how Umbargen went from being a small-time Baron to the first

Emperor from the Red Guards. Hamer wrote the whole thing up, first as a serious history, then as a ballad, or epic poem."

"The history didn't catch on but the ballad did. Trouble was, as time went on and real bards got ahold of it, Umbargen and the Red Guard stopped being a bunch of murderous thugs and instead became courtly knights, tall and fair to look upon and all that drivel."

"A lot, most, rulers wouldn't want the details of who they killed on their way to power recorded accurately, but Umbargen was an exception: he really liked Hamer's work. He ordered that the ballad in its entirety be engraved on the lid of his coffin, and every one of the Red Guard had it engraved somewhere in their burial places, too. These days, those are the only uncorrupted copies of Hamer's ballad that anyone knows about."

"Why not just visit Umbargen's tomb, then?"

"Because he's not in it, Umbargen III built it. Whatever else you can say about Umbargen and the Red Guard, the fact was they were tough men, the real steel. They carved the Empire out the hard way, and paid the price themselves. Umbargen was buried by the surviving members of the Red Guard in a cave, and the location is lost to this day. The Red Guard, those that survived the wars creating the Empire, were real leaders and died in out-of-the-way places, like this fellow we're after."

I thought about this. "So a member of the Red Guard died at this fort and was buried here. Later, before the fort fell, they got his body to safety. Provine Sael wants to find the tomb because there will be a copy, an original copy, of Hamer's ballad about the first Emperor carved in it."

"Yup. Providing the tomb is intact; the first one we found had been wrecked long ago."

"I've heard of the Red Guard; recently, I mean, not from long ago."

"Yeah, old Umbargen's descendant, Umbargen III, the one who built the huge fancy tomb that's got no corpse in it, he named the Emperor's personal guards the Red Guard. Thing is, the original Red Guard wasn't

Umbargen's bodyguards, they were his friends, advisors, generals…his inner circle. Umbargen III is the one who really got things going on making his namesake a great and noble ruler who was pure of heart and deed, and named his son, the current Emperor, after the old bastard, too."

"So if Umbargen the First lived hundreds of years ago, why is the current Emperor Umbargen IV? People don't live that long."

"There were a lot of Emperors between Umbargen I and the current Emperor; Umbargen II was actually the grandson of the first Emperor, and it was at least a century, probably more, before Umbargen III took the throne, and he ruled for nearly seventy years. The Emperors were all related, but they used their own names. Umbargen III took the founder's name when he was crowned, he named his son Umbargen, and built the tomb and all that as a way of reminding people of the Empire's origins and history. He was trying to build up pride and rekindle the spirit that made the Empire great."

"Did it work?"

"Some. It would have helped if he had had a son survive infancy earlier in his life, but that's how things go sometimes." She sighed and stood. "We're close; lets finish this."

Hatcher found one more trap before we turned down an off-shoot that didn't look any different than any others and entered a chamber. Or rather, approached a chamber which turned out to be full.

"What the blazes?" the little Nisker muttered, moving her torch in short arcs around the doorway. "It's full."

"Bags," I nodded. "Looks like burlap."

Neatly stacked, as a point of fact. After Hatcher was comfortable with the doorway's trap-free state I moved up and saw that the chamber was oval, about a hundred feet at the wide point, and at least sixty feet high. And almost entirely full of stacked bags, a great block of hundreds of sacks.

"You could dam a river with that lot," Hatcher kicked one near the bottom and swore. "Solid, feels like sand. No, gravel. What's this?"

"It drives away rodents and insects." I hadn't heard Provine Sael approach. She took the engraved tile Hatcher had found and examined it before handing it back.

"They must have opened it from the surface and slung the bags in that way," Hatcher speculated, peering up. "Nice job; looks like they left about six inches clearance around each wall. A lot of work went into this."

The Dellian thoughtfully tapped the burlap wall with her staff. "Grog, slice this bag. Hatcher, move back."

The pressure of the bags atop it forced me to work the blade of my knife into the slit before the contents started to come out. Provine Sael caught a couple of the dark blocks that spilled out, irregular chunks of some coarse, light material that made me think of plaster mixed with straw. She sniffed them, and then nibbled at an edge. "Compressed rations," she tossed them onto the floor. "Fifty-pound sacks, I would guess."

"Protected for long storage," Hatcher kicked the tile down the corridor. "A cache."

"I would suppose it is just one of several."

"Wonderful." Catching my look, Hatcher gestured towards the spilled contents of the bag. "You take cabbage, lettuce, sliced up turnips and spuds, all that sort of stuff, get it good and wet and then compress it into forms, and by compress I mean *hard*, squeeze all the water out with a thing like a wine press. Takes time. You end up with a block of material you chop into little chunks, and it lasts for years. You take a handful of those chunks and toss 'em into a pot of water and heat it up, you've got soup or mush, depends on the amount of water you use. Add in some salt and jerky, you've got sort of a stew. However you do it, it's healthy, keeps you going. Tastes like crap, and if you're using it to feed Ukar or Tulgs they'll get mean as blazes wanting meat, but it's light and it lasts. A pound of it, dry, would keep even a big'un like you for a day so long as you had time and the water to prepare it."

"Fifty-pound sacks, feed fifty for one day, or one for fifty days…," I muttered, looking at the block of sacks, my new-found numbers rattling around in my thick head.

"Yeah," Hatcher nodded. "There's enough to feed an army in there."

Hatcher and Hunter went back to tell Torl the news while Burk and I started shifting bags. We didn't need to empty the room, just move enough bags from the doorway so that Provine Sael could squeeze into the narrow open space that had been left along the wall. She had to leave her sword belt and cloak, but she fit. She slipped into the left side, trailing her haversack behind her.

Half a torch later Hatcher returned alone. "Where's Provine Sael?"

I jerked a thumb towards the chamber. "Along the wall."

"Well, damn," Hatcher examined our handiwork. "Move these bags here and I'll get up on top. I'm not going to try to fit into that space." She patted her bosom. "Not all of me is small."

Once we had cleared away enough bags I boosted her up, and she scampered off, returning shortly to report that the Dellian had found the ballad, which was carved into granite slabs set into the walls.

Hatcher fetched candles and water for Provine Sael over the next couple hours. It took about a half hour for a torch to burn out, and Burk and I burned out four each and made a good start on a fifth before the Dellian emerged from the right side of the doorway, dirty and grinning.

Hatcher scrambled down the bags without waiting for a hand. "So you've got it?"

"Indeed," The Dellian tried to blank her face, but the smile fought to hold its ground. "But there is a great deal of research yet to be done."

"Do we need to stay here any longer?"

"No, the slabs bearing the ballad were intact. Translation and cross-reference will take time, but that time will be spent elsewhere."

It was getting towards sundown when we emerged from the trapdoor, and I for one was very glad to be out of the place. We snuffed out our torches and gave the unused ones back to Akel, along with the rope.

"Success," Provine Sael informed Hunter and Torl; she had her face back on, the cool disinterested one. I thought she looked a lot prettier when she had been happy. "What did you find?"

"Three more chambers loaded, two of dried rations, one of dried meat in barrels. There's strap iron, planks, nails, rolled leather, and five hundredweight of good coal stashed in a half-building that still has a roof," Torl reported. "Can't say who put it there given the time that has passed, but my guess is Tulg, maybe five weeks ago."

"Those sacks were stacked with precision," Provine Sael stroked a horn. "Tulg would only have attended to such detail if they had exceptionally strong leadership."

"Dusmen," Hunter spat it like a curse.

"That would be my guess," Torl nodded. "Rations and repair materials positioned for a rapid and sizeable advance."

Provine Sael squatted and unrolled a leather sheet on the ground. "What is the target?"

"Too far south for it to be the Fist," Torl traced a finger across lines burned into the leather. "Merrywine would be my bet." He tapped the sheet. "Take it, and you've a navigable river heading south-southeast."

"A raid?" Hunter asked.

"Too big for a raid, too much preparation," Torl shook his head. "I'm thinking this is an incursion. A demonstration in force; they push the Empire to see how hard the Empire pushes back. It has been a few years since they really tested the Legions' mettle, might be they think it is time to see how things stand."

"Any sign that Imperial patrols are operating this far north?" Provine Sael absently smoothed the leather sheet.

"No. At the Fist they said they hadn't seen one in months."

"That's it, then." The Dellian stood and rolled the sheet up. "Torl, give us an hour head start and then set fire to those repair supplies in the half-building. We'll head to Merrywine and pass the word. I need to get there ahead the enemy because what I want might not be there afterwards."

Chapter Six

"What was that sheet of leather they were looking at?" I asked Hatcher after we got the captives moving again.

"What, the map?" The Nisker was riding again.

"I guess."

"It was a map, a map is like…let's see…like a drawing of an area, only everything is set out the way they really are, in relation to each other. I'll show you when we have time, it's easier to understand when you're looking at one. A good map is a valuable thing."

We marched for a couple hours before making camp, and Provine Sael set a brisk pace; Burk had to carry a girl who couldn't keep up. He kept his face set like stone but I could see he was uneasy: these sort of things never happened back at the barracks. I think it is the effect of operating in forests, where poor planning and a lack of order abounds. There's really nothing as useless as a forest.

When I woke up in the morning Torl was sitting by the fire looking like he always did. I couldn't imagine trying to move through the forest at night, but Torl was clearly a man of sterner material. I noticed the captives didn't mind the forest, and even girls who were frightened by Burk or me passing within six feet thought nothing of dashing off to fetch water or gather branches for bedding.

Torl kept the pace brisk, angling off the old road and along a creek or stream, some sort of random waterway flowing for no apparent purpose.

"If you ever get lost, follow the water downstream," Hatcher observed as we trudged along, seeing trees that looked just like the trees we had seen earlier.

"Why?"

"It is likely to lead you to people. People build along water sources, and the land is always flatter downstream."

"Always?"

She laughed. "Grog, water doesn't run uphill."

I hadn't considered that. I wasn't so stupid as to not to realize that water flowed down an incline, but I hadn't realized that the stream would be seeking out lower ground. I eyed the stream suspiciously, wondering what else it was up to that I didn't know about.

We started crossing cleared ground soon after that, and not long after mid-day reached the captives' village. Our timing was good: the entire village was preparing to move.

The captives and other villagers shrieked and cried and ran about hugging and exclaiming in a very disorganized fashion when we entered the village square, and there was a great deal of thanking and bowing to Provine Sael. Burk and I dropped back to the mules and tried to be inconspicuous.

"I guess they're happy to get home," Burk muttered.

"Seem to be," I nodded. "I know I would be glad to see the barracks again."

"Me, too." That surprised me.

"If we were at home we would have a match this week, I think."

"Yep. I like it better when you know when a fight's expected. This business of wandering around waiting for trouble to show up isn't very practical."

"It's certainly not how Master Horne did things," I agreed. "The forests are not proper, either. Very untidy. I've got nothing against trees, but you need some sort of organization."

"It was better closer to Fellhome: people there knew what they were doing. They had standards, and the trees were in rows. These people don't seem to be very well organized: look how the buildings are out of line with each other. No real streets."

"Even the Brocks are better situated."

"Why are they moving?" I asked Hatcher as we headed out.

" 'Fleeing' is the word," she advised grimly. "See that smoke?" she gestured to a faint plume to the northwest. "That was a village. Turns out Torl was right: we're smack in the path of an incursion. Tulg scouts are swarming all over the place, that's why everyone is heading south."

"So now what?"

"We're heading to Merrywine," Hatcher sighed.

"That's where the incursion is headed," I said slowly.

"Yup. How it works is the garrison and whatever the Legion has to hand will use it as a breakwater while the common folk head south. This is going to get very ugly."

I thought about it for a bit. "So it is going to be a siege?"

"Some siege, some fighting. From what I'm told Merrywine's defenses aren't the best, so even odds say they'll be doing a bit of the old street-to-street before it's over. The idea is to break the incursion, or hold it until help arrives. Either way, the dirt-grubbers need to get away safely. Provine Sael needs to get there and look at something, so we we'll get a front-row seat for the opening songs but hopefully not the entire opera. Hard to bet on how close a thing like that goes."

I wasn't sure what an opera was, but I understood what she meant. "I guess if help doesn't arrive in time and they don't break the incursion, then they die," I ventured.

"Yup."

"Will there be a way to send a letter in Merrywine?"

"Yeah, why?"

"It is important we get word to Master Horne so he will know we have conducted ourselves properly and upheld the barrack's good name, in case me and Burk get killed in the fighting."

She was quiet for a long time after that.

As we walked I thought about what she said. Make a stand, to act as a barrier between the incursion and the people like the captives, people with families and homes and little strips of land they planted things in.

Fighting was what I do, it is my purpose. Akel said I should not have a life that was just a trail of bodies, but I thought this might be different, that it might be considered helping people, the way we had kept those villagers from being sold to the Tulg. That could be a good thing.

I resolved to check my thinking with Akel at the first opportunity.

The further south we went the more villagers we overtook and passed, whole families on the move. A couple had carts pulled by horses or cows, a few had little carts or barrows they pushed by hand, and the rest just lugged what they could carry on their backs. Some herded goats or sheep or pigs or even geese. All looked worried and ready to panic.

To me, they looked the way I felt when Master Horne told me I was being sold to Provine Sael.

Maybe even worse.

Hunter was arguing with Provine Sael as we walked, but I didn't pay much attention, being too busy watching the people we passed and thinking on the possibility I would fight in a real battle. It wasn't until we finally took a break and Hunter confronted Hatcher that I found out what the dispute was about, not that I was much interested.

"You need to talk some sense into her," Hunter snarled at Hatcher as she stretched, having just gotten down.

"Why?"

"You know damned well she wants to stay over at Merrywine."

"What's wrong with that?"

"Don't be coy: there's a damned good chance of dying."

"The Tulg won't have siege gear, and even with Ukar they'll play merry hell trying to carry the walls. You got somewhere better to be?" The little Nisker grinned at him.

"There's no money in it," Hunter shook his head, scowling. "Leave it to the Legion."

"The Legion is going to need all the help it can get."

"I didn't hire on for this hero business. No one a hundred miles from here is going to even hear about this raid."

"I don't care who hears what, or where. You how it works: if you don't stop an incursion they'll over-run the peasants before they can get clear and carry off those they don't kill."

"The Legion will make a stand at Merrywine; that's their job."

"If the Legion has any troops there; otherwise it's just the city garrison."

"Still someone else's job."

"Every dirty detail is always someone else's job," Hatcher spat disgustedly. "That's why the Empire's in the shape it's in. There's always twenty with their hands out for alms, but no one when they're issuing blades. Someone has to step up."

"I don't."

"Your choice, but run and you can bet I'll tell everyone I know and any stranger who'll stand still that you're a coward, a fake, and prone to buggery."

Hunter stared at her for a moment, and then snorted. "I've done a lot worse than run, defraud, and bugger." He rubbed his stubbly scalp, watching the villagers trudge past. "No doubt I'll do worse in the future, too."

We lit torches so we could stay on the road a couple hours after full dark, passing small groups of people huddled around campfires who watched us with fear. Hatcher said they were refugees now, on account of them seeking refuge, and that they had good reason to be afraid as terrible things happened in times such as these. She didn't go into detail, but I could guess.

We pushed hard and reached Merrywine by mid-morning, a full day earlier than Provine Sael had initially planned, according to Hatcher. Merrywine was a town, probably a couple hundred buildings I guessed from the size, fully enclosed by a timber wall with square towers jutting out every sixty feet or so. The timbers had been scorched black; Akel said so it would be harder to set them on fire, and the lower third was coated in clay for the same reason. A ditch filled with stakes surrounded the wall, and there were stakes and abatis in front of the ditch, along with freshly-painted posts that Hatcher said were to mark the exact range at different points so the defenders knew how to adjust their fire for distance.

It made me uneasy, looking at the defenses and seeing the thought that smart people had put into them; I was trained to fight one-on-one, but this spoke of real battles, big fights of which I knew little. I am stupid, but even I could see that this was a business which would see a lot of killing before it was done.

Merrywine was built on the east bank of a river that ran mostly north and south, and the busy pace of the water renewed my suspicion now that I was aware of its nature. The town itself was on a slightly higher place so it had a wall but no towers along the river side, the base of the wall standing about twenty feet over the water and maybe thirty-five feet back.

The main gatehouse into the town was made of cut stone, and most of it looked new, like they had worked on it slowly over a long while and had finished recently. We didn't get too close to the gatehouse at first because soldiers had set up a barricade across the road and everyone had to stop. Nearly all the refugees were being directed to a dock where rafts and barges were ferrying them across the river, which was only about a hundred feet wide, to a road going south. Those with goats and sheep and other little herds were being diverted into a field where it looked as if men were buying the animals.

"Buying up food supplies," Hatcher explained when I pointed it out to her. "They make sure the refugees keep heading south, and secure any excess food. That way the garrison can hold out a lot longer."

"Why don't the Ukar and Tulg just go around the town?" I asked, having thought about that. I had to raise my voice to be heard even though she was sitting on my shoulders because we were in the midst of a long column of refugees waiting to reach the barricade, and there were a lot of voices and animals.

"If this was just a raid, they would," Hatcher drummed away. "But it's an incursion, figure at least a thousand troops. They'll need carts, wagons, and slaves to haul food and gear, and to carry away loot. Things with wheels need roads, and if you look at the map you can see that every road hereabouts passes through Merrywine. The troops could slip past, but not a supply train." She unrolled the sheet of leather and held it in front of my face. "See?"

Burk and I studied the burned lines. "Why did they build all the roads that way?" Burk asked.

"A road is made so wagons and carts can move things without beating themselves to pieces. Farmers grow food, and what they can't eat they haul someplace where there's people but not a lot of growing space; a city or town, in other words."

Like the water, this established a purpose in something that I had assumed just existed, and I found that to be unsettling. It was as if there was a vast conspiracy of purpose of which I was largely ignorant. Being stupid was proving to be more and more of an impediment with each passing day.

"So they have to take Merrywine to go south," I observed. "Look, after Merrywine the roads don't really come together again until way down here."

"That's Fellhome," Hatcher observed matter-of-factly as she rolled up the map.

Burk and I exchanged a look as we shuffled forward a few steps and stopped. "If they get through here, they could reach Fellhome?" Burk asked, in a way that suggested he knew the answer but didn't like it.

"If the Legion doesn't get enough troops into the area in time to stop them, sure."

Burk nodded thoughtfully, fingering the hilt of his sword. I drummed my fingers on my armored chest and stood on tiptoes to see the front of the line.

I wasn't surprised to see that Provine Sael had made her way directly to the head of the queue and was talking to an officer. It was also no surprise that despite being overworked, they were paying attention to her; she had that effect on people.

She came back with a soldier in tow and waved us out of the queue; an older man a bit better dressed than most around us started to protest, but I stepped up to him and he stopped talking, at least while we were within earshot.

We headed into the pasture where the animals were being purchased, circling around to stand near the buyers, who had some tables set up. Provine Sael spoke at length with some officials and some officers, showing them some documents and being shown some in return. After a while she came back over to where we were waiting.

The Dellian scowled at the ground for a bit before confronting Burk and myself, tapping her staff into her palm. "Do you understand what is happening here?"

"There is an incursion. They have to take Merrywine to get to Fellhome because of the roads," I gestured towards the town as if presenting proof.

"Very good. I have to look at something in the city, and to be allowed in, I have to agree to stay and help. Imperial troops have not arrived yet, and are not likely to before the enemy reaches the town; this will be desperate work, especially if they carry the walls, so I cannot in good conscience order you as slaves to take part in this. Yet I need your services afterwards, to complete the tasks I have undertaken. I am in a dilemma." She pulled her writing kit from the back of her belt. "I have already written your letters of manumission, and they only require a magistrate's seal; however, I would not expect you to pay such a price for your freedom. I am certain your master would welcome you back without question, so if you want, I could send you back to Fellhome."

The slender Dellian fixed us with her icy gaze. "What will you do? Return to Fellhome or stand here with me?"

For an awful, aching moment the thought of going back to Fellhome filled me with hope, but beside me Burk straightened to his Noble Ukar stance, and thumped his chest with a clenched fist. "We'll stand with you, mistress."

Standards, always with his Standards. I could go home, Master Horne would certainly be glad to put me back to escorts and fighting in the pit, for a wage because I was free now, or would when my letter was stamped. I could fight and die as was my place in life. I was Grog, a pit fighter of the High Rate.

But the Ukar and Tulg were coming south like blood running down the face of the leather map, and only Merrywine stood between them and Fellhome. My home.

The Ebon Blades are a proper barracks of the old school, and when you engage their services, you get a proper job. I thumped my chest.

I was surprised that Hunter agreed to stay; he didn't look very happy about it, but he didn't argue, either. He just shot Hatcher a sardonic look and nodded when Provine Sael asked him. Everyone else was willing, too. I wasn't terribly happy myself, having had the thought of going back to Fellhome, far from forests and untrustworthy water, but Burk was right: this was the proper thing to do. I was glad he was around to keep my mind in the right place.

Chapter Seven

Torl led us through the passage under the stone gatehouse into Merrywine, where soldiers and officials were waiting. I was struck by the strange notion that this was akin to our first meeting with Provine Sael as she came through Fellhome's gatehouse, only this time we were coming in and others were loitering, awaiting a duty. When you are stupid you think strange things; I'm sure Master Horne and Provine Sael never thought such things, having more important thoughts to weigh.

Provine Sael did most of the talking, explaining that we were here to help. There were others queued up to get in, mostly fighting men or young craftsmen with tools loaded aboard carts or mules.

"Mercenaries and journeymen," Akel nodded at our compatriots. "Come to earn gold or make their masters' mark on the quick. They're a sure sign trouble is coming."

"Why are they here quicker than the Legion?"

"Started out closer, and it is easier for a small group to move fast than a large. The Legion won't dispatch a cohort until they're sure it's a real problem, but a sell-sword goes on the drop of a rumor. No doubt the Lord Mayor dispatched birds requesting all manner of help."

"Why are the craftsmen here?"

Akel grinned. "It takes a journeyman quite a few years to work his way through a Guild's standards and get his title as a Master Craftsman. Thing is, there's an exception: a journeyman can be awarded his Mastership for a significant contribution to the Empire, such as aiding in a siege. There will be a lot of demand for workers of metal, wood, leather, and the like in the days to come, much more than would normally be available in a town this size. The garrison will be encouraging four out of five of the town's inhabitants to get out of the burg to reduce the number of mouths to feed, and will be checking this lot to make sure they'll be of use."

"Have you been in this sort of thing before?"

"Four years as a Legion accounts clerk, and then six years as a notary in a town much like this one." His normally cheerful face darkened. "We held out for two weeks, but the Legion never arrived."

Unexpectedly, our group split up, although Provine Sael was very clear that Hatcher would serve to keep us all in touch. Torl was going to be working with scouts and later, archers, while Provine Sael would be going about her errand here, with Akel to assist. Hunter had some arrangement of his own and was welcomed with enthusiasm by the officials inside the gate.

"Come on, I'll help you two get situated," Hatcher announced to Burk and me. "We've been attached to a decent outfit. Way it works is, when the rough stuff starts we'll help defend the town, except for Torl and Hunter. Those two will be used where their talents are best employed."

She led us over to a man sitting on a keg whittling on a stick, a carved bone toothpick in his mouth moving in time to the little knife-blade. A standard with a tan swallow-tail banner depicting a red and black rooster leaned against the wall next to him. He was a bit over average height and burly, a little soft in the gut but very solid across the shoulders, dressed in fighting leathers and a blackened mail shirt, a long axe leaning against his keg, close to hand, and a long dirk was sheathed at his hip. "The Barley Company, I take it?"

"So the bird says," the man rapped the stick against his knee to dislodge shavings, and I saw that he was carving a figure, it looked like a woman. "Yesten, they call me, Company Quartermaster. The Paymaster's around here somewhere."

Yesten had a greasy beard worn short, dark with plenty of silver, and a silver-threaded circle of dark hair around a bald pate. He looked thoughtful and tired, and I marked him as a one who would fight without flair but would be a hard man to kill.

"We have been assigned as auxiliaries to a reputable company for the duration of the siege," Hatcher hooked her thumbs in her belt.

"So it's a siege, then?"

"You know what I mean. These are hard lads, pit fighters with their own gear and a lake of blood behind 'em. Plus me as a sort of jack-of-all-trades, a Healer, and her assistant." It took a minute for me to realize that she was referring to Akel. "The last two will be delayed a couple days before joining."

"They look like slaves."

"Pit fighters from Fellhome, over a hundred death matches between 'em, and some rough business since."

"I heard that a brute beat a full-blood to death with his bare hands a short while ago, up in Ganter's Fist."

"Not quite bare-handed, but yeah, Grog here did the job." Hatcher jabbed a thumb over her shoulder. "Burk's the other, both good hands. I've seen 'em fight."

"Given the great respect I have for your opinion, I am very reassured," Yesten nodded to Hatcher. "All the more so because no woman has ever told me something that wasn't true."

"You've heard about the fight at Ganter's Fist," Hatcher grinned at Yesten.

"We don't have much call for beating Ukar to death with our bare hands," Yesten said to his carving. "We normally just hack at them." He looked up at me, and his dark eyes were hard and calm. "You mind killing Ukar, brute?"

"Not at all." Beside me Burk grunted an agreement.

"The Barley Company stands by their own," he sounded as if he were talking about the weather. "We distribute an honest share, both rations and loot, and expect obedience. We are professionals: we do a fair job and expect fair pay. No horseplay, no skylarking, and none of that business of badger the newcomer. You serve with us, you shoulder your share and stand firm when the steel sings, understood?"

We understood.

"Since you've your own gear there's nothing much for me to do with you, so grab a patch of barracks space and relax. We're signed on with the garrison for the duration. Veterans draw six shillings a day and rations, and all loot taken is turned in to me and shared out. We pay every fifth day, given the circumstances. We'll be in the thick of it once the dance begins, but otherwise they leave us out of the petty work. You're only signed on for the duration, but while you're under the standard you serve the Company, understand?"

Listening to Yesten was stilling my nervousness because he talked like Master Horne and the agents at the barracks: firm, straightforward, unexcited. Familiar ground for me.

"Six shillings a day?" Hatcher threw up her arms. "That's what they're paying farm boys who have to be told which end of the spear you point at the enemy."

"We have negotiated bonuses based on unit actions and performance," Yesten carefully peeled a spiral of wood off the carving. "The daily pay is just to keep us interested and out of mischief."

"Look at these two: they're a file by themselves."

Yesten didn't look. "It takes more than height and a mouthpiece to win acclaim in the Barley Company. Plus they have to make up for you."

"So you say," Hatcher grinned at the mercenary, hands resting on her knife hilts. "I'm hell in a fair fight, and I don't often fight fair."

"Amazing coincidence, there: neither do we."

She motioned for us to step away from Yesten. "It's a good deal; I've heard of this bunch before: very good reputation for fair dealing and good service. We'll do well with them, just keep our heads down and follow orders. Let's get a look at our quarters and find something to eat, and then we'll get your letter, Grog. You, too, Burk, if you want to send one."

The Barley Company was billeted in a warehouse and had set up a cooking area out back. We got straw and blankets from the billets master and picked out a spot along a wall. I was surprised that there wasn't anyone else in the building.

"This isn't bad," Hatcher surveyed the warehouse. "The stone floor's a bit rough, but it has a decent roof, and looks like it was a dry goods place." Catching my look, she explained. "No rats or fleas. A warehouse where they store foodstuffs or fleece, wool, hides, that sort of thing, is going to be rat-infested and lousy. Looks like Yesten knows his business."

"I thought we would be in a barracks."

"Those are for the regular troops. Mercenaries take what's left, and for the moment we're mercenaries. Let's see what we can do for food."

The cooking area was set up under a canvas roof held up by poles. A ruddy-faced fat man in a greasy apron sat in a fancy chair made of ox-horns and leather cushions, keeping an eye on a handful of skinny kids peeling potatoes and tending the fire in an oven. "You the master cook?" Hatcher asked the fat man.

"At the moment." The fat man turned to regard her with uninterested eyes. "Pushin. New-hires?"

"Hatcher. Sort of, auxiliaries for the duration."

"And you figured that I don't have anything better to do than to feed you."

Hatcher gestured towards us. "They've been on field rations for a while. Events kind of caught up with us on the road and we ended up marching all night to get here, and now we're in for a siege."

Pushin glanced at us, and I saw a quick, experienced evaluation made behind his eyes, which were in no way as sleepy-looking as his expression. "Pip, get this lot some stew and spuds. We're out of bread until the next batch rises," he explained to Hatcher.

"That's how it goes," she nodded, pulling her eating gear out. "How is this place looking?"

"Middling fair," the cook shrugged. "The defenses aren't much to get excited about, but there's some hard lads standing behind them, and the Ukar won't have heavy gear. It'll come down to cold steel, I figure."

Hatcher nodded as the boy called Pip ladled out stew and slid a tray of cold baked potatoes onto the serving table. "House to house?"

The cook shrugged. "Hopefully not, but the lads are sorting out a few places on the off-chance. Where are you coming from?"

"Most recently Ganter's Fist, then some digging about to the north. Ran into some slavers, and then signs of the Ukar heading south."

The cook looked at where me and Burk were spooning down a better-than-fair stew. "I heard a brute killed a full-blood at the Fist, bare hands."

"Grog, on the left. Wasn't exactly bare-handed, but it wasn't hard for him, either."

"I would like to have seen that," Pushin produced a fancy pouch and extracted a small wizened black thing which he popped into his mouth. "I never mind seeing an Ukar get what's coming to it. Pip, get those two another bowlful. Slavers, you say?"

"Yeah, grabbed up some farmers."

"Strip-farming," the cook shook his head. He had tucked whatever he had gotten from the pouch between his gum and lip, where it bulged out like a tumor. "Damned locals; what can you do? You kill all the slavers?"

"Yeah, we like things neat. These are good potatoes."

"They do well in this soil. Myself, I like the little red ones, but these big brown spuds are best for feeding troops."

After we ate Hatcher wrote a letter for us; she used it to give us an idea of putting the symbols for letters into groups to form words, and use the words to build a sentence. It was just a kind of quick look at the business of writing, but it made a lot of sense.

The letter said that we were well and hoped Master Horne was well. It described our actions and that we intended to make a stand here in Merrywine to protect Fellhome, and would do everything we could to uphold the good name of the Ebon Blades.

It was good to send word, and nice to know that Master Horne would hear of our actions. Our departure would have left a gap in his fighting roster, and I was concerned that the barrack's reputation might suffer a bit until some of the younger fighters hit their stride. Burk and I discussed this at length, debating whether to include our estimates of some of our younger comrades in the letter, but decided against it because Master Horne knew the business better than we did.

"You think Master Horne...worries about you?" Hatcher asked after we returned from paying a messenger to deliver the letter, hoisting herself to sit on a handy rail.

"Well...that we conduct ourselves properly. The Ebon Blades are a well-established barracks of the old school. When you commission a job from the Ebon Blades, you get proper service."

"The Ebon Blades trains children and then sends them into the pit or on escorts," Hatcher pointed out.

"Yes, that's true."

"Slavers, like those we killed a few days ago."

"Slavers, but not at all like those a few days ago," I objected. "Those people were being kidnapped and were being taken to the Tulg. I was born a slave, and raised by my rightful master. Master Horne raised me, us, from a cub. That cost a lot, so it's only fair he see a return on his investment. Some of our age block died in their first death match and were a complete loss."

She grinned at me. "I'm listening to a slave defend slavery."

I nodded slowly. "Yeah. It's just...Master Horne made me who I am."

"Sixty went into the pit with you. None came out."

"But I did come out, because of Master Horne."

"True. But he sent you into the pit in the first place."

"He had raised me, and he needed a return on his investment."

She nodded thoughtfully. "You ever think of the sixty or more you killed in the pit?"

"The fights? Of course, Master Horne was very strict about recording the details."

"No, the dead, not the fights themselves. Those you killed. Someone put them in the pit."

"Yeah." I looked at Burk, but he was staying out of it. "Some were free, some slaves, some captives. I killed them; once in the pit, only one comes out, that is the rule. It was our place."

"You really believe that?"

"Yeah. You believe my place is in the fighting line," I pointed out. "So does Provine Sael."

Hatcher scowled. "Not in the pit." She shrugged. "There's a point there: slave or free means squat if you catch a blade. It just seems cleaner when it's for money, your own money."

"I suppose." A thought occurred to me. "It's like you said: I am an expensive slave. Probably I don't see things like most slaves do."

"Good point." She sighed. "Free people end up having to do terrible things to keep body and soul together as well. We do what we can and go on."

The next couple days passed very quickly. The Barley Company had taken on an equal number of militia and auxiliaries like ourselves, organized in files of eight, with four veteran mercenaries and four militia. Five files made a block, three blocks made a century, and the Company had two centuries.

We rose at dawn, had a hearty if simple breakfast, and set about our duties. Most of the militia and auxiliaries, which the mercenaries referred to as fillers or new fish, spent the day in drill and weapons-training. Hatcher was assigned as a runner for our Block, and after watching us go through a single weapons drill the block-leader put Burk and me with a veteran to learn fighting within a unit.

It was drill until noon, eat, have an hour's explanation on military subjects, then drill until sundown, get a large meal, clean your gear, stand inspection, and then to bed. The Company was very focused upon cleanliness, another aspect Burk and me found to be a comforting reminder of the barracks.

During this training I learned that when people referred to 'the Legion', they were actually talking about the

Imperial Army; the Army had twenty-three Legions, each a military unit of seven infantry and three cavalry Cohorts; a Legion had about five thousand warriors at full strength, but none of the twenty-three were at full strength. The Red Guard was also the size and configuration of a Legion, and it was always at full strength.

The mercenaries who were not in charge of training were assigned to details of some sort; I wasn't clear on what they did, nor did I really care. They didn't need to teach me and Burk anything about weapons or fighting, but we knew almost nothing about combat in a group. The mercenary assigned to teach us was also our file-leader, a short brute named Gareth who had small tusks coated in gold. He reminded me of a belligerent bullfrog, and he made it very clear he wasn't impressed by us, which was fine with me because I was ready to feed him his own face five minutes after I met him.

He knew his business, I will give him that, and by the second evening we could drill better than any other fillers and were getting a real feel for fighting in formation. I still wouldn't mind gutting Gareth, though.

The fillers bunked apart from the mercenaries; Burk and I had established a corner for ourselves and Hatcher through the simple process of being bigger than anyone else. The fillers were mostly farm workers and day laborers in their early twenties, tough from hard work but not any sort of fighting men. They shied away from us and I was fine with that; they might be free men, but that wouldn't mean a thing when the steel came out. I have killed enough free pit fighters to not be impressed by status. Steel didn't care if you wore a collar or not.

We had finished the evening meal, and had touched up our equipment; Burk and I were always ready for an inspection because Master Horne had pounded that into our thick skulls, but we had to get Hatcher set up proper. She was clean and tidy in her habits but stopped short of the correct 'just-so' attitude. I was putting a quick buff on her spare boots while Burk used a straw on the embossed pattern on her leather gear, and Hatcher worked us through our letters.

"So how does it work: one at a time or both together?" The speaker was a big filler who went by Mountain, big-bellied and as tall as me, hard and scarred by work, the lash, and manacles. I figured he had either been a slave or more likely a convict on the road gangs the Empire used to keep the roads in good shape. He was standing just out of quick reach with a couple cronies backing him up.

I had talked it over with Burk and we agreed that there would be trouble at some point: Hatcher was pretty, and the only female in the Company, so this was not a surprise. I had pegged Mountain for trouble because he liked to bluster and push smaller Men around. I was surprised to see Gareth leaning against the wall within earshot, watching but not showing any sign of getting involved. That wasn't expected, but not a factor at the moment.

Hatcher bristled, but before she could get a word out her boot caught Mountain on the jaw; I didn't throw it very hard, just enough to put the big Man off for a second while I got to my feet.

Mountain was a veteran brawler: he threw a punch while backing off to get some room, but I just took the hit to my shoulder and bored in, looping a good right roundhouse to the ribs and following it with two sharp jabs to the face. Burk was piling into Mountain's back-up, but I remained focused on the big Man.

He might be a veteran brawler, but Mountain was facing a trained and experienced pugilist. His style was to knock down a foe, ideally with help from comrades, and then put in the boot; if that wasn't possible, to get a grip on his foe and let his weight and strength do the rest.

I didn't let him do either. I had my gloves on, and used my longer reach and experienced footwork to keep him at arm's length. I didn't stand on pride, moving, feinting, and ducking as needed, nor did I try for any showy put-downs. I fought as Master Horne had taught me: simple, clear workmanship. I pounded Mountain's gut until he dropped his guard, and then I jabbed at his face and throat until he raised his guard, and then I went for his belly again.

The big man staggered and gasped and threw wild swings, taking punishment but dealing none out. Bruises on my blocking forearms were nothing to the way his ribs flexed under my punches and the blood flowed freely from his mashed nose and broken lips. The fight had started before he had expected it, and the tiny lag in adjusting to the new circumstances cost him dearly.

Simply knocking him out of the fight would not do, Burk and I had agreed previously: when someone decided to raise the issue, the best thing to do was make an example of them. So I rationed my breath and ducked, weaved, and jabbed, reducing Mountain to a lurching, bleeding, wheezing hulk who gasped in agony with every shot to the ribs or jab to his swelling, ruined face. Pride kept him on his feet, and I used that to beat him within an inch of his life.

The sudden roar of the Company battle-horn at close range jerked me from my fighting-focus, and I instinctively hopped back two steps and raised my hands to shoulder height, palms open.

The Captain was standing nearby with the unit horn-man, the big curved ox-horn still at his lips, and a couple fully armed veterans. The Captain, referred to as 'the Bear' by the veterans, was an older Man, his close-cropped hair gone steel gray. The left side of his head looked like a plowed field, and the ear on that side was a stub, but he was hale enough. He wasn't a large or tall man, but he had a way about him that reminded me of Master Horne: he could put you in your place with a look.

"What is going on here?" the Captain asked mildly. He was the sort who never bothered to raise his voice.

"Adjustment, sir," Gareth spoke up before anyone else could say anything. "Just the new fish sorting out their living arrangements."

"I see." The Captain studied the scene with a thoughtful look on his face. "Rather a noisy adjustment. The usual venue for this sort of business is not in the barracks, I might add. Dismiss that fellow," he gestured towards Mountain. "Put the others on water detail for two days."

"This is absurd," Hatcher groused, even though she was just sitting on a barrel watching Burk and me fill kegs and load them on a cart. "Extra work for a fight we didn't start."

She hadn't fought and wasn't working, but I didn't point that out.

"That's not why we got the detail," Burk explained, passing me a bucket. "It was part of proving a point."

"What point?"

"The point of who is in charge and how things are supposed to be," Burk moved a full keg onto the cart, lifting with his legs to protect his back. "Happens all the time."

"I don't see it."

"Mountain was trouble: anyone can see that," I explained. "Types like him always are. Sometimes you can whip them into shape, sometimes you can't. Mountain was one of the 'can't', at least in the time that the Captain had. Along comes a couple recruits who are big enough, and Gareth nudges things along. Mountain tries us because he's that way, and gets drummed out whether he wins or loses."

"Why not just kick Mountain before all this nonsense?"

"Because it's not nonsense," Burk stopped to mop sweat. "Mountain starts trouble, and ends up beaten bloody: there's a message. Mountain starts trouble, and gets kicked out: another message. The ones who were in the fight all get extra work: a third message."

"Moral of the story is, the Captain is in charge and toeing the line is a good idea," I nodded. "And all us new fish getting along, that's a good idea. See?"

"Yeah," Hatcher admitted. "This happen in slave barracks?"

"Yup," I nodded. "S'why me and Burk hang together. We made our place in the Ebon Blades barracks. Thing is, the Captain hasn't got a lot of time, so he had to work it out fast. But the principal is the same: people need to see how the rules work. Now there won't be any trouble in the barracks."

"So you two knew this would happen."

"More or less," Burk took over the winch. "Wasn't sure which one it would be, but since you're the only girl we figured someone would start something. We wanted to send a message, too: mess with us or our friend, and see what you get."

Hatcher bristled. "I can take care of myself."

"Sure. But it's easier this way."

She relented a bit. "I suppose."

The morning after we were done with our extra duty they mustered the entire Company in full battle gear. Yesten, who commanded our century in addition to his other duties, addressed us. "The enemy's main body is close and our lords and betters want to demonstrate their displeasure, so the Barley Company will advance north and skirmish a bit. Remember what you have been taught, stay in your ranks, and listen for the horns; think of this as a bit of a proving opportunity. I know each of you is eager to show how well he can fight."

As we marched out the main gate I caught a glimpse of Provine Sael with the command group, dressed in plain homespun garments so as not to attract missile fire. She didn't see me.

A couple other mercenary units fell in with us as we reached the gate, and we made a good show as we moved out as the new fish had learned how to march fairly well. Most were white-faced and sweating, terrified of the coming fight. A few had drawn blood in tavern brawls, but that was done in an alcohol-fueled haze, while this was something else entirely, being marched calmly into a match with enemy who would be trying to kill them. Burk and I were easy; while the venue was new, violence itself was not, and to be honest I enjoyed the Barley Company, it felt good to be in an organization again, with nothing to do but follow orders. My only concern was for Hatcher.

We moved about a half-mile north of town and then deployed into skirmish lines across a well-trampled pasture, veterans in the second rank. Burk was to my right, and a husky farm hand who went by Tulley was to my left, a good-sized lad with broad shoulders and blond-white hair he wore in a queue while working and loose while hunting women. Right now his face was nearly as pale as his hair.

Catching him glancing back as I unsheathed my sword, I hissed to get his attention. "Run, and I'll see to it you die slow," I muttered with my best scowl. I spun my sword through a few warm-up swings. "There's nothing in front of us that can't be killed."

He nodded weakly.

I did not like all this waiting around; my usual style is a brisk march into the pit at an expected time, or the sort of tension erupting into violence such as the toughs in the Burks. A fighting coming to me was something new.

Bone whistles shrilled in the tree line opposite us, which was a neat, orderly windbreak arrangement that I thought should be implemented in all forests, and then the Tulg burst into the pasture in an untidy howling mob. They were wiry and short, a bit shy of five feet, hairless and ruddy colored, with faces like a bat's, tall forward-facing ears, and mouths full of needle-like teeth. They screeched and yammered in their chirping language as they came, clad in furs and leathers decorated with bones, trinkets, feathers, and the like.

They were raiders and ambushers for the most part, mean little bastards who bred fast and true. The Ukar used them for skirmishers and scouts, just as the Dusmen used the Ukar as line combatants. They might be short, but Tulg would fight if they thought they had an even chance.

The Company horns blew 'hold in ranks', and Tulley stood his ground, sweating and scared, but steady enough. I gave my sword one last spin and set my feet, blade held in low inner guard, ready, breathing deep and easy. Ready.

The veterans let fly with crossbows and throwing weapons, and then the Tulg hit. I twisted to let a spearhead scrape across my armor and swung low, taking off both the creature's unarmored legs below the knees. Instead of a full recovery I stepped into the swing and brought the point up, punching through a hide and horn-plate tunic to impale a second Tulg.

To my right Burk was an engine of destruction, and to my left Tulley was fighting fairly well; I lopped off the head of a Tulg who was trying to double-team the blond Man as I stepped back to dress the line. It was unusual for me to have to hold a place in line while fighting, I was more accustomed to maneuver, but I was quickly seeing the utility of the practice: the cloud of Tulg hit our line like a volley of eggs thrown at a wall. Forced by our formation to fight toe-to-toe, the smaller Tulg fared very poorly.

Settling down to the stationary application of my blade, I focused on the targets and weapons in front of me and concentrated on holding my position and supporting my comrades to either side. At one point a blood-spattered Hatcher raced past behind us, grinning madly, and Yesten roved up and down the line behind us, effortlessly projecting his voice in short, sharp words of instruction and encouragement.

The Tulg were tough and willing, but they were not going to break our line, and after losing a quarter of their number they pulled back. Immediately the horns sounded, signaling to tighten ranks and prepare to march.

"Let's go, boys," Yesten bellowed. "Time to head back."

We could see the reason as we moved away at the quick-step: a column of armored Ukar deploying into battle line on the far side of the trees.

"The hard lads," Burk observed as we trotted towards the walls, looking back over his shoulder. "I would have liked to bag one or three."

"Their turn will come," I muttered. "You can count on that."

Chapter Eight

For the rest of that day and all the next we drilled all day and stood a turn at watch at night. The drill was responding to horn signals while defending a wall; the calls were made softly because in a battle, we were told, it would be hard to hear over the din. Everyone put their back into it: the skirmish had made the business real to the new fish. Most of us, anyway: two new fish had been killed by the Tulg, and one had broken ranks during the skirmish, only to be cut down by a veteran.

The enemy moved up to just outside the war engines' range of the walls and set up an untidy series of camps; they were concentrated to the north, with a couple little outposts to the east. I had expected them to surround us, but they didn't seem interested.

Once they had their camps set up they started cutting down trees. I wasn't sure why, but veterans explained that they were going to use the trees to build equipment for attacking the walls.

We drilled until noon on the second day after the skirmish, and then were called into formation and given the remainder of the day to rest.

"They'll be hitting the walls at full dark," the Bear announced. "Get some sleep, get a good meal, and stand to at sun down. The Eighteenth Legion has a couple cohorts close by and more behind them, so the Ukar won't be messing around with coy looks and sweet touches, they'll be coming at us hard, fast, and mean. They'll try to break up the defenses on the first assault and finish the job on the second, so our job is to prevent that. We hold on the walls because it's a lot safer than fighting in the streets, although we're not afraid of that should it come. Dismissed."

"Let's grab something to eat. Better not to fight on a full belly," I advised Hatcher. "Then we'll get some sleep."

"Sleep?" Hatcher's eyebrows shot up "Seriously?"

"Going to be a long night," Burk shrugged.

I dropped off easily enough; I noticed nearly all the veterans were settling into their bedrolls when I was heading for mine. Being rested would save some lives tonight, and a lack of rest would kill others. Like Master Horne always said, a fight can be won on small things.

There was a thin soup waiting when we woke, barley in salty beef broth that warmed the belly and anticipated a need for replacing sweat. I don't know how it works, but salt was really important when you work very hard.

I had drawn a shield after the first day's drill because I figured that my sword would not be very useful in a formation. It turned out I was wrong, but after training on defending a wall I established that the hammer was a better choice there. My shield was round, with a banded iron rim and an iron center boss, a little bigger than usual, which suited me fine.

Our section of wall was to the west of the gatehouse, hard against the tower that anchored the corner next to the river. The corner tower was held by troops from the city garrison, while the one to our east was held by militia. Our section of wall, like the others, was about fourteen feet high, with archer positions every five feet and torch sconces every two feet, each of which was now fitted with a flaming brand. A wide walkway allowed us to move about easily.

Tulley, Burk, and I were stationed at one archer's notch watching the lights moving around in the enemy camp. Gareth was roving around checking on his file, and stopped to peer out at the lights. "Won't be long now," he grumbled. "When they come, we'll be in the thick of it."

"Why?" I asked. "Why here, I mean."

"The river," he jerked his chin towards the water, glossy in the light of a nearly-full moon. "They broke down farm houses for the timbers and floated them down here. So the best equipment will have been assembled closest to the river. Plus there's fewer towers that can bring fire to bear. That's why we're here, and most of the regulars. The hammer will fall here."

"We could die here," Tulley observed.

"Yup," Burk nodded.

"I don't mind the place, but I would rather it waited a few years," Tulley tried to grin. We both chuckled weakly.

This was worse than the pit, I discovered. Waiting for your turn was tough, but you knew what the match was, and that you would go out there, kill your foe, and then get a rest, maybe even be done for the night. Here was company after company of Ukar forming up, with strange angular machines to aid them. There was no telling how hard they would come for us, or whether we could stop them.

At the same time, it was better than the pit. There, you waited alone, and you fought for the honor of your barracks and the entertainment of the cheering crowds. Master Horne had trained us to ignore the audience and focus upon the task, but now I looked back and saw the faces twisted in excitement, the waves of cheers and howls, the eyes watching while my age block went down under blades and claws. Here you were part of a group, a company, and we were standing between those Ukar and Fellhome, and all the people in their little villages planting things in strips.

For a moment I was filled with a sudden, painful longing, a burning desire to know what it was to live in a cottage, to plant things and see them grow, to know what it was to be in a village. It burned like a cauterizing iron, but I focused the way Master Horne taught me and pushed it out of my head. I was a brute, a tusker, and I had to prove my worth every day I lived. I was a member of the Ebon Blades, a proper barracks of the old school, and my place was here, to fight, to die if needed. When you retain the services of the Ebon Blades, you received proper service, that was the rule.

It was important to keep my head in the right place.

Patrols had scattered powdered chalk across the ground a hundred feet out from the wall and dumped piles of wood at various range increments; as we heard the Ukar start moving archers fired flaming arrows to ignite the oil-soaked wood piles to give us a little more light. It would help with the shooting, although the bright ball of the moon was plenty to see the battle lines step through the stumps of the last windbreak and begin their advance upon the city.

Ladders sloped up from the ranks, and little walls mounted on wheels were rolled in front of some units. Mantlets, the little walls were called. They had siege towers, too, which were a kind of timber framework tower on wheels, each tower slightly taller than the walls, the ladders inside hidden by sheets of wicker attached to the frames.

The attacking force looked like a single creature, a single being rolling across the field fully as wide as our entire wall, the towers shifting side to side and the ladders wagging like a living creature's fur and ears. It looked like a wall of death creeping over the ground, an atrocity on the march. I looked at it and knew that I was going to die here; it looked completely unstoppable.

If you looked close you could see lighter markings on the dark rows of bodies: skulls hung in clusters from belts, skeletal torsos nailed to shields, lower jaws lashed together like a staircase and used to form a helm crest. The Ukar like to wear the proof of their deeds, to show what happened to those who opposed them.

Gareth came by to peer at the enemy. "If we get overrun, make sure you don't get taken alive," he reminded Burk and me. "They hate us worse than anything. They'll just kill or enslave captured Men, but they torture brutes." That stiffened my spine a bit: it is easier to fight people who hate you.

The big trebuchets set up in the town square let fly, and soon the war engines in the towers started to hurl rocks, smashing mantlets and punching holes into the enemy ranks. The Ukar line leaned forward like they were marching into a hailstorm and kept advancing. There was a lot of courage on display out there.

Burk, Tulley, and me were the only three in our file with crossbows, so when the enemy closed we took turns firing;

given the reloading time we had no problems sharing the position. Firing was a relief, a distraction that helped dispel the tension that built with every step the dark lines took. I forced myself to concentrate solely on the business of cocking, loading, aiming, and firing, trying to make every bolt count. Flocks of shafts rained into the Ukar ranks but the line ground on, a second and third line following on behind. They were leaving a carpet of bodies, and ladders were being lost, but they kept coming, stepping faster as the walls drew nearer.

Their armor was good quality and they held their shields for best effect, but missile fire got through the gaps. They closed ranks professionally and I was surprised at that. I had always thought of Ukar as half-mad animals, so seeing them dress ranks under fire was startling. Holding a formation at night and under fire was very hard, and I hadn't thought the Ukar were capable of it.

The Ukar roared as they charged the last dozen yards to the wall, a sudden explosion of sound that caused more than one new fish to break and run. I fired one last bolt into an upturned tusked face as the other members of the company stepped up to hurl ten-pound rocks down onto the enemy. Hanging my crossbow on a post on the inner side of the catwalk I heaved a few rocks down, mostly to loosen up. I knew that no amount of rocks were going to break that charge; these Ukar would take a deal of killing to stop.

Then ladders were banging against the walls, each with crudely forged iron hooks (that looked like they had been made from barrel hoops) fastened at the top to hold them in place. Settling my shield, I worked my arms and wrists and stepped up to meet them as the Ukar were coming up fast; a few ladders had been broken free and pushed away, but not enough.

I caved in a helm and the skull beneath it, and half turned to knock an Ukar warrior off the top of another ladder. It was easy for a few minutes, but the Ukar kept coming, and the ones waiting to ascend hurled javelins up at us. Not many hit, but we couldn't spare anyone.

The Ukar came to the top of the ladder swinging, usually without much skill or style but having a lot of energy and enthusiasm. I quickly realized these were young Ukar warriors, green seeds sent first to weaken the defenders before the veterans closed.

Young or not, they were tough and willing, and unimpressed by the losses they had taken getting to this point. They hurled themselves off the ladders, swinging and hacking for all they were worth in a ferocious effort to gain a foothold on the catwalk. We met them with an equal ferocity, determined to stop them. I still felt that I was going to die here, but it was overlaid with a grim determination to make these animals pay for the privilege of killing an Ebon Blade. Master Horne would have had no use for these savages, and neither did I.

They were attacking the length of the north wall, although I could only see my little piece of the battle between the two defensive towers, and that only in flashes of movement and half-glimpsed figures in the weak light of torches and fire baskets.

When I had a second I glanced out and saw yet another wave of Ukar advancing across the field towards us, taking few losses as everyone was focused on the attackers already at the walls. The second assault, I realized, the killing blow the Bear had predicted. Those would be the veterans, the hard lads coming to sort us out, the ones who had taken other towns.

Sucking air deep, I hammered at the current attackers, hoping I would last long enough to face the second assault and kill some veterans.

I saw Tulley catch an Ukar's cleaver-like sword blade in the neck and stagger blindly off the walkway, blood leaping in jets from the wound; Burk killed the Ukar who had gotten Tulley, but our file-mate was hardly the first of our Company to die, and some Ukar were getting off the ladders before we could deal with them. One of the siege towers, partially on fire, had bellied up to the wall-tower to our right and heavy fighting was raging up there.

Not that it was particularly easy going on our section of the wall; I smashed an Ukar from a ladder while deflecting a wild swing from another with my increasingly-battered shield. The light was bad, the footing made uncertain by puddled blood and discarded weapons, and javelins swept in at random times just to keep things from getting dull. Our file was down half its strength, mostly new fish being gone, and the Ukar kept coming in unending numbers. My chest was getting tight and my muscles were burning, but I wasn't going anywhere: we had to hold. Fail here and Fellhome, my home, was next.

It was looking bad, but the war hammer is a simple weapon perfectly suited for these quarters, and I was wreaking considerable havoc. There are worse things to do of an evening than kill Ukar.

Then something smashed a six-foot gap in our section of the wall. One minute we were hacking and brawling, and the next there was an otherworldly shriek and a six-foot width of wall-timbers smashed inward in the same fashion as a man kicking a lath fence. Bodies, both Ukar and defenders, went flying at the point of impact, and the timbers under our feet heaved and groaned like they were alive.

I was a dozen feet from the breach when it occurred, and in a distant corner of my mind I wondered how it happened because there hadn't been any sign of a rock or projectile. I saw the timbers fly and the catwalk sag at the new gap, and then I was running, dumping my shield and shoving my bloody hammer under the back of my belt as I went.

My sword was in hand when I jumped down into the gap, careful of the broken timbers; lucky for me the Ukar outside the wall were just as surprised as we had been. I had time to discard the scabbard and check my footing before the first enemy clambered through the gap, the two feet of jagged stumps still sticking up preventing an all-out charge.

In the lead was a bull Ukar, a much-scarred veteran with a fanged beast skull affixed to its helmet and four clusters of yellowing skulls hanging from its war harness. Our eyes met for an instant in the flickering light, and I think I saw surprise there that it was a brute who faced it. I knew from the barracks talk that the Ukar were outraged when they encountered their bastards facing them in battle, as if it were some sort of betrayal. It made sense, because they were too stupid to understand anything. Nothing more than animals, really, no matter how well they held formation.

It roared and crashed its graceless cleaver-sword against its shield before leaping the stumps in a mad rush. I waited with my sword at middle guard; gestures are for impressing the crowd before the horn sounds, not during a fight. I took advantage of the bull's pointless drama to pull in more air and to set my feet better, because in a fight small things can win for you. My sword point took the bull in the throat, getting the windpipe and the big artery in a long thrust with a twisting withdrawal. Ukar always think with the edge, what little they do think. I was sure Master Horne would hold such linear tactics in contempt.

There were plenty more behind the now-dying bull, and it was hot and heavy for a few seconds as I plied my sword with all the skill and speed I possessed. My sword was the perfect weapon for this sort of action, but the Ukar hurled themselves at the gap, and a dying veteran is still dangerous, for unlike the tales they tell in taverns Ukar and Men do not simply drop dead when mortally wounded. I was dead and I knew it: I could hold for a couple seconds, but numbers would soon tell.

Then Burk was alongside me, and the odds suddenly changed drastically: I covered the center and he worked the edges, crushing helms and skulls with his star. We couldn't hold the gap long, but with Burk's help we might go a full minute before being cut down, and in this sort of fight a minute meant a lot of dead Ukar.

I wasn't really thinking of time, though; what little thinking I was doing behind the combat focus was centered on killing Ukar. They were nothing more than animals, and nothing mattered but to kill as many as I could, kill them until too few were left to threaten

Fellhome. I am of the Ebon Blades, a proper barracks of the old school, and these damned Ukar would have to kill me to take this gap.

A horn bellowing behind me cut through the combat focus and air-loss haze that filled my mind, and I reflexively staggered back: it had been 'recall'. Two files of Barley Company troops were behind us, reserves committed to the gap. They charged the gap as Burk and I fell back, weak-kneed and gasping for air.

The gap was too narrow for the Ukar to force against the reserves, all the more so when they brought up a couple cart frames with stacked rows of long spears attached which they positioned as a sort of temporary barrier.

After we caught our breath and gulped a cup of water Burk and I returned to the wall and helped hold our section. We threw rocks and sandbags down onto the Ukar when we had a spare moment.

The Ukar couldn't carry the wall, not at our section or anywhere else; quite a few got in, but never enough at any one point to do anything but die. They took defenders with them as they died, but the wall held.

Hatcher found us sitting on an over-turned cart taking turns drinking from a bucket of water. Gareth and one other veteran, all that remained able-bodied of our file, were with us. She was a bit sooty and smudged but otherwise fine, and under the crushing fatigue and several minor wounds I felt glad that she was all right.

"Glad you two are alive," she said by way of a greeting. "Everyone else is, too. Provine Sael and every other healer will be busy for hours with the wounded, though. I heard you lads had it hot and heavy."

"Half my file," Gareth mumbled wearily. "Only four new fish in the whole Block still on their feet, counting these two." He was clearly pained by this, and I found myself feeling less homicidal towards him.

"Yeah, the garrison took a beating," Hatcher produced a skin of ale and handed it around. "But the Ukar lost at least two for every one we lost. It doesn't do our dead any good, but the Ukar won't be coming at us again tonight."

"They knocked a hole in the wall," I mumbled, tying a bandage around a cut on my right thigh which hurt like blazes now that I had noticed it. I had no idea when or how I had gotten it.

"Three, in fact, two with sorcery, one with a lucky catapult shot. They over-ran a fighting tower, too, but the reserves stopped all the breaches."

"Good for them," Burk muttered.

The reserves, who hadn't seen as much action, manned the walls while the survivors of our Block fell back to our barracks and cleaned our gear. I was stunned to learn that the action, which had seemed like hours, had lasted only a few minutes from start to finish. I certainly felt like I had fought all night.

A weary-looking Healer checked my cuts, smeared ointment on them, used a healing poultice on my right thigh, and pronounced me fit for duty. We were told that food was available if we wanted it, and to fall in at first light.

Burk and I ate three bowls of stew apiece and collapsed into our bedrolls.

From first light the Barley Company and several other mercenary units formed a skirmish line just outside the walls while crews of workers gathered up the few dead the Ukar hadn't carried off, burned the siege gear that had gotten close to the walls, and patched the breaches. Since we were not fully enveloped, they hauled the enemy dead to a field south of town and burned them.

Being stiff and sore, not to mention wounded, I was glad to just stand in ranks and watch. Besides the usual bruises and over-taxed muscles, the fairly deep cut on my right thigh (which had been swiftly healed by blacksap last night) ached, and my head hurt.

The area stunk of sour blood, corpses, burnt wood and leather, Ukar, and hot tar, none of which were making my headache feel any better.

"We'll reform later today, drop one century," Gareth advised us as we watched the enemy camp. "No point in deploying understrength Blocks."

"The Company lose that many?" Burk asked.

"Some, our Block is below half. We'll end up with six Blocks instead of eight. I'll still have a file. Mostly we lost new fish, and those that survived aren't new anymore. Not exactly veterans, but a long stride towards it. You two, now, all you need is a couple weeks of field living to qualify. You ought to give it some thought: this is a good Company, we take care of our own. You two showed us something last night."

I wouldn't mind being part of an organization again, but our time was not our own. "We'll think about it," I nodded, and Burk immediately scowled in concentration to indicate that he was seriously contemplating it. "Why didn't the Dusmen join in the attack last night?"

"There aren't many," Gareth scowled. "I've always wanted to kill one, but I've never been at the right place at the right time. You can figure there's about one for every hundred Ukar in any given force, a lot in command positions, the rest in small elite units. There's never many Dusmen, but I don't know why."

We stood in skirmish order until noon; groups of Tulg shadowed us but didn't seem to be inclined towards starting anything, and I for one was glad to do nothing. No one in our Block looked any more eager for a fight than I felt, and the rest of the Barley Company looked pretty tired as well. We would fight if we had to, one look at us certainly made that plain, but for today we weren't looking for trouble.

I didn't think much about the fight, for while it had been a lot different than the pit, it was still blood-work, nothing terribly new. Part of being a slave is not having to choose your own path in the world, mostly. I suppose jumping into that breach last night was a choice, but it had been done on instinct. Master Horne had trained us to act without hesitating.

Maybe he would have gotten the letter by now. That would be good.

We marched back in a little after noon, work parties having done everything they needed outside the walls. We got a decent meal, stew, bread, and baked potatoes, and then helped pile stones on the ramparts and haul timbers for more repairs until the evening meal. The units that had worked before noon rested and stood watch while we worked, so it seemed pretty fair, although some of the veterans grumbled.

Hatcher re-joined us in time for our evening meal, having been busy running messages and performing other chores.

We were washing our eating gear when Gareth found us. Motioning us off to the side, he kept his voice low. "There's word that your mistress is going to get picked up tonight." He gestured as if describing a fight to anyone watching would be misled. "The Barley Company has no part in this, but the Bear feels that since you fought well and your mistress tended our wounded, that Company honor demands we not stand aside. How it works, we give you your discharge papers tonight, and a gate-pass that says your lady is checking on a supply request for us. Tomorrow morning we adjust our daily report. This will give you a jump on whoever's plotting harm."

Hatcher hissed and shook her head. "In the middle of an incursion we have old trouble catch up with us. Look, tell the Bear we're grateful."

The tusker nodded grimly. "The Barley Company stands by its own. Good luck."

"Get our gear together, quietly, and get over to the Red Banner grog-shop, don't go inside, stay where you can see the front door. I'll go grab the others," Hatcher re-tied her head-scarf. "Fuggin' idiots: I thought we had given them the slip."

Waiting for the others at the entrance to an alley a half-block down from the grog-shop, I started to regret that we hadn't gotten a chance to say goodbye to our file, only to realize that nearly all were dead or in the hospice, which was an unpleasant thought. I hadn't been with the Barley Company long enough to really make any friends, but it had felt like the barracks. Like home, I realized after a moment.

Maybe that was how you felt if you had a cottage and strips of ground you planted stuff in, I guessed. If you ended up in another cottage with other strips you would feel like I did in the Barley Company.

It was an interesting thought, so I slouched against a wall and pondered it while we waited. Burk stood in his Noble Slave stance in keeping with his Standards.

After a while I saw Hunter wander out of the 'shop and trudge down the street towards our alley. He passed us, and I was about to call out to him when I saw his hand twitch in a 'come along' gesture made real small. I elbowed Burk and we walked out casually, like we were strangers who just happened to be going the same direction.

"Akel just came out," Burk muttered, having glanced behind us.

I nodded shortly. "I think we're avoiding looking like a group."

"Makes sense."

Hatcher, Torl, and Provine Sael were waiting in an alley near the gate; we followed Hunter, while Akel had not followed us, but showed up not long after we had, leading the mules. Without a word Torl led us out the alley and around to the gate. Since we were not invested it was still used, although it was closed and heavily guarded by regular troops. This gatehouse was still timber, although they had laid the foundations for a stone gatehouse.

The gate captain wasn't enthused about seeing us, and looked over the paper Provine Sael presented with great care, but in the end they opened a small sally port and we scrambled through the ditch and headed south. I was a little nervous during the proceedings, but Provine Sael was as calm and sure as always and nothing was said.

Merrywine wasn't surrounded, but there were Tulg patrols roving around south of the town keeping an eye on things and picking off whoever they felt was worth the fight, so we didn't light torches and stayed alert. Hatcher was silent for once, riding my shoulders with an axe in hand. We moved at a brisk pace, a bit faster than normal but with the usual rest stop every hour. There was enough moon to make staying on the road easy enough, and the open fields to either side made ambush unlikely. The Tulg had been burning the farms and anything else that would catch fire so we were seldom out of smelling distance of ash and wood smoke, which was a sad smell.

The idea that a smell could be sad was interesting and I thought about it while I walked. The people who grew things in their strips would come back and their cottages would be gone. But they would have the things they carried on their carts, and maybe they hid some other stuff, too. And there were still too many trees, so they could get wood to make new cottages and get rid of some of the clutter at the same time.

It occurred to me that the Tulg couldn't affect the strips the peasants grew stuff in; they couldn't burn them down or steal them. The Legion would make the Tulg leave, and then the people could go back to growing stuff. Torl had mentioned that people would go through a lot to have their own farm land, and I could see why: you can't steal or burn down farm land. It was security.

That was an interesting thought, and I pondered it as the miles trudged by. Slaves don't have security, not really; on the one hand, our masters take care of us, on the other, we can get sold without warning. Although I had only been sold twice in my life, and I couldn't remember the first time. Being free meant you were on your own, unless you belonged to an organization like the Barley Company.

"Hatcher?"

"Yeah?"

"How are you secure?"

"What?"

I thought about the wording for a moment. "What makes you feel secure, you know, like farmers with their land?"

She chuckled. "Farmers aren't secure, not like you mean. They have taxes, too much rain, too little rain, blight, that sort of thing. Just because you plant a crop doesn't mean one will grow."

"Oh." I hadn't considered that.

"But for me, my security is in my reputation. My skills and abilities are known."

I nodded: she must be like a High Rate in her field. I understood that.

"But how I get security for the future is putting money away so that if I fall on hard times I have something to tide me over."

"I thought this trip was very thin. Hunter said it was."

"It's not the best-paying job I've had," Hatcher conceded. "But it's not the worst, and if we pull it off I will have a huge boost in my reputation. And it's a good cause."

Helping people, and improving your standing: I understood those, too.

"Thinking about your future?"

"I suppose," I said slowly. "Sort of, anyway. I was thinking about those farmers coming back to their cottages burnt down, and I realized that's why people take risks to get farm land like Torl told us: because no one can steal land."

"Well, they can, but it's harder," Hatcher mused. "Dirt-grubbing isn't a sure thing, and it's a bastard load of work. It's good you're thinking along those lines, though, because too many free men don't plan beyond the next job." She drummed with her free hand for a moment. "Look, I know Provine Sael said you'll be free when this job is over, but don't think that means you and Burk will be alone. Odds are real good that she'll have more work for us, and if not you two can work with me. Plenty of things we can get into, stuff I've had an eye on but never had the reliable muscle needed to pull it off. You two have skills, Grog, skills that are in high demand. More importantly, you have friends. She may not show it much, but Provine Sael likes you both."

"Oh."

"You don't complain," Hatcher explained. "Provine Sael hates a whiner. She's so nervous that griping really wears her down."

"Nervous? Her?"

The little Nisker chuckled. "She is as jumpy as a cat in a strange house. She hides it well, even I bought the whole ice queen line for a while, but it's harder for her to hide it from a girl; you male lunks see a pretty face and get all mushy-brain. Don't get me wrong, she's no coward, you've seen that for yourself. But this business is really hard for her."

"So why is she doing it?"

"Because it needs to be done. That's another reason I'm along on this job: it's hard for me to stand aside when someone else is setting that kind of example. There's lots of blowhards with a mug in their hand sounding off on what needs to be done, but there's damn few actually putting their butt on the line. Provine Sael could be home sipping tea and eating little pastries right now if she wanted, telling people what's wrong with the Empire these days, but instead she's out here on this fuggin' road trying to do something about it."

That was a lot to think about, so I broke it down into bits. Firstly was wrapping my mind around Provine Sael being nervous, well, I couldn't see it. She was always cool and calm, always so sure of herself. I put that one on a shelf and turned to the idea that she liked me and Burk. That one was a little easier to work with. We were both good workers, and High Rates, so being appreciated wasn't so hard to grasp.

I liked the idea of working with Hatcher after this was done; I understood how reputation worked, and was sure

Burk and I could build ours up fast: look at how many had heard of the fight at the Fist.

Thinking on all this made the miles go faster and my heart rest easier. I was still a little uneasy because it was dawning on me that being free would mean being responsible for things that other people had always done for me.

"One for the brute, there, that one." Master Horne paid the cart-owner and gestured for me to take the fried pork pie.

"Thank you, Master."

"Shut up."

I followed Master Horne down the street, munching the pie, which was very good. It was a knack he had: he could look at a push-cart laden with identical foodstuffs and pick out the best one. We had all seen him do it more than once; he never had a kind word, but Master Horne very seldom took one of us out without buying a snack or two along the way. Never for him; he mostly lived on fried bread, pickled cabbage, and strong dark tea.

We stopped in front of an ordinary-looking shop when I was just finishing the last flaky bit of the crust-rim, because I always saved the rim for last, like a dessert. Burk always mashed his into the pie, but I never did.

It was a cobbler's shop, but not the one we used, just a little workroom with a door that opened onto the street with a big wood boot hanging on a hook next to it.

Master Horne shook his head as he mopped his brow with a kerchief, even though it wasn't a warm day. "Listen, brute: we are here to do a job. It is business, nothing more. I want you to do exactly what you are told, no more, no less."

"Yes, Master."

"There shouldn't be any risk," Master Horne brushed his bald pate with an unsteady hand. "None, really. But this must be done. The Ebon Blades…come on."

I had to duck to get in the door. There was a skinny man working a piece of leather at a bench to the right, and a rack facing the door that had some footgear, belts, and whatnot on display. A small boy was dragging a broom around without a lot of skill.

Master Horne didn't speak; the cobbler looked up as we stepped in, looking like he was about to say hello until he saw who it was. His mouth sagged, then closed with a click.

We stood there looking at each other for a while, sweat breaking out on the man's face, which had gone deathly pale. The little boy stopped sweeping to look at us, interested at first at my size, but the cobbler's silence made him fearful. He had the same red hair as the cobbler, and I guessed him to be the man's son.

"You changed the marker you put up," Master Horne's voice was strange: soft, even gentle, not like him at all. "Smokey didn't clear you for that much. Now you owe me."

The cobbler sighed and looked down at the little tack hammer in his hand. "I didn't think…Bent Ed's brute seemed like such a sure thing…"

"The Ebon Blades are a proper barracks of the old school," Master Horne's voice remained soft. "We don't often lose."

I realized they were talking about my last match, where I had faced a brute from the Scarlet Wind barracks, which was managed by a man known as Bent Ed. The brute had been a High Rate for quite a while, whereas I was new to the title. Veteran or not, he hadn't prevailed.

The silence returned; I waited patiently, while the boy crept to his father's side.

Master Horne finally broke the silence. "Five Marks."

"I don't have it," the cobbler absently put his arm around the boy, who buried his face into his father's shirt. "Not now. With some time…"

"Time." Master Horne shook his head. "In time you'll lose even more."

The cobbler shrugged helplessly. "I don't have it."

"Ten shillings each week, eight to the principle," Master Horne sighed. "I'll send one of mine to collect. Until you are square you make no wagers, and do not set foot at the pits. Violate either rule and fifty Marks won't save you. Understand?"

"Yes, yes I do," the cobbler nodded shakily. "Thank you."

"Send the boy away," Master Horne mopped his brow again. "No need for him to see."

Later, as we waited for a line of loaded carts to pass so we could cross the street, Master Horne spat a curse. "Things have to be done in a proper fashion," he snarled at me.

"Yes, Master."

"It's not the individual case, damn you, it's the principle of the thing. Let word go out the Ebon Blades are going soft, and we'll be out of business in a year."

"Yes, Master."

"Check the markers closer, you say? Damned hard, says I. When the bets are coming in fast, these things happen. There's always some piker who thinks he can slip a fast one."

"Yes, Master."

"It wouldn't have mattered if he had won. It wouldn't have mattered if he had five Marks in gold ready and waiting with a nice bottle of wine as a bonus, the matter would still have gone the same way. You can't look weak in this business."

"Yes, Master."

"There's men sitting over ale wondering how Horne conducts his trade, speculating that maybe Horne is getting too soft for the business, that maybe the Ebon Blades are heading for the trash heap. Well, I'm not, and we aren't, understand?"

"Yes, Master."

"Damn right. I didn't tell him to bet, I didn't tell him to alter a marker, and I certainly didn't tell him to wager that kind of money with the resources he has. Never bet more than you can afford to lose, that is the rule."

"Yes, Master."

"Everyone knows what happens when you try to pike a bet. Everyone *knows*. So why does everyone think their situation is different?"

"I don't know, Master."

"Pig-headedness, pure and simple. Finally. Come on, I haven't got all day."

I woke, startled to find it had been just a dream; of course, it wasn't really a dream, but a dreaming memory. That visit to the boot-maker had been several years ago, back when I had first made High Rate. We hadn't done much of that sort of thing, and that time was the only time I had personally had to do it; Master Horne did not rent his fighters out to the collections-trade, preferring escort jobs, and after that day I understood why.

Nor did we have much trouble with markers because most of our bets went through agents, but as Master Horne says a custom is harder to change than a law, and some people insisted on wagering directly with the master of a barracks. It made them feel special, Master Horne said, and a man who needs to feel special generally loses, so taking those bets was good business.

That day had bothered me a lot, and looking back I can see it bothered Master Horne as well. The cobbler had changed his marker before placing a bet, and that sort of thing could get a man killed, and often did. Afterwards he was still able to work, and broken ribs wouldn't scare his boy as much as if he had lost teeth.

Hatcher had asked if my kills in the pit bothered me, and I had been truthful: none of the men, brutes, or creatures I had killed in the pit or out of it had ever warranted a second thought except as a study of method, but that day, that cobbler, still weighed on me.

"This is stupid," Hunter announced as we ate breakfast. "Provine, you're coming at this all wrong."

"Really." She didn't look up from her greens.

"Watch your tone," Burk growled, surprising everyone. "She commands here."

Hunter shook his head. "Get your brute on a leash and listen to me: you're working towards failure."

Provine Sael nodded to Burk, a simple chin dip that set him back to eating. "Explain yourself, Hunter."

"You have a group that includes four non-Humans, including a very well-dressed Dellian and two massive brutes, both accomplished pit fighters. It's no wonder the Sagrit are dogging our heels: you've a group that stands out wherever it goes."

"I used what was to hand."

"You're on an undertaking that has predictable movements. When they failed in Fellhome the Sagrit knew you would head north into the wilds, and that if you were successful the nearest place to seek reference would be Merrywine. So they waited there, and now they're back on our heels. You're predictable and distinctive, and that is going to get us all killed."

I didn't like his tone and I had no idea who or what the 'Sagrit' was, but Provine Sael was listening so I listened, too.

"Do you have a suggestion, Hunter?"

"Yeah: stop making the obvious next move. There's not much we can do about standing out, but we can choose a better route."

She ate her greens thoughtfully. "What do you see as the obvious next move?"

"The Grand Library in Fellhome. No doubt they have people following us, but I'm certain they already have plenty waiting in Fellhome, too."

"So you suggest we seek a library elsewhere?"

"No. I suggest we avoid libraries entirely. The Sagrit have a decent idea of where we are, and if we don't show up at Fellhome, they'll just cover the libraries that are the next closest."

"Are you suggesting we quit?" Hatcher asked with a touch of belligerence.

"I've given up on that. What we need to do is disappear from sight so that the Sagrit become unsure of where we are and have to cover many possible destinations; they are numerous, but finite. Then we need to seek the knowledge from an unconventional source; if we complete a step in your mad scheme without the Sagrit realizing it, they might not catch up."

"So where do you suggest we hide? We've got trackers on our trail, so just finding a discreet copse won't suffice," Torl pointed out.

"We head due west for a couple days until we hit Greenward's Way, and then follow that southwest to the Conclave."

The others seemed to ponder this; why, I did not know because none of this made sense to me.

"Even as a group we would not stand out at the Conclave," Hatcher admitted, sprinkling a little more of her dark sauce on her food.

"Even less if we joined up with another band heading there," Hunter pointed out. "And it is a place where minding one's own business is respected."

"The Conclave is not a place for the thrifty," Provine noted. "My funds are not unlimited. They may not be sufficient for the delay and added expense."

Hunter jerked a thumb towards me and Burk. "They have a pit at the Conclave…"

"No." With a single word Provine Sael established that there would be no debate.

"That would be a bad idea," Hatcher said slowly. "Easy money, but it would attract a good deal of attention. I don't doubt the Sagrit know we have two ranked pit fighters with us; neither were unknown in Fellhome. But there's other ways to make money."

Provine Sael shot her a stern glance. "Honest ways?"

"Honest enough," the Nisker shrugged. "We are on an honorable, even noble, undertaking, and no honest person would be harmed. Best of all, it's unlikely the Sagrit would hear of it; for all their murderous ways, they do not travel in criminal circles. Look at the attack in Fellhome: they used common street thugs rather than any organizations' blade-boys."

Provine Sael ate her greens for a bit. "I expect violence would be involved."

"Against persons of evil bent," Hatcher countered.

"I am disinclined to send Grog and Burk into violence for profit, be it a pit-fight or some…suspect undertaking that sprouted from beneath that mop of hair."

"We do not mind violence, mistress," I assured her. Burk nodded.

"So we cut them in for a share," Hunter shrugged. "Say half of the proceedings goes towards your grand quest, and we divide the rest equally among ourselves. If you're going to cut those two free at some point, they'll need a stake."

Provine Sael tapped her fork against her plate. "We will head for the Conclave," she said after a bit. "That is wise counsel. I will think on the other suggestion." She shot Hatcher a sharp look. "I suspect this financial undertaking is something you have had in mind for some time."

"They don't call me 'Hatcher' for nothing," the Nisker grinned. "I've got *lots* of ideas."

"Find one that involves very little killing."

"I can do that."

"You're still going at this backwards," Thol observed thoughtfully.

"How so?" Provine Sael's tone was polite, but she forked up the last of her greens with unnecessary violence.

"The Conclave is a good idea, and Hatcher certainly can find money, but there's a simpler way to go about this: we head north."

Hunter grinned. "That's brilliant."

"If we turn around and head north…oh." Provine Sael bowed her head and stared at her plate.

"The Sagrit are well-funded," Hatcher nodded thoughtfully. "And they won't go crying to the authorities. We lose the trackers, unless they have a group coming up from Fellhome."

"They'll wait in Fellhome," Hunter shook his head. "After they missed their chance there the first time, they'll spend the time and money to hire real killers, probably pit fighters of the same rank as our boys. You've never turned and faced them, so the group to the north will be complacent."

"I did not want unnecessary violence," Provine Sael sighed.

"They chose the dance," Hatcher shrugged. "They can't complain."

Provine Sael nodded slowly. "I do not like this, but we will retrace our steps."

Chapter Nine

"What is a 'Sagrit'?" I asked Hatcher as we started back north.

"'Who', not 'what'," she corrected absently. "It is a secret society devoted to the downfall of the Empire."

"Why would they want the Empire to fall?"

"Pick your reason: it allows slavery, it's too big, it has some corrupt officials. About half the membership are idealistic fools who somehow think that tearing down the existing political structure can be done quickly and a replacement structure installed without any imperfections before any of our many enemies can react. The other half plan to make up the power structure that replaces the Empire."

"Huh."

"They want Provine Sael dead because she won't give up on her quest."

"To get a set of cymbals?"

"A set of…no, to get a *symbol*, something that belonged to the first Emperor. Preferably his helm, but anything of his, really. Such an item would help the current Emperor maintain power, which goes against everything the Sagrit stands for."

"Huh." I pondered this for a while. "But Provine Sael hates slavery."

"So do I, but just because you oppose slavery doesn't mean you want to pull the entire structure of society down. The Emperor has passed two edicts recently that will, over time, reduce the number of slaves. You want to get rid of slavery you have to make it a gradual process, otherwise you get a war. Slaves are worth a lot of money, and you can't just go taking away peoples' property without getting a fight. No, you nibble away at the institution, using the law to erode away the slave population until it fades away or is small enough to simply ban outright."

"So how does this symbol help the Emperor?"

"Part of it is politics, part is tradition, but either way it makes his hold on the Empire greater. Just as important, old Umbargen, the bastard who built the Empire, and his Red Guard had special gear, magical stuff."

"Huh."

"You know about magical swords and what-not, right?"

"Sure, but I thought they were just stories; it's always someone's friend who saw one."

"No, they're real enough, but they're rare. You need special materials to bind enchantments permanently, and the only source for the metal needed to make enchanted weapons is far to the north; the Dusmen have controlled it for generations. Provine Sael's staff is enchanted, and Hunter has an enchanted ring, but they're arcane focuses; for a weapon you need northern steel. Back in Umbargen's day, Umbargen the First, I should say, you could still trade for the metal, and naturally he and his Red Guard were at the head of the line when they issued it out."

"Can't the Emperor get a magical sword some other way?"

"It's not the weapon, there are hundreds of enchanted arms in the Empire; my sister has an enchanted short sword, in fact. But legend suggests that what Umbargen the First had was part of the reason he was able to build the Empire. Me, I don't believe it, because he had most of the Empire built before he started carrying enchanted gear, but still, having something of his would give the current Emperor a boost, because back in Umbargen I's day they made weapons out of the pure metal, not alloys like they do today. They don't even know how to work the pure metal anymore, so there's no way to fake something from back then."

I trudged along for a bit, thinking hard. "So Provine Sael uses the ballad to find Umbargen the First's tomb in order to get something that belonged to him, and then gives it to today's Emperor, and his having it will make things better."

"Yeah, basically."

I pondered it some more. "So why did Provine Sael have to buy me and Burk? Why didn't the Emperor just give her some of the Red Guard?"

Hatcher thumped her heels against my chest. "Because officially Umbargen the First is in the great tomb in the capitol. And because I doubt the Umbargen IV has ever heard of Provine Sael, or her quest."

"So…wait, then who told her to do this? Find the symbol?"

"Nobody told her, she set off on her own; she's been working on it for years."

"Huh."

Hatcher chuckled. "Yeah. She's a true believer; she's been risking everything on this undertaking just to make the world a better place. Go figure."

I wasn't sure what I was supposed to figure, but my respect for Provine Sael, which was already high, went up still higher.

Not that my opinion counted for anything.

Torl selected a spot on a rise overlooking the road and assigned each of us a position. I was with Burk behind some bushes, and as the morning went on I told him what I had learned from Hatcher.

"So it's definitely not a musical instrument?" Burk studied a group of refugees trudging past, unaware of our watching eyes.

"Yep."

"Too bad; I really thought we were onto something. So we're trying to find a magic helm or something, and that's somehow better?"

"So I'm told."

Burk scowled at the road. "I still think a musical instrument would be the better plan."

"I do, too, because people *like* music. But apparently Provine Sael has given this a lot of thought."

"Well, she's a lot smarter than we are." He checked his crossbow. "At least now we know who is after us."

"And why. Come to think of it, the Sagrit are taking the whole magical helm thing serious, too."

After a couple hours Hunter, Torl, Hatcher, and Provine Sael gathered for a quiet discussion, and then Hunter moved down to the road and started talking to refugees as they went by. It wasn't long before he headed back to Provine Sael and the word was passed to form up on the road.

"What happened?" I asked Hatcher as I lifted her onto my shoulders.

"The Sagrit left the road yesterday afternoon after press-ganging some refugee labor."

"Why?"

"That's an interesting question, because they're supposed to be hunting *us*. My only guess is that they got wind of something more important than our band."

"What would that be?"

"I haven't a clue. They've been dogging us since before you and Burk joined, so whatever it is, it must be pretty damn important. Of course, the Sagrit have a lot more irons in the fire than just stopping Provine Sael."

"We're still heading north; why don't we head west while they aren't following?"

"Good question. Because the fact that the Sagrit broke off pursuit is so interesting that instead of doing the obvious smart move, we're going to double back and find out what they are up to."

"Huh."

"Huh, indeed."

After an hour's walk we turned off the road onto a little trail and followed it for the rest of the day; Torl stayed a few hindered feet ahead of us and spent a lot of time studying the trail.

We finally made a cold camp an hour after dark, and were up and on the trail before dawn, but instead of heading out we stood around and waited for the sun.

Hatcher kept falling asleep and laying across my head so that I was wearing her like a hat, so I finally just held her in the crook of my left arm with her head on a folded blanket on my shoulder. Provine Sael passed us, a ghost in her white fur cloak that seemed to glow in the dark, and gave the sleeping Nisker a cool glance, but didn't say anything.

    Burk and I hung back with Akel and the mules when we finally started moving. "Why did we get up early and then just stand on the trail?" Burk asked the mule-tender.

    "A confusion of intents," Akel smiled. "Provine Sael is in a hurry to find out what the Sagrit is up to, but Torl wouldn't move until it was light enough to see."

    "What's Torl worried about? We've moved during the dark before, and we're have a trail here," Burk pointed out.

    "Ah, but this area is what they call karst," Akel swept an arm to take in the lumpy terrain with scattered clumps of scraggly trees. "The place is honeycombed with caves, underground streams, sinkholes, and the like. Trail or not, the ground can fall out from under your feet without warning. Torl is being careful."

    "Akel, how is it that a man as smart as you are is taking care of mules?" I asked, keeping my voice low so as to avoid disturbing Hatcher. "You're an educated man."

    "Life leads us into strange places," he smiled. "I had many plans as a young man, and made choices with careless ease, and decades later I find myself here, leading mules and chatting with two expert pit fighters. Tell me, boys, why are you still here? You have skills which are in high demand."

    "We're slaves," Burk scowled at Akel. "Where else would we be?"

    "You are heavily armed warriors," Akel countered. "I've seen you fight. There have been a half-dozen points in our travels where you could have taken your leave of the group and lived as free men."

    "We are of the Ebon Blades, a proper barracks of the old school," I shrugged. "When you employ the Ebon Blades you get quality service. That is the rule."

    "Ah, yes, the rules. We follow the rules, don't we?" Akel smiled sadly. "The rules that are written, the rules that are expected, and the rules we make for ourselves."

    "You have to have rules," Burk said, a touch uncertainly.

"Indeed."

Hatcher had finally woke up and was riding on my shoulders as we were following the trail up a hill when Torl appeared as if he had stepped out of the shadows of a rock and motioned to us to halt. Burk and I moved up as the scout trotted to Provine Sael. "The Sagrit are headed this way." Torl kept his voice low. "Six fighting men, a couple cart-drivers, and four agents travelling without scouts or outriders."

"The refugees they press-ganged?"

The scout shrugged. "Dead, I expect. You know the Sagrit."

Provine Sael nodded quietly. "Six fighting men are too many; we will let them pass."

"Counting Hatcher, that puts us as six to five, not involving you or Akel," Hunter protested. "With surprise that's no great odds."

Provine Sael hesitated, glancing at me and Burk. "This seems rather cold-blooded…"

"You want to see cold-blooded, look at the refugee labor they spirited away," Hatcher observed. "The Sagrit don't bother with the rules."

"All right," the Dellian nodded. "Torl, make it so." As the others bustled about to the scout's directions she turned to me and Burk. "I am sorry to order you into combat yet again."

"It is our duty, mistress," Burk shrugged.

"You are free."

"We are in your service." Burk was in his Noble Ukar stance.

"Thank you."

Torl had us withdraw a quarter mile to a clump of scrub trees and brush where Hunter deployed us as the scout carefully cleared away any sign of our passage on the trail.

"This is a good spot," Hatcher noted, weighing a throwing axe in her hand. "Not the very best place for an ambush so as not to put them on alert, but we're upslope and have better cover than you might guess, looking at this clump from a distance." She jabbed the butt of the axe into the ground. "Man, this place is just a thin layer of dirt on top of…what is this? Chalk? Limestone?"

"It is karst," I kept my voice low, watching the nearby rise for the first sign of the enemy. "A place honeycombed with caves and caverns."

"Listen to you," she grinned. "Akel is rubbing off on you; another couple months…," she stopped and jerked her chin at the road. "Here they come."

The Sagrit band didn't look much different than a lot of travelers; the fighting men were in good mail and carried themselves in the manner of warriors who knew their business. The four agents were dressed in the style of well-to-do merchants, the sort who frequented the pits with pretty young women on their arms, but as they drew closer I could see they were leaner and hard-faced in the manner of men who traded in lives. The two carts were not heavily loaded, and the drivers looked bored.

Hunter and Torl had been explicit in their instructions so there wasn't much I had to consider as we waited for the Sagrit band to enter the ambush; I just knelt and watched them walk to the end of their lives, not thinking about much.

I had seen a lot of men and brutes walk to their death in my life, generally emerging into the pit from the hatches opposite the one I was walking through. Only one leaves the pit alive, that is the rule. I thought about the people crowding around the walls of the pit on the raised platform: the poorer sorts, the professional gamblers who wanted a close look, and the blood-lovers who thrilled at the sight of death. Behind them on the raised, tiered rows of seats were the wealthier patrons and their companions, reclining in comfort to watch the sport.

Everyone has their place, and I had been born to the sand-covered dirt of the pit, at least until Provine Sael had bought me and Burk. It suddenly struck me that by selling me, Master Horne had saved me from death in the pit. That was a new thought, and I filed it away for serious consideration, but the thought of Master Horne's kindness filled me with a warmth and a strong sense of homesickness.

Then Hunter caused a bright burst of fire amongst the foe, and I reflexively raised and fired my crossbow, hitting one of the warriors. Discarding my crossbow, I caught up my sword and trotted down to the road, Burk about ten feet to my left.

Three guards were down, but the other three were undismayed, and moved to meet us. The one that came at me had a bearded axe with a fire-scorched haft that had been strengthened with four brass bands and a heater-style shield painted a fading green; I caught his axe-swing with my sword and ran the blade up under the axe's down-swept curling edge (it's 'beard') and twisted, trapping his weapon as I threw a shoulder-block into his shield.

My being a head taller and broader, the Sagrit warrior staggered back from the impact trying to recover his footing, but he had a leather wrist strap on his axe which let me jerk the captive weapon up and away, throwing him further off-balance. Pivoting on my left leg and leaning away, I kicked him hard on the left thigh, spilling him onto the ground.

The wrist strap finally broke; I tossed aside the axe with a flick of my blade and clove his helm and skull in two with a single stroke as he clawed at the hilt of the long dirk at his belt.

Bringing my sword up to the ready, I checked both sides: Burk was hammering on the last Sagrit warrior still standing, and Hatcher had cut down one of the agents and was squaring off with a second; a third agent was down with an arrow jutting from his chest, and the fourth was racing away. One cart driver was sprawled across his seat, dead or unconscious, and the other was standing and holding up empty hands with an urgent look on his face.

I realized someone, I think Hunter, was yelling to '*get him*', and I realized that the 'him' was the fleeing agent. Why Torl didn't just pick him off crossed my mind, but I obligingly set off after the man, despite not having too much optimism. I ran a lot in training, but it was to build endurance, not speed, and the man I was pursuing wasn't wearing armor. Nevertheless, I gave it my best, hoping to wear him down over a distance.

The agent charged over an irregular mini-ridge or mound about twenty feet high, and I thundered along in his wake, losing ground steadily but controlling my breathing and stride. As I crested the mound I saw the agent about a dozen feet off the slope on his hands and knees, and hope flared: he had tripped.

I leapt halfway down the slope in a single bound; hearing me, the agent, still on his hands and knees, turned and shouted at me, but I couldn't hear what he said and didn't care anyway.

Crashing down into flat ground, I charged the agent who was desperately shaking his head and yelling, but on the second step the world seemed to be moving around me, and then I was flying in a cloud of dust as night swept across the sky.

Instinctively I held my breath against the dust because coughing killed a lot of fighters in the pit, and that saved my life when I hit water and plunged into its cold depths, my armor dragging me down until my boots hit gravel.

Kicking off the waterway's bed, I clawed my way back to the surface, erupting from the water into pitch darkness, but at least the darkness contained air. After a moment I realized that I was being pushed by a strong current; looking back over my shoulder I saw a dust-choked beam of light falling away into the distance.

Swimming with weights was part of our endurance training, and it didn't take me long to work out how to keep my head above water despite my boots and armor; as I got situated I realized I had lost my kettle hat and sword at some point, but those were concerns for another day. It dawned on me that the agent hadn't tripped: he had realized he was standing on a potential sinkhole and was trying to crawl away before it collapsed. He hadn't been shouting for mercy, he was trying to keep me away lest my weight and motion drop us both into the pit, which is exactly what had happened.

The current kept dragging me along, and it was rough enough that I couldn't do anything but struggle to keep my head about the water, and in any case I had to keep one arm out ahead of me at all times to keep from meeting a stone head-first.

It was pitch black; I had heard that term used a lot, but I had never experienced such absolute darkness before. The sound of the rushing water meant I couldn't hear anything else; I only had the pressure of the current to orient myself, and I quickly lost all sense of distance and of time.

Over and over I tried to get a grip on to one of the rocks the water drove me against, but they were smoothed by the passage of endless water and slick with growths, and I failed again and again. As the chill of the water crept into my body I struggled against the thought that I was going to drown in this endless darkness.

It would have been easy to just let go, to stop struggling and accept fate, but in the back of my head Master Horne was shouting at me, the same voice that had led me from childhood to becoming a High Rate with sixty killed: "Quitting is for the dead! You are of the Ebon Blades, a barracks of the old school! You die when you are told to die, and not one second before! There is always one more strike left in your body because the mind is weak and always quits first. Many who die in the pit do so because they accept death, and many have survived the pit because they refused to accept death. NEVER accept death. Never quit. Never stop fighting. If death comes to you, make it have to work for you. Force death to remember your name."

So I kept struggling to keep my head above water, to catch onto something solid, to live. I was of the Ebon Blades, a barracks of the old school, and I would fight until the bitter end. That was the rule.

There is no telling how long I was in the water; it felt like I spent days fighting the cold and the current in the darkness, days sustained only by the honor of the Ebon Blades and the teachings of Master Horne. It was a nightmare, the worst thing I had experienced in my life, and a part of me argued to simply drown and end the horror, but I fought on. A High Rate does not go easily, that is the rule.

At first I thought I was seeing things, that madness was creeping into my thick skull just as the cold was eating into my body: up ahead I caught flashes of blue light as I struggled to keep my head above water. But as the seconds dragged past I realized there was in fact a point of blue light ahead, and to the right of the light, a red glow that illuminated a section of cavern wall. As I drew closer, I realized the blue light was perched on an old log that thrust out over the water.

Hope is a terrible thing: seeing the chance of survival filling me with an aching dread that my efforts would fail. I kept dog paddling to my right as the current pushed me, too heavy and weary to risk swimming lest I simply sink. It seemed to take forever, but finally I was lined up on the blue light and the log as the water swept me along. A desperate lunge let me lock my arms around the water-smoothed trunk, and for a moment the dead tree shifted and leaned slightly, but then it stopped and for the first time since the ground gave way from beneath my feet I was motionless.

For a long moment I hung there, gratitude flooding through my entire being, and then carefully I began inching to my right. A half dozen careful arm-shifts and my feet hit a graveled bottom, and I could move faster. Then the water level dropped with each careful side-step, and hope turned from sick fearful desperation into a glowing warmth. Stumbling up onto dry stone, I fell to all fours and crawled to the source of the red glow, which was a sizeable driftwood fire blazing in a fire pit twenty feet from the water's edge.

Collapsing dangerously close to the crackling blaze, I dropped my head onto my forearms and either passed out or slept.

Chapter Ten

When I woke or regained consciousness the fire had burned down to a mound of glowing embers; my armor was steaming in the heat, and my trouser legs were nearly dry.

Growling at the stiffness in my limbs and back, I struggled to a sitting position and laboriously removed my belt and armor, arranging the latter so it would continue drying. I debated removing my shirt, but decided to let it dry on me; my boots had to dry on my feet or I would never get them back on. My war hammer and all my crossbow bolts were gone, but I still had my dirk and work knife, and the contents of my belt pouch had weathered my swim.

I was buckling my belt back on when I realized I wasn't alone: a Man sat on a rock across the fire from me, at the far edge of the embers' light; the blue light I had seen on the log was resting on the ground at his feet, only now it was hardly more than a firefly. It wasn't easy to make out details, but I couldn't see any weapons, and if he meant me ill I would not have regained consciousness.

"Hello," he said quietly.

"Hello." I finished getting my belt adjusted. "Thank you for putting that light on the log."

"Another mile and the stream goes deep," he observed. "But even had you managed to get ashore, you would have died in these lightless warrens." His voice was thin, formal, and spoken in the manner of a man used to giving orders.

"Again, my thanks."

"It was a minor task. Unfortunately, I have no victuals to offer you."

"That's all right. Can you show me a way out of here?"

"Certainly. And perhaps you would be inclined to undertake a task for me." It wasn't really a question.

I rubbed my face, wondering if I were still dreaming. "I have limited skills, but I would do my very best."

"I expect you are suitable to the task: I require the services of a gravedigger."

"I can dig," I nodded. I scraped a boot heel against the floor of the cavern. "But this appears to be stone."

"The burial will take place outside."

"No problem, then."

"Good."

The silence stretched until I stirred uncomfortably. "How did you come to be in this place?"

"Much the same as you, I expect: through the ceiling."

"Have you been here long?"

"Long enough, but such matters do not concern me."

"I guess I'm very lucky you heard me coming."

"The strength of your will to live and the lives you have taken shouted your presence far and wide. I needed to make no haste to have a fire ready. The other man drowned before he reached this point, not that I would be inclined to help his sort."

It took me a moment to realize he was talking about the Sagrit agent. "I'm not a murderer," I said, feeling stupid the instant I said it.

"I know. A warrior does what he must." The man looked off into the darkness for a moment as if distracted, and in the thin light I could see that he was much older than I was, with a shaved pate and a mustache and goatee gone iron-gray, thin-featured and conveying a sense of hardness.

"My name is Grog," I offered.

"I have a multitude of names," he said thoughtfully. "But my mother called me Fall when I was young."

"Well met, sir. How far must we travel to leave this place?"

"Hmmmm?" He had been staring into the darkness again. "Oh, not far, an hour or two, perhaps. We will leave when you are ready."

I climbed to my feet and stretched, working my shoulders and arms while my joints popped and crackled. "I suppose that I'm as ready as I am likely to be." I removed my belt and pulled my armor back on; it was still wet, but at least it had been warmed by the fire. "Sooner started, sooner finished."

"Good. Follow me." He stood, revealing himself to be only half a foot shorter than me. The blue light rose of its own accord and floated above his head, lighting the way and revealing that he was wearing a dark cassock with a belt of dull metal plates, perhaps silver.

We walked for a goodly distance through narrow passages that meandered through the crumbling stone, most too narrow for more than single file. Fall moved with grace and ease no matter how rough the floor was, and never hesitated as he led me through a labyrinth of passages, the dim blue light floating over his shaven scalp our only light. He said nothing and I asked no questions; I wasn't certain if he was a spell-weaver or just a madman, but he was clearly right about me dying down here without help.

In addition to the terrible sense of stone and darkness around me, I was painfully aware that I was completely alone but for Fall. Other than in the pit, I was used to there being someone around to tell me what to do at any given time, and having someone to follow, no matter how strange, was a comfort.

Keeping an accurate track of time was impossible given the poor light and oppressive conditions, but I could guess based on how long it had been as my clothes, armor, and boots dried out. After what seemed to be a couple hours Fall ducked through an opening no more than four feet tall and stopped. "Here."

I squeezed through the opening, finding myself in a roughly oval chamber whose roof was lost in darkness. "What is here?" I was looking around for an exit.

"I need the services of a gravedigger." Fall moved forward to stand next to an oblong shadow. "This is what must be interred."

I moved forward and saw that he was standing next to a wood coffin lying in the smashed wreckage of a cart; the box had been crafted from a smooth-grained dark wood that looked hale and strong despite the dry-rotted wreckage it rested upon. "But I thought…well, this is all stone."

"Yes," he nodded. "You must take it outside this place. I will show you the way out."

"All right." I stepped up to the coffin, and realized it was no more than four feet long. I tapped it here and there, but the wood was thick and seemed thoroughly solid. I lifted one corner to judge the weight. "This won't be a problem."

"There are men at the exit," he said abruptly. "Five men. Common road-murderers."

"Well, is there another way out?"

"No."

"We could just wait until they leave."

"They have made camp there, and five guard while the rest of the band prey upon passers-by."

I couldn't see how he knew that, but I wasn't inclined to argue. "That is a problem; I expect they will challenge my passage."

"You must kill them."

"Can you help fight?"

"No."

"I'm willing, but I lost most of my weapons in the water; I can't kill five men with a dirk, even from surprise."

He stared off into the darkness as if he were studying something. Turning back to me he steepled long, pale fingers. "I have a sword. Will that suffice?"

"That would help a great deal."

He pointed. "It is over there, in that crevice."

Trying not to think about spiders, I gingerly fished out a scabbarded sword from the recesses of a deep crack in the wall and carried it over to where Fall stood in order to examine it in the blue light.

It was in a hard scabbard hung on a back-carry baldric; I slid the weapon free and examined it as best I could in the blue light. "Sharp enough, and no rust," I muttered, half to myself. "Decent balance."

"So it will suffice?"

I spun it through the basic manual of arms. "It's an old-style longsword." I tossed the hilt to my left hand and repeated the manual of arms. "Intended to be used either one or two-handed, often called a bastard sword. A bit longer than the average longsword, a bit over four feet of blade with wide strong crossguards. I'm used to wider blades with ricassos and better hand protection, but this is a very fast sword. I just hope that narrow blade doesn't snap when it hits a helm or meets a strong parry."

"That blade won't break."

"I hope not. Five to one are long odds, but I expect those are better odds than trying to find another way out. Give me a bit to get the baldric adjusted and settled."

Fall waited in silence as I got the baldric set so the scabbard rode right. I was doubtful it would work, because a back-carry is seldom practicable, but whoever made the baldric was clearly a master craftsman: once I had it adjusted to my size it was no problem to settle it into the proper angle for a smooth draw. "This is a very fine weapon and harness," I observed as I slid the sword back into its scabbard.

Fall shrugged. "So long as it serves to clear the path. Pick up the coffin and follow me."

Nothing moved or rattled when I heaved the box onto my left shoulder (the sword's hilt projected over my right) and it didn't smell of corruption, but I wasn't inclined to ask questions.

We walked for another hour, perhaps closer to two, before Fall halted. "That passage leads to a cave in which the bandits shelter; the cave is shallow, and is open to the surface."

I set down the coffin and examined the six-foot crevice he called a passage. "Does it get any narrower?"

"No."

"All right. How far to the cave?"

"Three hundred yards. The bandits are unaware that the crevice leads deeper into the karst."

I nodded, trying to think. "I'll leave the coffin about a hundred yards short so it won't get in the way, and come back for it once the fighting is done."

Fall frowned, the first time he had really changed expression. "You *must* bury this."

"I will, but I can't carry it and fight. Or I might get killed, and then what happens to it?"

He stared at the coffin for a long moment. "All right. You will return."

"I will. And I'll bury it properly."

Fall was right that the crevice didn't narrow any, but it also didn't get any wider, either. I had to take the baldric off and carry the coffin at waist height to get it through the passage, and still it was a tough walk. Torl had taught Burk and me how to measure distance by counting steps each time our left foot hit the ground, and when I estimated we had covered two hundred yards I set the coffin down with a sigh of relief.

"I'll rest a moment, and then go deal with the bandits," I whispered to Fall, who nodded once.

Five to one was bad odds, but I felt easy with it; after the nightmare in the water and hours of following Fall, killing felt comfortable. It was what I knew best, and when you engage the Ebon Blades you received quality service. That was the rule.

Stretching as best I could in the tight confines, I drew the sword and left the baldric on the coffin. "I'll come back when the way is clear."

It wasn't much further before I caught the smell of wood smoke and porridge; another thirty yards and I could make out a faint glow ahead.

What the crevice led to was less a cave and more just a bare indentation in the side of a hill or ridge, but I don't suppose there was anything else you could really call it; I was able to examine it unobserved because there was a bushy short tree or tall bush with waxy green leaves growing in front of the crevice opening. The sun had just risen, to judge from the light outside the cave, and the simple sight of the outside world filled me with a feeling I could not possibly explain.

But I tore myself from the sight of the early morning light on the grassy fields beyond the cave opening; Master Horne always said to count a victory after you were back at the barracks, and as always, he was right.

The broad 'cave' had around twenty bedrolls scattered around, but most were rolled or folded up and set to the side. Sacks and bags lined the walls, an unshaven man knelt at the campfire at the cave mouth stirring a pot of porridge, two more lay in bedrolls in the manner of men summoning up the will to get up and start the day, and a fourth bandit, a brute, leaned against a glaive a little further out from the fire, on watch. The brute and both men emerging from their bedrolls wore the marks of a slave collar.

As the two men rolled out of their bedrolls and fumbled around for clothes and boots, I noticed a skinny young man with dark hair and his left eye swollen shut sitting with his back to the wall across from my tree or bush, one wrist manacled to the lifting handle of a battered old traveler's trunk.

I wanted to go in before the man at the fire and the other two donned armor, but I didn't know where the fifth man was; relying on Fall's count was risky, but he had steered me unerringly through to the surface and I figured he would be right about the bandits' numbers.

Finally another bandit, a tall lean man in fighting leathers, came into the cave, a short-hafted axe thrust under his belt and a gold ring in his left ear. He had a confident air and the bearing of a man with faith in his own abilities.

"Nothing moving," he advised the man stirring the pot, who grunted by way of a reply. He took a few steps and kicked what I thought was a pile of bedding. "Get your lazy ass up."

A pale girl under a tangled mop of blond-ish hair emerged from the bedding, feeling around for a dress that lay nearby. I am not smart, but one look at her face told me everything I needed to know about how she had come to be associated with trail-robbers, and what her life had been like since. She had the marks of a slave collar, same as the young man chained to the trunk.

Crouching, I examined the bush/tree in front of my crevice for the best way to get past it into the cave; after some consideration I decided to push past to the right. It wouldn't be quiet, but it was my only decent option. Flexing my hands, I took several deep, slow breaths and then jammed my body past the branches into the cave.

Gold Earring heard me and looked in my direction with an expression of mild curiosity which was transformed into wide-eyed shock just before my first swing lifted his head off his shoulders. I was shocked by how easily the blade cut; I had decapitated men before, and seen blades bend or edges roll from the impact with the spine, but other than a mild back-shock the cut was smooth.

The cook was fast and decisive; he flung a scoop of boiling porridge at me and dove for his weapons. I brought the hilt up so the hot goop mostly hit my gloved hands and armored forearms, but a couple drops scalded my bare scalp.

The two late risers were not as quick, and I moved through them with a pair of hard strokes that took them out of the fight, but by then the brute was coming at me and the cook was arming himself with a shield and a spiked club.

Settling into a middle guard, I grinned at the brute. "You might want to run."

He came in fast, thrusting low, going for a thigh, but I parried and stepped inside his reach to slam my right elbow into his head, but he ducked and the hit just was a glancing blow.

The cook was boring in from my right, but he was leading with a roundhouse swing that would have pulped my skull, except that I dropped to a knee and thrust around his shield, which wasn't properly positioned, and spitted him, going in about an inch below the sternum. I stood and put my shoulders into a leftward heave; I could feel the blade flex through the tang as the man was tossed to the side, sliding off my blade with an agonizing shriek, and then I had the blade up to deflect the descending glaive.

Taking a half step back, I returned to middle guard, impressed by my last maneuver: I had never handled a sword this fast or strong. My dopplehander could have handled the way I had tossed the cook, but its weight and balance meant that I would have never gotten it back into play in time.

The brute shifted his grip forward on the haft of his weapon and eyed me cautiously; I kept my eyes on his leather-clad center torso, and saw his knuckles whiten and his arms tense just before he struck. Even as he swung I was side-stepping, bringing up my blade to deflect the strike and then continuing into an high thrust that put my point through his throat. Twisting the blade as I withdrew, I leaned at the waist to side-kick him away as he dropped his weapon to paw at the blood flowing from the gaping rent in his throat.

"I'm a High Rate of the Ebon Blades, a proper barracks of the old school," I told him as he thrashed away his final moments.

The cook, one hand clutching his wound, was crawling away; I followed and lopped his head off to ensure he didn't get ambitious. Glancing around to check that the others were dead, I inspected the pot, but bright drops of arterial blood were soaking into the porridge, so I upended it over the fire with a swipe of my boot.

"Where are the rest of the bandits?" I asked the girl, who had dove under her blankets during the fight. When she didn't answer I nudged her leg with the toe of my boot and repeated the question.

"Looking for travelers," she said, poking her head out. "Are you going to kill us?"

"No. How many more bandits are there?"

"Ummmm...more than ten."

"When will they be back?"

"Near dark. They go out for four days at a time."

"Will you let me loose?" the young man in manacles asked.

"Where is the key?"

"He has it." He avoided actually looking at Gold Earring's corpse as he pointed. "In his pouch."

I found the key and stood, then knelt again and gathered the coins that had been in the pouch. I might need money soon; after a moment's thought I stuck his axe under my belt as well. Standing, I bounced the key in my palm as I tried to form a course of action.

"Girl, do they have money?"

"Just what is in their pouches," She sat up and adjusted her dress. "They aren't having much luck."

"Gather the coins and put them…in this cup," I pointed. "Do they have any more food?"

"Some dried sausage, cheese, and trail bread."

"Set the food out, and stay put. I'll be back in a moment." I started away and then caught myself. "See if they have a shovel or a pick axe, too."

"What about me?" the young man asked.

"You stay put, too."

Fall was standing exactly as he had when I left; I thought it was possible that he hadn't even moved. "The bandits are dead," I advised as I put the sword, which I had wiped clean on a blanket, back in its scabbard. "I'll take the coffin now, and you can show me where you want it buried."

"No. Bury it on high ground away from the karst. Do not mark the grave."

"How do I know where the karst ends?"

"We are on the south edge of this region of karst. Simply continue south at least a mile."

"All right." I paused. "Aren't you coming outside?"

"No."

I thought hard. "Would you happen to know where Greenward's Way is?"

"No."

"All right. Thank you for leading me out; I would have died down here if you hadn't helped."

Fall, staring off into the darkness, didn't reply, so I just held out the sword and baldric. "Thanks for the loan of the sword, it is an excellent weapon."

He glanced at it. "Keep it. I have no need of a weapon, and there may be further dangers nearby. Do not waste time."

"I'll bury it as soon as I find a spot." I put the sword on top of the coffin and settled the entire load across my chest.

"Goodbye, sir."

"Farewell."

The blue light vanished before I had completely turned to go.

Back in the cave the girl was sitting by the cup of coins, the food laid out on a blanket. I set the coffin down and carefully strapped on the baldric.

"What is that?" she asked cautiously as I moved around tossing the weapons into a pile next to the bush covering the crevice.

"A coffin."

"It is small for a coffin."

"That is true." I didn't care for the looks or smell of the bedrolls, but I found a couple tanned steer hides I could use as a ground sheet and makeshift blanket, and a sack of new mess kits, which was the extent of the camp gear that I was willing to use. None of the weapons interested me, so I dumped out a haversack and put the mess kit, a tin cup, and half the food into it, tying the rolled cow hides to its bottom. Dumping the coins into my pouch, I tossed the key to the girl. "You can let him go if you want."

"Can I come with you?"

"Do you know where Greenward's Way is?"

"No."

"Neither do I, so it isn't going to be an easy journey."

She shook her head. "Nothing is ever easy."

"You're an escaped slave, aren't you?"

She touched the calluses on her neck. "Yes."

"Have you been gone long?"

"A couple weeks. I'm Burya, he is Willen, we ran together."

I didn't know what to say; no one had ever tried to run from our barracks. Finally, I shrugged. "I'm not free, I am a pit fighter. I fell into a sink hole and was separated from my mistress. I'm going to have to find her, and she has enemies. If you come with me you may be in danger at some point."

"Wait, you are a *slave*, and you're going to *look* for your owner?" Willen was unlocking his manacles with the key Burya had given him.

"Yes."

"But *why*?"

I scratched my cheek. "Because that is the rule. Now shut up."

"You don't have collar scars," Burya pointed out.

"Pit fighters don't wear them very much, and when we did ours were leather, and loose. Plus brute skin is tough."

"So can we come with you?"

I tried to weigh the options, then shrugged. "If you want. Did you find a shovel?"

"Over there, a pick and a spade."

"Gather up what you need, and be quick. No weapons; Willen, you carry the pick and shovel."

We walked for about an hour before I saw a hill that seemed suitable. I took the pick and Willen the shovel, and it didn't take long to excavate a proper grave. I positioned the coffin in its bottom and then clambered out. "Start gathering rocks," I advised the other two.

"Why are we doing this, exactly?" Willen asked, wiping away sweat and leaving a smear of dirt on his forehead.

"Because I said to, so get moving." I picked up the shovel and started filling the grave in.

A layer of rocks about a foot down, and then the sod carefully tamped back into place completed the effort. I stood back a few feet and examined our handiwork. "That should work; in a little while no one could tell it is a grave."

"That sort of defeats the entire purpose of a grave, doesn't it?" Willen observed.

"Let's go."

From the hill we headed west; I had no idea where we were, but I guessed that a road wouldn't be too hard to find if I kept walking. I felt worn to the bone after my experiences underground, but I had grown up training to push through fatigue, and I kept moving.

"I never heard of Greenward's Way," Willen shrugged.

"I never was off the master's holdings." Burya admitted.

"Neither was I," Willen nodded. "But he's not our master anymore."

"We didn't get far, though," Burya sighed. "The bandits grabbed us a day's walk from the…place we ran from."

"Why were you in irons, Willen?"

The young man flushed. "Because I objected to the way they treated Burya. The only reason I'm alive is because they wanted someone to do the scut work."

"Most of the bandits looked to be escaped slaves."

"Most are. Why are you looking for the woman who made you a slave?"

"I've been a slave since I was born; I only met her a few weeks ago."

"So why are you trying to return to her?"

I scowled. "Because that is the rule. Anyway, she needs me: there are violent men after her."

"So you would fight for a slaveowner?" Burya asked.

"I was a pit fighter; I won sixty death matches for my barracks," I shrugged. "Now I fight for her. She'll set me free if we survive this business."

"Or you could be free today," Willen pointed out.

"Shut up."

"How can you fight for a slave owner?" Burya persisted.

"She's a good person."

"She can't be a good person if she owns slaves."

"What would you know?" I snapped.

"Only bad people think that people can be property."

How did those ex-slaves treat you? I thought, but I didn't say it. "You're wrong, and don't say it again."

She blanched and blinked rapidly. Willen put a hand on her shoulder. "You shouldn't say things like that," he scowled.

I scowled at him. "I am a High Rate from a barracks of the old school. Who are you to tell me what I can or cannot say?

He looked away. There was no way that Master Horne or Provine Sael were bad people, and I wasn't going to have a slave saying anything bad about either. If either of them didn't like that, they could lump it. I didn't have to stand for that sort of talk from ordinary field slaves.

The time underground had left me bone-weary, but I kept walking until not long before sundown. I couldn't be sure how long I had been separated from the group, or how long it would take me to find Greenward's Way, so there was no time to lose. When you engage the Ebon Blades, you get quality work, that is the rule.

The area we were traversing was pretty wild; we saw a few ruined farmhouses, but no people or roads. We crossed a couple tracks, but they were clearly not used enough to rate a name, and they weren't running in the right directions.

I had Willen dump the shovel and pick axe about two hours before we made camp; we hadn't needed them after the grave, but I made him keep carrying them because I didn't like his attitude. Then I had him dump them because I didn't want him having anything he could use as a weapon, although I was pretty confident that for all his talk there wasn't much fight in him.

"We're leaving," Willen advised me with great dignity the next morning as we broke camp. "We're heading south."

"All right." I rolled up my cow skins and tied them to the bottom of my haversack.

"I think we should get half the money," he continued.

I rubbed my chin. "You didn't do half the fighting. The money goes to my mistress."

He scowled, but he didn't have any way to force the issue. I briefly considered getting his head right, but dismissed it as not worth the effort.

"You'll never be really free," Burya said sadly.

I didn't know what she meant, so I just focused on getting my baldric to sit right.

"You could help us," she continued, wistfully.

"I killed those bandits," I pointed out. "You've got collar-calluses and no papers; you're not going to get very far." As I said that it occurred to me that that was probably why so many bandits were escaped slaves.

"Our master was a bad man."

"There's lots of bad men." For some reason I thought of the master of the Fist. "I have to find my mistress. She would probably help you because she hates slavery."

"If she hates slavery, why does she own slaves?" Willen frowned.

"She needed fighting men."

The two conferred quietly. "We'll help you find your mistress," Burya announced.

I wasn't certain that was good news.

Chapter Eleven

The day before I had been moving in a fog of fatigue, but I felt a lot better now, and a lot more uncertain. It was one thing to say I was going to find Provine Sael, and another to actually come up with a plan to do it. I knew that Greenward's Way was a road to the west, and you followed it southwest to the Concourse, which from the way it had been mentioned I figured was an event rather than a place, like a fair. I didn't know how much time I had to work with, and I did not know how the location of the sinkhole I fell into and the cave I emerged out of related to each other.

What I needed, I decided after much pondering, was someone to ask. The problem was, I was travelling with two escaped slaves. I studied on this situation as we trudged along.

"Why aren't there any people around?" Burya asked as we walked along.

"Look at this ground," Willen advised, kicking at a tuft of grass.

"Oh."

I covertly studied the ground as we walked, but it just looked like dirt to me, maybe a bit redder than I was used to, but that wasn't special. Finally I asked. "What do you mean about the ground?"

Willen looked startled. "Huh? Oh, the ground." He stopped to scoop up a handful of dirt and let it trickle through his fingers as he walked. "See? Clay cut with sand; that's why the grass is so thin. You can't grow crops here, and you couldn't graze cattle on this for long."

"Willen clerked for the land-keeper," Burya noted with a touch of pride.

"So if there's no people here, who were the bandits robbing?"

"They were working a stretch of road to the east, an old road built by the Legions," Willen shrugged. "They would go out for four days at a time because it was nearly a day's march to the road."

"Did the road have a name?"

"The Old Mill Road. It served a number of holdings raising sheep, one of which was where we came from."

"Huh." I stopped and studied the surrounding terrain. I wished I could remember if they had mentioned how far Greenward's Way was going to be. "How long until we get to better dirt?"

Willen gave me an odd look, but pointed south. "You see the line of trees? That's likely a large stream or small river. The ground is sloping away from us in that direction, so I expect the further south, the better the land will be."

"You follow water to people," I muttered; Hatcher had told me that. "All right, let's look at this water."

"There might be slave-taker patrols," Burya protested, looking fearful. "Or bandits."

Our group had passed slave-takers in our travels, tough men mounted on horses. I thought about that, then shook my head. "I don't know how long I have, or how much time I lost. Do what you want." I set off towards the trees, which looked to be a couple miles away; after some discussion the pair trailed after me.

As I walked, I tried to think ahead; no matter who I ran into, they would have questions for a lone brute, much less one travelling with escaped slaves. For the hundredth time I wished Burk was with me so we could talk this out. He wouldn't know any more than I did, but he would be company. This business of freedom was very taxing, I thought for the tenth time since rising this morning; things were very disorganized and unplanned. I couldn't say that I was enjoying it.

It didn't help that I didn't like the pair I was with; they were the whiny sort, which was something Master Horne had never tolerated. I had grown up in a barracks with a proud reputation, and although the training was tough, it hadn't been unpleasant, and we had had time to ourselves and seldom suffered punishment. It occurred to me that my version of slavery was much more like being in the Legion than the sort of slavery that Willen and Burya had experienced. That was an interesting thought, and I filed it away for future study. That was another trouble with freedom: there were a lot more things you needed to think about, so many in fact that you had to put some off. I didn't like that, either.

The ground turned darker as we headed south, and the grass grew thicker and longer, or maybe it was a different sort of grass, if there were different sorts of grass. I suspected that there were since there are different sorts of trees, but I wasn't sure and I certainly wasn't going to ask.

As the line of trees drew close I stopped and listened: I could hear little metal bells to my left, west.

"Sheep," Willen said, pointing west. "I would guess just beyond that rise."

"They put bells on sheep?"

"Just the lead sheep."

"People herd sheep, right?"

He gave me a strange look. "Shepherds, yes."

"Are they free or slaves?"

"The shepherd will usually be a free man, with a couple dogs and a couple slave helpers."

"Good. You two stay behind me and look humble. Keep your mouths shut." I had a vague idea in mind that might work.

Cresting the low rise, I saw a vast swarm of black-tailed sheep ambling in our direction, guided by three men, two wearing collars. They had a couple of black and white dogs that seemed to be trained, and the free shepherd was carrying a short bow and a knife. He watched me as I circled around out of the way of the herd and approached him.

"Good day," I sketched a salute.

"And to you," he nodded.

"That is a lot of sheep," I observed, mopping my scalp with a kerchief. "Did you happen to see three slave-takers, one a brute, the leader having red hair?"

"Afraid not. We see few folk out this way."

"Such is my luck. We split up and I caught these two, but now I'm lost."

He grinned. "City boy, I take it?"

"Born and raised," I said with genuine feeling. "I hate the country. Do you know where Greenward's Way is?"

He nodded and pointed west. "About thirty miles west of here. There's a road on the south side of Edder's Creek," he indicated the line of trees. "Follow that; it passes through a village, Mule Yoke, and then runs into the Way."

"Thank you. I got turned around a day ago." I looked back at the pair, who were looking suitably downcast. "Is there any chance I could buy your slaves' collars? They're less likely to run when they're wearing a collar. I lost all my ironwork when I fell into a sinkhole chasing these two. Well, three, but one tried to be a hero."

He clucked his tongue, looking thoughtful. "Well..."

I jingled my purse, having seen Master Horne work this way. "A Mark apiece, in small coins. What you tell your foreman I paid is your business."

"I hate wearing this," Willen announced for the third time.

"I don't care. Keep your eyes peeled for that ford the shepherd mentioned."

"A slave-taker with two captured slaves does look believable," Burya offered.

"Until it becomes the truth. He killed people in a pit, and is a loyal slave."

"You don't like it, feel free to go your own way." I spotted a place where the bank was worn by sheep feet, or hooves, whatever they had. It led to a place where the water was shallow enough for even Burya to wade.

Seeing the road was a big relief to me, even though it was just a rutted track, because it lifted the burden of decision-making from my shoulders: all I had to do was follow it until we hit Greenward's Way.

But freedom's endless decisions would not let up; my story of having captured two escaped slaves while separated from my group was thin, especially since real slave patrols usually had handbills listing escapees from the area. I could fool a shepherd, but not another slave-taker or a road patrol.

Studying at this filled the next hour, but not in a good way. It made my head hurt, having to look for ways to get things done; no wonder Provine Sael was nervous: being in charge must be a terrible burden.

As we took an hourly rest break, I turned to Burya. "Did you bring some empty sacks?"

She looked surprised, but nodded. "I thought they might be useful."

"Let me see them." After examining them, I chose the two largest. "You two fill these with leaves, not just dumped in, but like you were transporting them." I had seen leaves like that for sale in markets, usually dried, but we had to work with what they could find.

Willen nodded. "You're guarding two slaves delivering a cargo."

"Safer than my slave-catcher story. If you're asked, say you're from a steading near your actual one." I wasn't pleased that he has sussed out my plan so quickly.

"East Haven," Willen nodded. "We can gather ferns from the creek banks, and put some small branches in to give it weight. Where are we supposed to be going?"

"A slave doesn't know where he's going."

"Good point," he nodded. "We stick to the truth."

It took two hours to fill the sacks properly, but they were out of sight in the creek bed, and I waited in a clump of trees. A couple of wagons passed during that time, both heading west, but we went unseen.

"How much further are we going to walk today?" Willen asked as they rejoined me.

"Ten miles or so."

He rubbed his face. "Look, I was a clerk, and Burya was a maid; we're not accustomed to walking all day."

I hadn't considered this. "How far can you walk?"

He shrugged. "At your pace, maybe two hours. Any more and we're going to be useless tomorrow; yesterday took a lot out of both of us."

This was not good, as I had planned on covering twenty-five miles a day; certainly Provine Sael would be moving at that speed. "Well, let's walk for two hours, then." I needed time to think. Freedom certainly involved a lot more thinking than I wanted to do.

The two hours were nearly up and both slaves were clearly flagging when I heard a wagon coming up from behind us. I still had found no solution to my problem, but as I waved the pair to the side of the road and stopped to watch the wagon approach, I had a thought.

The wagon was actually two wagons being towed by three pairs of oxen, both bearing tall canvas-covered loads; the lead wagon had a driver and a man next to him, and the second wain had a young man sitting on the wagon seat. All three were armed with short swords and bills, but one look told me they spent more time riding wagons than training with arms.

Asking myself how Hatcher would handle this, I stepped into the road and waved at the driver, who expertly brought his animals to a stop when I was at a proper talking distance.

"What do you want?" he asked; he was a big, bluff sort, no doubt used to brawling in a grog shop and considered by his fellows to be a rough man.

"I'm escorting two of the laziest slaves that ever drew rations," I gestured to Willen and Burya, who were sitting in the shade of a tree. "If you let them ride, I'll stand with you if bandits attack."

He glanced at the pair. "We're heading to Limerock, that's about thirty miles south-southwest along Greenward's Way."

"Fine with me."

He studied me for a moment. "All right, but you'll have to walk; you weigh more'n both of them put together."

"I expect that I can keep up."

He barked a laugh. "I would guess so. All right, you two can sit on the tailgate of this wagon; move sharp now."

"What are you carrying?" I asked as the two scrambled aboard the wagon.

"Clay for the lime quarries at Limerock," the driver cracked his whip to get the oxen moving, and I started walking. "I'm Leonardo, but most call me Ox. This is Uven, and the lad on the second wagon answers to Bird."

"Burk. Have you come far?"

"A day to the east. You?"

"Closer to four. A donkey would have served better, but no, they gave me slaves."

"What's the cargo?"

"Leaves."

"Leaves?"

"Leaves. I have to see them delivered to the Concourse." I glanced at the rear of the wagon and lowered my voice. "And sell those two, as well."

"Huh. Well, I expect people buy leaves and twigs and all sorts of odd stuff at the Concourse. You ever been there?"

"No, but they tell me I can't miss it."

"That's the truth; think of a faire that is over a mile across. I hauled a load of wine there two years ago, and..."

As Ox described his adventures at the Concourse I listened intently and ventured a few questions. Apparently the Concourse was an twice-yearly gathering or faire for strange people, to include exotic cults, spellcasters, merchants of oddities, and far more. It lasted for at least a month, and a lot of gold changed hands. Most importantly, I learned that it was forty miles southwest of Limerock.

Ox turned out to be the sort for whom every event in his life was an adventure, and he felt compelled to share this treasure, which worked out well for me: after years of Burk I could pursue my own thoughts while keeping half an ear on the monologue so as to grunt in the right places. For his part, Ox was glad to have a new audience, and so the miles rolled by at a walking pace.

As I walked I pondered my sword; it had spent time underground, enough so that despite two cleanings and being worn for two days the baldric still had traces of gritty deposits here and there, but the leather was neither cracked or mildewed. The leather was thinner than I would expect for a combat harness, but it did not lack strength. The scabbard was rigid, two leather-covered strips of light but strong wood that the sword laid in, the upper side of the scabbard open for nearly all its length; the sword was held within the scabbard by the angle and a broad flap near the top that went over the open side and was secured to brass pegs.

The sword had not been stored in wax or grease, yet there wasn't a speck of rust on it anywhere; I had been practicing with it at every rest break since I had gotten it, and despite careful examination I had not found a single chip or mark on the weapon; that wasn't unusual for a weapon fresh from the maker, but the hilt of the weapon was some sort of wood with a cross-hatched pattern carved into it for a secure grip, and the wood was age-darkened with sweat and grease.

I wondered if it were enchanted, as I had heard that enchanted weapons took no battle damage, but Fall had seemed very intelligent and well-informed, and he certainly wouldn't have given away an enchanted weapon as casually as he had given this blade to me. And I always heard of enchanted swords being richly decorated, while this blade was a simple device for killing, without any excess effort wasted on anything but the mechanics of battle.

We came to Mule Yoke as the sun was setting; the village had about forty buildings enclosed in a log palisade and ditch.

"Now, let me show you a trick a good caravanner learns early in his travels," Ox advised me. "You don't waste your pay buying watered ale by the mug in some ratty tavern. No, what you do is learn which goodwife in any particular burg brews well and frequently, buy her product for pennies, and drink better for less." He rambled further on the subject but I drifted away again.

The woman who sold us two buckets of good dark ale had a travel tankard which I bought, mine being still on my pack which was off somewhere with the rest of my group. Just thinking about that made me feel a little sad.

Ox parked the wagons in the commons across from the town's only tavern, and we sat on the grass and drank ale. I had told Willen and Burya to sleep under the lead wagon, and hoped that the night would pass quietly.

That didn't happen. Not long before closing time four armed men came out of the tavern and headed our way, walking like men who had been drinking hard but weren't completely drunk. Draining my mug, I rose and leaned against the side of the wagon. As they headed for the lead wagon I set my mug atop the nearest wheel and moved to intercept them, Ox trailing in my wake.

"You need something?" This was like an escort job, I decided.

The leader of the four was a heavy-set man going bald, with what was left turning gray and worn long; he had a brute and two more men, none looking particularly impressive. The leader jerked his chin towards Willen and Burya, who were wrapped in their blankets. "Gonna check their brands."

Some slave owners banded their slaves in addition to the collar, normally on the hip.

"You think so?" I stepped squarely between him and the first wagon.

"We're slave-takers," he blustered. "We have the authority."

"You're hunting the bounties on escaped slaves," I said. "That doesn't mean you got any authority with any other slaves. We're not playing any games tonight; I've got a delivery to make, and I don't need some half-wits pawing my employer's goods, or trying some scam." I knew this one from Fellhome: slave-takers would grab some slave out about on his or her master's business and try to extort money out of their master to get them back. Or outright kidnap them to sell elsewhere.

"Who are you calling a half-wit?" Baldy snapped.

"You." I reached up and unfastened the scabbard-flap on my sword. "Go play your road-robbery games on someone else."

"This is no game, tusker: those slaves are likely runaways." He pulled out a well-thumbed sheaf of handbills for emphasis.

"They belong to my boss, and that is that. I know how to read, and how to gut four piles of crap." I was bluffing on the extent of my ability to read.

"Maybe we should get the bailiff," one of the men backing Baldy suggested.

"Good idea," I kept my eyes on Baldy. "I would like to tell him about some road thieves trying to steal slaves. My employer is a man of means."

Baldy was furious, but I was growing confident that he wasn't the sort to resort to steel; lots of men wore weapons every day, but weren't inclined to use them unless they were truly desperate. I've never understood that, but I've seen it enough to know it to be true.

"Do you have papers for them?" Baldy snapped.

"Do any of you have papers? Maybe I need to start checking brands, anyone can collect a bounty."

"There's *four* of us," the man who suggested getting the bailiff pointed out.

"Not for long, once the fight starts."

Baldy stepped back, shoving his handbills into his shirt. "This isn't over." He led the others back into the tavern.

"You don't budge, do you?" Ox grinned, stepping up beside me.

"You give bastards like that a minute, and they'll take an hour." I had heard Master Horne say that.

I settled down to sleep, sitting with my back to a wagon wheel and my sword across my lap in case Baldy and his crew tried something after drinking some more courage. After a moment Willen crawled over.

"Burya and me are going to slip away; this is too risky."

"No," I whispered back. "I would have to report you as runaways, and go after you, or I would be exposed. You can run after we leave these wagons at Limerock."

"It's too risky."

"You don't want me coming after you: I'm not interested in bounties." I was bluffing, but he didn't need to know that.

"Why would you do that?"

"Because I'm supposed to be a man-at-arms escorting two slaves, and the three waggoneers will report suspicious behavior for the bounty. Wait until we part ways with them after Limerock and you can do what you want."

"It's too risky," he repeated.

"How would you know? You got caught a day into your first escape attempt. I've gotten you further, and if you're smart you'll stick with me until we find my mistress. But you're stuck with me until Limerock whether you like it or not. If necessary, I'll leash you to the wagon."

He was silent for a bit. "All right, until we're past Limerock."

I bought more food before we left Mule Yoke, enough to get us to the Concourse. Ox was less talkative, but he still said his share and another man's as we rolled to Greenward's Way and swung south. Traffic along the Way was steady: we passed wagons, Legion patrols, merchants with a line of carts, peddlers leading a single mule, carriages, and more. There were travelers both ahead of us and behind us, and the fields to either side were cultivated, without many wild patches, which was fine with me.

We traveled until dusk and made camp in a meadow. "We'll make Limerock before noon," Ox advised cheerfully as the oxen were unhitched. "I know a goodwife there who not only brews, but makes a duck pie you won't believe."

"I wish I could, but I am supposed to deliver those two and the leaves by sundown the day after tomorrow. I'll have to flog those lazy buggers and march after dark to have a chance to make it as it is."

"Too bad. Still, we do what we must."

That night I laid on my cow skins and thought about things. So this was freedom: moving around doing things for money, making decisions, constantly planning and worrying over the future. Frankly, I didn't see it as any great improvement over the barracks. In fact, if I couldn't find Provine Sael, I decided, I was going to go back to Fellhome and see if Master Horne would let me fight for the Ebon Blades. I needed a place in the world, and if that was the pit, then that was the way it would have to be.

Still, being out here had made me think about slavery in ways I hadn't before. Hatcher was right: I had been a very well-treated slave because I had expensive and productive skills. Willen and Burya had no such skills, and weren't worth much more than unskilled labor.

But on the other hand I felt no kinship or respect for either of the two; they were complainers and not competent at anything useful. They hadn't been able to go two days without getting caught by bandits. I was used to being in the company of people with skills, or people learning skills; even though we were slaves we had pride and respect in being part of the Ebon Blades.

Slavery was terrible, I knew that, but I could not see Master Horne as a bad man; he had raised me, trained me, and built me into a High Rate of a respected school. I frowned into the darkness: Master Horne was smart, very smart, and he had talked to Provine Sael a long time. Could it be that selling me to her was his way of giving me freedom? I studied on that, and could see that working: Master Horne gave Burk and me our freedom while getting payment, the best of both worlds. That was exactly the sort of thing he would do, and I resolved to get another letter sent to him at the first opportunity.

Limerock was a rough little town that was covered in an off-white dust that put a sour taste in your mouth; we parted ways with the wagons just short of the town as Ox and his crew headed for the quarries. It took no urging to get the pair to step lively passing through Limerock: it apparently was shift change and the streets were busy with work crews of skinny slaves coming and going, those returning to the barracks coated with white, their eyes red and weeping and often with blood leaking from their noses making purple mud on their face. The crews heading to work still wore traces of the dust, and moved like men being herded into a battle that was doomed before it began.

"And you think slave-owners aren't bad people," Willen observed once we were out of earshot of the town.

"I said my old master and my mistress are not bad people," I corrected him. "You keep talking that way and I'll knock you flying."

"Violence doesn't solve anything," Burya said softly.

I thought about that for half a mile. "That's stupid," I finally observed. "Violence solves everything. Willen just shut up because I threatened him. Back in Mule Yoke Baldly backed down because he wasn't willing to fight. The only reason you two are free from the bandits is because I killed them. That quarry behind us relies on people hitting rocks with hammers. Violence is what makes things work."

"It shouldn't."

That made no sense to me, but I was having too much trouble learning how things actually worked to bother with the idea that they should work differently.

The pair slipped away before dawn the next day. I heard them going, but they weren't trying to take anything of mine, so I just pretended to be asleep until they had left. I could move a lot faster without them, and if they thought they had a better plan than relying on Provine Sael, well, that was their decision. Freedom was all about making decisions.

Traffic picked up steadily the next day, most of it bound for the Concourse, and it was pretty cheery: strangers waved to each other and called out greetings and comments as the faster passed the slower; a few even waved to me, although most avoided noticing a large brute in full battle rig. As for myself, I kept my head down and avoided eye contact; I didn't want to draw attention to myself. The Sagrit could be anywhere, and I didn't know enough to recognize them or their ways. Freedom means having to worry about things beyond the immediate.

I kept walking past dusk; the sky was clear and the moon was nearly full, so following the road was no problem. Walking felt like an accomplishment, and every step was one closer to rejoining my band. I was eager to see Hatcher and Burk and have simple duties assigned to me.

Campfires dotted the fields to either side as I walked along the moon-lit road and the sounds of conversations, music, and laugher came from the circles of light.

Finally I reached the crest of a low ridge and stopped in awe: before and below me a sea of lights swept away and to either side, extending as far as the eye could see. It was as if they had built a city on the plains below, a tent city of many-colored lamps, lanterns, and torches. As I watched a ball of green fire arced into the sky and burst into numerous smaller balls that drew fiery lines in the night sky; a second later the '*pop*' of an explosion reached me. Further away and to my left a cloud of luminescent mist rose and shaped itself into the a dragon before gently dissipating.

The lights were organized in a vast hollow circle surrounding an arrow-straight tree that thrust into the night sky, taller than any tree or building I had ever seen. It was hard to tell in the moonlight and distance, but I guessed that the trunk must be at least twenty feet across, perhaps more.

I had found the Concourse.

Chapter Twelve

I spread my improvised bedroll on a patch of meadow grass not long after sighting the Concourse, and slept until well past dawn. I washed up at a handy creek, and figured out a way to strap my armor to my haversack, as I expected that the local guard would not appreciate armor being worn.

My supply of food was running low, so I counted my money with care: five Marks from the fight at the Fist, and three Marks, two shillings, four pence left from what I had taken from the bandits. Not a lot of money, but not a little, either, but the problem was that I did not know how long it would have to last me. I sat beside the road and thought hard about this for a while; if I hadn't found them in two days, I decided, I would go to the pit and bet on the fights, perhaps even take a challenge if need be. Provine Sael would not like that, but I had no other way to earn money quickly.

Watching the flow of people into the Concourse's thronged streets, I reminded myself that I was a brute, a tusker, and I had to prove my worth every day I lived, and that I was the product of a respected barracks of the old school. I needed to keep my head in the right place, and return to my mistress, because when you engaged the Ebon Blades you got quality work, that was the rule.

Rising, I headed into the huge tent city.

It quickly became apparent that this wasn't anything like the faires I had seen before: as I approached the outskirts a man wearing only a leather codpiece and a long wooden nose stalked across the road on stilts that were taller than I was, and no one seemed too surprised to see him.

The fairs I had experienced had tents with games and contests, acts, and performers wandering around doing…well, performances. The entire activity was geared to extracting money from the herds of people who had come to be entertained and amazed; all in all, they had been pretty straightforward enterprises. I understood those sorts of faires because the pit was just a bloody version of the same. Pit fighters fought beasts, captured foes, and other pit fighters, pugilists battered each other, acrobats risked life and limb cavorting with hostile animals, and the like, all to entertain the paying customers and to serve as a venue for gambling. I was rather proud of the word 'venue', as Master Horne had explained it to me in some detail while I was escorting him to a meeting at the Desert Abyss. That had been a good day.

The Concourse wasn't anything like those faires, and it was more than just its size, The booths, tents, and stalls that lined the streets held no games of chance or challenges; some were clearly selling things, usually strange items of no apparent use or value, but others seemed to be just displays of art, or places where performers did entertaining things without hucksters urging the crowd for money. The crowd was made up of as many performers as ordinary people, and even the 'ordinary' people looked to be wealthier than you normally saw at faires, and a lot looked as if they had come here for serious business.

Moving into the Concourse I turned down a side 'street' for no particular reason and paused to get my bearings in front of a lot which had a statue of a big wolf made out of rough-hewn logs; the wolf was at least ten feet at the shoulder, and numerous people lounged on its back and head. What its purpose was, I couldn't guess, nor did I really care.

Crossing my arms, I leaned against a post that supported a cluster of unlit lamps and pretended to watch the crowd while I tried to think. I had to find Provine Sael in this place, but there were thousands of people here; it would be no easier than finding someone in Fellhome, except I had grown up in Fellhome. Thinking about it, I realized that I couldn't ask for her by name because the Sagrit might have people here on other business, and word might get back to them; I knew how fast rumors and loose talk moved in the circles that made money off the pits, and I didn't doubt that it would work everywhere else. People like to talk.

A couple Dellians passed as I stood there, and I had seen more than a few brutes, which explained why the group had been heading this way: even as mixed a bunch as we were would not stand out here.

"Are you troubled, friend?"

I realized the speaker was addressing me; a slender woman who had lines around her mouth that suggested she was older than she looked, with gray-streaked ash-blonde hair dyed blue and purple at the bottom; her eyebrows were dyed green and tiny gems drew arcs across her forehead above her eyes. She was wearing a deeply cut green dress that matched her eyebrows and hid very little of the tattoos that swirled across her arms and between her breasts, or much of anything else; a fine silver headband supported a twisted horn of burnished silver and copper just below her hairline.

"No," I managed, rather startled by her appearance, as well as the concern in her eyes.

"This place can be overwhelming when visited for the first time," she assured me, brushing at a strand of hair that had escaped the silver circlet.

"I'm looking for my comrades." I cursed inwardly: I should have said I was *waiting* for my comrades; being stupid was a serious handicap.

"Ah. That can be difficult here. If you need help seek people wearing these," she tapped her metal horn. "We are the Unicorns; we deal with problems and issues that may arise."

"What about a Watch, or guards?"

"We perform those duties as well."

"You?" She was alone and slender.

She smiled. "In a place like this, other skills are needed rather than muscle and steel."

"All right." Clearly she was a madwoman; you couldn't keep order without hitting people, of that I was certain. "I'm not troubled."

"Good." She patted my forearm, which was as thick as her thigh. "Be well, friend."

She moved on, and I returned to pondering my situation. Two days to find Provine Sael now seemed hopelessly optimistic; I wasn't sure I could see everything in the Concourse in that amount of time. Provine Sael would have our group lying low, and it occurred to me that they probably would not be watching for me because they would think I was dead. The odds against me just seemed to be getting worse and worse.

But when you engage the Ebon Blades, a proper barracks of the old school, you get quality work, that is the rule, I reminded myself; I was not going to give up. I had to keep my head in the right place and figure things out. I was sure that if Master Horne were here he would sort this matter out quickly and efficiently.

So how would Master Horne find Provine Sael without drawing the Sagrit's attention? I pondered that carefully.

"Excuse me, do you know the location of the Street of Unguents?" a genial-sounding man asked, speaking with a thick accent. He was a burly figure with a shaved scalp and a gray beard whose square-cut end touched his chest, which was largely bare as he was only wearing sandals, a leather kilt, and a necklace of thick polished sticks. Two words were tattooed in an arc across his hairy belly, but the letters were not from the alphabet Hatcher had taught me and Burk.

"No, sir. I just arrived." Inspiration struck me. "Do you know where the fighting pits are?"

He scowled. "Stay away from the blood-pits, friend. They are the death of culture and a poison of civilization." He stamped off into the crowd, his appearance drawing no attention.

After some thought I set forth as well; at the next intersection I studied the boards with street signs and directions painted on them, but I didn't know how to assemble many words yet. Casting about, I approached a woman with her waist-length hair worn in countless thin tight braids; she was wearing a dress made of tiny mirrors held together with silver wire, and nothing underneath. She was standing in the shade of a booth drinking a glass of wine and watching the crowd. "Excuse me, my lady, can you give me directions to the fighting pits?"

She took a slow sip of wine, studying me. "You are a pit fighter?"

That wasn't much of a secret. "Yes, my lady."

"I'm no one's lady. Why do you seek a place of death?"

"Money, m…, ah, for money."

"Many die in the pits."

I already knew that, having done a lot of killing in the pits, but I nodded as if it were news. "Yes. Can you direct me there?"

"We should not have pits here. Not in this place." She took another slow sip, then shook her head and told me the way.

Finding my way was easier than I expected: the streets following the long curve were named, and the short cross streets were numbered. I made my way carefully, aware of the possibility of pickpockets even though most of my money was tucked away in my boots. The variety of manners of dress in the crowds did not diminish as I moved through the Concourse; if anything, it grew stranger.

I tried to watch for my comrades and still get a feel for this place, but didn't make much headway towards either goal: there were just too many weird sights, sounds, and smells. I did see several people wearing the same sort of horn as had the crazy woman who said she was an enforcer; the horns weren't identical, but I guessed they all had the same dumb idea.

The fighting pits were actually a quarter mile outside the circle, but I found them without difficulty; like in most places the actual fighting arena was sunk into the earth to ensure that no one got to watch for free. The pits were surrounded by stands filled with seats, stacked so every customer could get a good view.

Men and brutes were practicing in the open areas around the pits, and animal handlers were feeding their caged charges; the air was rich with the smell of sweat, blood, and viscera, which struck a warm chord in my chest. It was like coming home.

I stood on the fringes and let the sights and sounds soak in; this was what I had been bred for, a place where I understood everything I needed to understand. Closing my eyes, I could hear Master Horne's voice calling me an idiot, or passing on some sour advice or admonishment.

My eyes snapped open: Master Horne had always told us that confidence and comfort killed, that the winner was the one still standing after the fight, and he was right. If the Sagrit were hunting Provine Sael here, the hunters would know she had bought pit fighters back in Fellhome. In fact, one of their people had seen me during the escort to the Desert Abyss. They might think that those pit fighters might end up at the fighting pits, and in fact Hunter had suggested something along those lines. I had sixty kills to my name, and was close to seven feet tall, big even by brute standards, and Burk was not just a High Rate, but a strong up-and-comer; there were pit fighter barracks who worked the circuit, and a large number of travelling gamblers as well. Master Horne didn't bother with the circuit; he always said that only the capitol hosted better games than Fellhome.

So there would be people here who knew the top killers of the Ebon Blades by sight and reputation, and that could be bad. The plan had been to lose the Sagrit by ambushing those following us and then going to the Concourse instead of a library, but that didn't mean that there wouldn't be Sagrit here on other business, and they might not have been fooled by our change in plans. From the pit I knew that feints did not always work, and tricks didn't always deceive.

But I knew the pits; I rubbed my jaw and tried to think like Master Horne. Talk moved fast in the pits, but it didn't always move far outside certain circles. Play your strengths, was what Master Horne often said.

Turning away from the pits, I spotted a washing station and headed over to it. Cranking up a full bucket of water from the well, I curled it a few times with each hand and then poured the water into the basin hollowed out of the top of one of the blocks of stone that surrounded the well. Digging out my sliver of soap from my pouch, I washed my shirt and spread it out to dry as I washed my head and torso.

As I washed up a sweaty brute wearing a simple tunic, trousers, and a loose canvas collar came up and cranked up a bucket of water. He poured it into a low basin and sat to remove his sandals. Given that he was unsupervised I guessed him to be a trusted High Rate or an advancing Medium.

"Training hard?" I asked, rinsing off my scalp.

He dunked a rag into the basin and started scrubbing his left foot. "You know it. You fight here yet?" He didn't have a brute's usual slur and choppy speech; clearly his master had paid for lessons.

"Not yet. I might, if I can find the right odds. Things were easier when the barracks handled that end of the business."

He nodded. "How long since you shed your collar?"

"A few months. Freedom hasn't been what I expected."

"I've heard that. A couple more wins and I'll find out for myself."

"What's your count?"

"Forty-two. My master says forty-eight and I'm free."

"That sounds fair."

"I'm ready."

"What will you do?"

He grinned mirthlessly. "What have you done?"

"Escort work, tried a mercenary company."

He nodded. "That's what I figure. Fighting is all we know."

"There's plenty of work."

He nodded and started on the other foot. "That's what I've been told. I may stick with the pit."

"Nothing wrong with the pit; you can make serious money there."

"True. Still, you wonder what else there is."

"Brutes are brutes," I shrugged and wrapped my soap in its oilskin. "We don't change when we take the collar off. Kids throw rocks sometimes."

"Yeah. If you don't fight in the pit, what will you do?"

I leaned against the basin-block, waiting for the sun to dry my skin. "I had a Nisker offer me a job, but I don't know how to find her; this place is weird."

"You can say that again." He wiped down his sandals. "And the little folk change names all the time."

"I figured," I nodded. "You don't see many around the pits."

He gestured towards a line of pavilions next to the training field. "You might talk to old Harmous, he works as trainer. He knows everything about everyone; look for a brute who is older than dirt and who is missing his left ear."

"Thanks."

"Don't mention it." He put his sandals on. "Does talking like a Man help, once you're free?"

I shrugged. "Maybe. I haven't been free long enough to really tell; it isn't as uncommon as I thought."

"My master thought it would help make others underestimate me."

"That's what they say. It helps with escort jobs, I think. People don't feel safe around a brute who talks like he has a mouthful of rocks."

Harmous was a short, broad brute with stubby under-tusks who was running to fat with age; he was sitting on a hogshead behind the pavilion drinking ale from a gallon mug and watching the clouds.

He had bulging eyes like a frog's, and they swiveled to track me as I walked up. "Grog. Ebon Blades." It came out as '*gwog, ebben bles*', pure brute-speak. He wasn't wearing a collar, but no free-born brute spoke like that, that was the patois of a slave upbringing.

"We met?"

"Nah. Seen you fight, lost a good brute to you last year."

"Would I remember him?"

"Nah. Heard you got free, been watching for you to surface. Looking for a trainer?"

"Not today, but who knows?"

"Me, I'm the best." '*meh, immna bess*'.

"I'll keep you in mind, but right now I need to find specific people."

"That's a good sword," he noted shrewdly.

"Found it along the road. You know any Niskers here at the Concourse?"

He slurped up ale. "Tricky, Niskers."

"Yeah."

He drank more ale, and I waited patiently. I knew Harmous' sort well: men and brutes, often ex-slaves, who kept the system running. They were the trainers, the recruiters, the equipment-masters, the fight planners. Most were ex-fighters, never great in the pit but smart enough to get side-tracked into non-lethal positions where they made themselves indispensable. They lived by cunning, guile, and knowing everything that happened in or around the pits. He probably had only seen me fight once or twice, but he recognized me at a glance a year later.

"Niskers don't show up at the pits." '*nicker no may da piss*'.

"But they like money, and in the pits there's more silver than blood." I had heard Master Horne say that.

He bobbed his head. "Yeah. And they all stick together." He slurped more ale. "They back the play."

He meant they bankrolled gambling operations. That had occurred to me while I was washing up; I had known that the pits were built around gambling long before I had ever stepped into one, and while I had never seen too many Niskers, everyone knew they loved money. Or at least that was what everyone said, which meant there was probably some truth in it. They also were reported to stick together, which made sense because they were small.

"So who is a good Nisker to talk to in the Concourse?"

He slurped ale and rubbed the scars that welled up around where his left ear had been. "Dunno, me."

"Huh." I looked around. "All right, I guess I heard wrong. See you around."

"You heard I know everybody," he grinned. *'Oo hed muh gob all-roun'*.

"I did."

"Maybe I do, but not for free."

I nodded. "I'll pay a full Mark."

He slurped ale thoughtfully. "You going to remember Harmous?"

"If a Mark buys me help, win or lose, I will definitely remember you. The pit lives on silver, and is run by the honor of a handshake." Another of Master Horne's sayings, but it was true.

He grunted and held out his hand. I dropped one of Marks I had gotten at the Fist into his palm. "I wasn't here, by the way."

Harmous grinned. "Nobody ever is."

Harmous didn't know street names, but he didn't need to: there were numerous timber beasts scattered throughout the Concourse to act as signposts for those who couldn't read, or only read other languages. With his directions I didn't have much trouble finding a stall whose rafters displayed a flock of haversacks, packs, and similar bags. It was staffed by Niskers, more than you would think were necessary to sell leather goods.

"Can I help you, sirrah?" A young Nisker bustled up as I approached. "A new haversack, perhaps? We have a selection."

"I'm looking for Berlon Torho."

He studied me for a long second before turning to the rear of the stall. "Master?"

"What?" An older Nisker came out from the back of the stall; he had the same mop of walnut hair and clear blue eyes as the youngling, but his eyes were hard and confident despite the fact he was shorter than my sword's blade. "Can I help you?"

"I'm looking for a friend of mine, a specialist," I had worked out the words on my hour-long walk here. "A container and traps specialist, female, with red hair. She wears a lot of green, is good in a fight, and goes by Hatcher sometimes. She's somewhere in the Concourse."

He pursed his lips in thought before shaking his head. "Never heard of her."

"Tell her that her horse has found his way back. I'll be at the badger down the road."

He looked down the lane at the statue. "I thought that was a muskrat."

I looked as well, and then shrugged. "Well, that statue, anyway."

"Huh." He studied the shape as if it were a problem that had to be solved. "Well, I don't hold truck with people who engage in that sort of work, but if anyone who meets that description stops by my stall, I'll pass the word."

"Thanks. She will be glad to see me."

He cocked an eyebrow at that. "Hard to imagine that, no offense intended: you look like trouble and bloody mayhem on legs."

"I am," I admitted. "But only when I'm getting paid for trouble and bloody mayhem."

He nodded thoughtfully. "I'm but a simple shopkeeper, so don't expect much."

The creature's neck was built at such an angle that I could stretch out comfortably and still be able to watch the traffic on the lane. It was so comfortable that I dozed off, my sheathed sword across my chest and my haversack beneath my head.

"You! Large half-breed person: wake up!"

I sat up, wiping my face and peering around. The sun was low in the sky and lanterns were springing to life across the Concourse. My nap had been ended by a dark-haired young woman who was remarkably thin; she was wearing tall, very thick-soled leather boots and a mass of twisted and burnished brass wire that enveloped her torso. "Me?"

"Yes, *you*." She pointed a small umbrella made from brass-colored paper decorated with green birds in flight at me for emphasis. "You are disharmonizing my turtle."

I stared at her. "I'm…what?"

"You are disharmonizing my turtle! My *turtle*," she thrust the small umbrella at the log sculpture, and a young woman dressed in loose gauzy linen tunic and trousers who just happened to be passing by had to duck to avoid getting stabbed in the face.

"Watch yourself," the girl observed mildly, straightening the white bunny ears she wore, getting a glare in return from the wire-woman.

"I thought it was a badger." I sat up and turned so that my feet hung down.

"This is *intolerable*!" she spun on her heel and strode off. I guessed that with those built-up soles she would nearly be able to look me in the eye, although she was so thin I figured she wouldn't weigh as much as one of my legs, if that. Her hair was the thickest thing about her, nearly reaching her waist.

A vendor passed and I called him over and exchanged four pennies for a mug-full of sweet cider.

I was still sipping the last of the cider when the wire-woman returned, her long dark hair swinging with the urgency of her steps. She had a Unicorn in tow, a solidly-built man wearing white boots, a yellow and red kilt, and his horn of office.

"*There*!" she pointed at me with her umbrella. "He is *disharmonizing* my *turtle*!"

"It's a turtle?" The Unicorn eyed the statue.

"I thought it was a badger," I offered. "The shopkeeper down the way said it was a muskrat."

"It is *clearly* a turtle." The wire-woman snapped.

"I can see it now," the Unicorn nodded slowly, rubbing his close-cropped beard. "A turtle."

"Now do your duty and *stop* him!"

"You want this gentleman to stop disharmonizing this turtle," the Unicorn clarified.

"Yes!"

"Will you?" he asked me.

"I had no idea I was disharmonizing this; I didn't even know it was a turtle," I advised. "I thought I was just resting here while I was waiting for a friend." I jerked a thumb over my shoulder towards the five or six others who were relaxing on what I now knew was the turtle's shell. "No one told me."

"This seems fairly straightforward," the Unicorn observed. "This gentleman will cease disharmonizing the turtle."

"I never meant to," I added.

"Do not presume to *speak down* to *me*," the wire-woman snapped, closing her umbrella with a brisk snap and tapping its tip against the Unicorn's hairy chest with each word. "I did not create this art only to have it *debased* in such a manner."

"These artworks are intended to be used as rest points and providers of shade," the Unicorn noted mildly.

"But not by blood-drenched creatures of the death-matches!"

The Unicorn's face hardened, but his voice remained even. "Here at the Concourse all conflicts, both national and personal, are set aside."

"I *know* that." The wire-woman tossed her long hair. "But this is an *artistic* issue, not a personal conflict."

"I don't plan to fight in the pits here," I offered. "And I had a bath yesterday and a wash-down today."

The wire-woman spun face me. "You *see!*" she pointed at me with the umbrella. "The brute admits it!"

"We are all free folk here," the Unicorn fingered one of the pendants hanging on leather cords around his neck. "And will be spoken to with respect."

"I *am* a brute," I pointed out, feeling a need to be part of the discussion.

"Be that as it may…," the Unicorn began, but the wire-woman snapped her umbrella open in his face. He brushed it aside. "Madam, you will respect my personal space."

"You are a *disgrace!*" she snapped. "My poor turtle!"

A second Unicorn joined us, a slender young woman wearing a simple sleeve-less white dress and with her blond hair pulled back into a pony tail. She wore a piece of silver jewelry in the center of her forehead right below her horn of office and a few pendants on silver chains, but otherwise was quite plainly dressed. "May I assist, Cama?"

"This is Lady Migarun," the male Unicorn, who apparently was named Cama, indicated the wire-woman. "She created this way-sculpture, and objects to this pit-fighter using it." He indicated me. "I am sorry, I did not get your name."

I had thought about this on the walk here. "Sharcul. I didn't know I was disharmonizing it."

"And I am Aramar," the new Unicorn smiled.

"Aramar is a senior member of our group," Cama noted; to me she didn't look old enough to be a Unicorn.

"So, Lady Migarun, you feel that Sharcul is disharmonizing your depiction of an opossum?" Aramar smiled brightly.

"It…is…a…*turtle*," Lady Migarun said through gritted teeth.

"I thought it was a badger," I said helpfully.

"Said de-harmonization is based upon Skarcul's occupation," Cama noted.

"A pit fighter," Aramar nodded. "Surely you do understand that all are welcome at the Concourse, Lady Migarun, and that when you were commissioned to erect this structure you were made aware that it was for public use?"

"I was," Lady Migarun admitted. "But I certainly never imagined that the masses would include his *sort*."

"His sort?" Aramar's smile remained, but now it was just a formality.

"I'm a brute," I noted in case anyone was blind. "And a pit fighter in the past, although now I serve as a bodyguard."

"He is a *killer*."

"I am," I agreed.

"But you are not a killer here," Cama noted.

"The Concourse exists in its own sphere, my lady. All law is suspended save that which has been proclaimed by the Twelve. All manner of feuds, judgements, and debts are left outside. Here Sharcul is just another visitor, albeit rather larger and better-armed than most." Aramar pointed out.

"So long as the pits are allowed here, so are their denizens," Cama added. "Each year the subject is raised, and each year they are allowed to remain."

"I can tell you that I will not grace another of these farces with my *art*," Lady Migarun snarled and stomped off in her tall boots.

"So, should I go someplace else?" I asked when she was out of earshot.

"Better not," Cama sighed. "No telling how many of these she made."

"I can see the turtle now," Aramar said thoughtfully. "But I wouldn't be bragging that I made it." She looked up at me. "Your name isn't Sharcul," she smiled. "And you're not long removed from killing. Remember that this is a peaceful place."

"I will," I assured her, a little uneasy.

After Unicorns left I found a stall where a silver shilling got me a bowl-full of some sort of stew, a half-loaf of stale bread, and a mug of very good ale. After washing out my eating gear I gave three copper pennies to have my mug re-filled and headed back to the turtle.

Freedom's decision-making was weighing on me: how long should I wait to see if the Niskers really kept in touch with each other? At what point should I look to earning more money? The only place I could do that was at the pits, and I had already been recognized once. The agents and staff at the pits worked the circuit, and more than a few would know Fellhome's top fighters, by name if not sight.

Choices, choices, choices: I was really getting sick of them.

Back at the turtle I stood in the growing twilight debating reclaiming my spot on the neck-head, or just wandering around for a while. The quandary was solved when a whoop erupted overhead and then Hatcher dove off the turtle's shell and landed on the back of my neck, neatly avoiding the sword's hilt.

Chapter Thirteen

"You're ALIVE!" she shouted in my ear, doing her best to strangle me.

I reached around and lifted her so she was sitting on my shoulders. "I am. And I'm glad to see you."

She gripped my left hand in both of hers and drummed her heels against my chest. "We thought you were dead: Torl and Burk both went down ropes into the sinkhole, but the water was too fast to wade through, and it filled the passage to both sides. We spent *hours* trying to figure out a way to go after you. How did you survive?"

"Luck, and some help. I came out miles from where I went in, and had to kill some bandits. Lucky for me, I knew where you were going."

"Burk didn't believe you were dead; he said you would show up. Provine Sael was so depressed she could hardly speak. Even Hunter was mildly put out."

"I am hard to kill. Is everyone all right?"

"Yes, we've been here for several days. How long were you underground?"

"I don't know, but I got my bearings when I got outside and came here pretty fast."

She let go of my hand to hug my head. "I'm so glad you're all right."

I didn't know what to say, so I patted her back.

"All right," she sat up. "We better get back to the others. Head the way you're facing and take the next left. How did you know how to get word to me?"

"I always heard Niskers stick together; I went to the pits because I knew the staff there always know everything about anyone with money."

"You mean everyone in crime," she chuckled. "Not all Niskers are that way, but those of us who leave the homeland are either cooks or rather shady sorts."

"I was recognized at the pits; just one brute, but I can't say if he'll keep quiet."

"Don't worry about it. Once the…the people looking for us realize we doubled back and took out our followers, they'll sent word to every place where Provine Sael can get the knowledge she needs, and the Concourse will be on the list. But suspecting we're here and finding us are two different things. Berlon will pass on a message, but he had a couple of his lads keep an eye on you until I responded."

"What if the people following us get rough with him?"

She giggled. "How intimidated did he seem when you talked to him?"

"Not at all."

"And with good reason. We're small, but we can fight, and Berlon doesn't just employ Niskers. He's not one of the happy, friendly Niskers; I don't like him personally, but he's useful."

"But will he keep your secret?"

"Yeah. Berlon is the head of a criminal organization, and in that sort of situation you have to have a reputation for keeping your word. And he's married to a distant cousin of mine. But the surest safety comes from the fact that he loathes those who are following us. Take the next right."

It took nearly an hour to get to the others, partially because Hatcher took us on a twisting route; she said it was to make sure that no one was following us.

"Only in the Concourse could an incredibly cute Nisker girl ride on the shoulders of a well-known seven-foot pit fighter and not draw attention," she observed as we navigated the crowd.

"What do you mean 'well-known'?"

"Hmmmm? Oh, people knew you back in Fellhome; when you were escorting us I met a number of people who knew who you were."

"Hunter didn't know me," I pointed out.

"Hunter isn't from Fellhome, he was just laying low there. And his judgement isn't the best on a lot of subjects, which is why he was laying low in Fellhome, and why he took the job with us: Provine Sael was able to clear his name on a couple things."

"I thought it was just for money."

"He is getting paid, but not the sort of coin that would motivate him to cross the sort of people who are following us." She was silent for a bit. "So why didn't you head back to Fellhome? That would have been the smart move."

"Provine Sael is my mistress, so coming back was only proper."

"She wrote out your papers back at the Fist."

"When you engage the Ebon Blades, you get quality work, that is the rule."

She hooted and slapped the top of my head. "You're something else, Grog, a child inside a killer's hide."

I started to object to being called a killer but caught myself: I really was. "I don't feel like a killer," I said eventually. "I just do what is required."

"That you do, my friend, and you're living proof that there are two types you never want to cross: those who love killing more than living, and those who see killing as just a job to be done."

I thought about that. "I suppose."

"So, what do you think about the Concourse?"

"It is *weird*,"

"That it can be," she drummed on my scalp. "And pretty, and funny…I never feel like the same person when I leave."

"Why?"

"I guess because I learn something about myself each time I come here."

"Huh."

"You're happy the way you are, aren't you, Grog?'

I thought about that. "I don't know what you mean."

"You don't dream of being someone or something else."

"My life was pretty well sorted out," I said slowly. "At least, until Provine Sael bought me and Burk."

"You're lucky: you know who you are."

"How can anyone not know who they are?"

She sighed. "Lots of people wish they were something else, or someone else. They would like to be braver, stronger, smarter, prettier…that sort of thing."

"Oh."

"Me, I'm pretty happy with myself, but I know a lot of people who spend their lives trying to be, or at least pretending to be, what they're not."

"That's good. You being happy with yourself, I mean."

She drummed on my head. "But I wish I had hair like Provine Sael; red hair is so common. I could dye mine, but it would still look like a cheap mop after a lot of use. Hers stays exactly just so, did you ever notice?"

"No."

"Of course you didn't. Men get out of bed, rub some water on their face, and wander around feeling handsome. A woman has to *work* to be pretty or stay pretty."

"Maybe that's a Nisker thing?"

She snorted. "Nope. There's a shared sisterhood that cuts across the races, trust me. And let me tell you another thing…"

I hadn't realized how quiet it had been since I had fallen into the sinkhole.

Akel was brushing down one of the mules outside a big tent at the end of a sort of alley; he broke into a huge grin when he saw us. "Grog! Hatcher sent word you might be alive. It is good to see you!"

"Good to be seen," I shrugged, a little embarrassed.

Hatcher summersaulted to the ground. "Is everyone here?"

"Provine Sael and Burk are still out." He said 'out' in such a manner as to indicate something important.

"Her research," Hatcher noted to me. "C'mon."

She led the way into the big tent, which was a lot taller than I was, and inside the material of the tent seemed to glow with what remained of the sunlight. About half the inside was screened off into individual sleeping areas, leaving a common area dominated by thick tent poles and a big wood table. Torl and Hunter sat at opposite ends of the table, the scout sharpening arrowheads while Hunter drank brandy and read a book.

"Look what the cat dragged in!" Hatcher exclaimed and hopped up to stand on a chair so she could help herself to a swig from Hunter's bottle.

"Use a glass if you are going to steal good brandy," Hunter shook his head, setting the book in his lap. "I would have lost good money betting on your survival," he toasted me with his glass.

"Welcome back," Torl said, but he stood and came over to shake my hand.

"Gah," Hatcher shook her head and took another pull from the bottle. "You are such *men*. Grog returns from certain death, and you act as if he just came back from buying food."

"Well, he brought *you* with him," Hunter pointed out. "You're more annoying than any three people I know."

Hatcher winked at him and took another swig from the fat-bellied bottle before thumping it down onto the table top. "There's your bunk," she pointed. "Burk put your gear there. He insisted you were coming back."

"Correctly so," Torl sat back down and returned to his arrows.

"You were supposed to be fetching our supper," Hunter noted. "Grog is welcome, but so would be our food."

Hatcher threw up her hands. "What a bunch of disloyal bastards. Fine, fine, I'll go. Grog, rest your feet, I'll take Akel." She swept out of the tent.

"It is good to see you," Hunter advised when she was gone. "I didn't think anyone could come out of that blackness."

"I had help," I sat at the table and shook my head when Hunter offered a glass.

"I had a good look at the channel; if you didn't drown I thought there was a chance the water would lead you out," Torl observed as he stroked a stone along an arrow's edge.

"It wasn't deep, and Master Horne had us wear weights in water to build up our endurance," I nodded. "The problem was getting out of the water, but I got lucky."

"Your old master hammered luck into you," Hunter poured more brandy into his glass. "I saw that at the Fist:

the mind gives out before the body." He regarded me over the rim of his glass. "What I do, the use of the Arts, is much the same: the fight doesn't always goes to the strongest or even the most skilled; it often goes to those who have lost the concept of defeat."

That was the most he had ever said to me, and it was true: muscle and reflexes are good, even great, but you win in your mind. A fighter who enters the pit expecting to lose is seldom found to be wrong, Master Horne often said. The great ones, he had always added, never really believed that losing was an option.

Hatcher and Akel returned with two kettles filled with rice and meat, a half-dozen fresh-baked loaves of bread, a small keg of ale, and a bowl of greens for Provine Sael. While they had been out I had washed up and donned clean clothes from my pack.

We had just finished laying out the food and eating ware when Provine Sael ducked through the tent flap, Burk on her heels. Her face lit up as she saw me. "Grog! Hatcher sent word it was possible." She swept around the table and grabbed me in a fierce embrace. "I hardy dared to hope."

"I'm back," I noted, uncomfortably patting her back, unsure how exactly this should handled, and wishing it was over. I was extremely glad to be back, but I would prefer to have this part over and forgotten.

Finally, she stepped back, wiping at her eyes. "How did you find us?"

"The Concourse was easy to find; I checked with the staff at the pits, and found out who among the Niskers knew everyone. But I was recognized."

She brushed that away. "The Sagrit may not consider the pits, and in any case they will find us sooner or later. What is important is that you are back."

Burk stepped up and punched me on the shoulder. "I put your stuff there," he jerked a thumb towards my sleeping area."

"Thanks." I slugged him on the shoulder.

Out of the corner of my eye I saw Hatcher rolling her eyes. "Enough heart-warming displays of comradeship," the Nisker observed. "Let's eat."

"So how go your studies?" Hunter asked as we all dug in.

"Good," Provine Sael stirred the greens on her plate with her fork. "It is all coming together."

"Will the muscle we have be sufficient?"

"Grog is back," she favored me with a small but warm smile. "And that will have to do. The Sagrit's efforts have spread: I doubt anyone worth having would go with us."

"What about buying more pit fighters? With all the coin we captured from the Sagrit ambush, money's no problem."

"I dislike that." She ate a forkful of greens thoughtfully. "And in any case few schools train their fighters to be as loyal as the Ebon Blades."

Burk gave me a pleased look at that, and I nodded: when you engage the Ebon Blades, you get quality work, that is the rule.

"A small group is better protection than a larger group of uncertain value," Torl observed. "I doubt we could hire or buy enough blades to be completely safe."

Hunter nodded and poured himself more brandy.

"Grog, I have been explaining to the others how my process has been developing," Provine Sael noted after the meal was over. "With the pieces finally gathered, I believe I now know where the bones of the first Emperor were laid to rest."

"Unfortunately, since he now has a tomb in the capitol, that knowledge, or even the bones, isn't worth much," Hatcher inserted.

"True," Provine Sael nodded. "But he was laid to rest with his sword and helm, both of which were powerfully enchanted, and cannot be mistaken for anything but what they are."

"Why did they leave such powerful things with his body?" I asked.

"It was a different time; the metal for such enchantments was more commonly available. In any case, my plan is to recover the first Emperor's remains, his helm, sword, and anything else buried with him."

"And give them to the current Emperor?"

She stared into the distance, absently stroking one horn-nub. "In a sense. They certainly would shore up the authority of his throne."

I wondered why he didn't just build a new throne, but let it pass. "I expect he will be grateful."

"No doubt. But it will not be a gift." She saw me watching her and put her hand on the table. "I intend to trade the items to him in return for the end of slavery."

That was a surprise, but I just nodded.

"And that's how you know she's crazy," Hunter grinned. "She could have a title, lands, or enough gold to fill a couple wagons to the brim, but *nooo*..."

Provine Sael glanced sideways at Hunter. "If I accomplish this, not only have we eliminated a grave evil, but the Sagrit will lose their rallying issue and be reduced to nothing more than a group who wants to pull down the existing order."

"The Sagrit's true believers will never forgive or forget you," Hunter sighed. "You'll spend the rest of your life dodging assassins."

"She'll spend the rest of her life protected by Ebon Blades," Burk growled, and Hunter held up a palm in gesture of peace.

"The Sagrit who love anarchy are mostly nothing to worry about," Hatcher said from where she sat cross-legged on the table shaking sauce onto her rice. "The dangerous ones are the ones who joined to stop slavery and are blind to the senseless methods the Sagrit endorse. End slavery and what will be left of the Sagrit won't amount to much." She took a pull from her mug. "But you had better stay mobile for a couple years," she added.

"I'll worry about that after the deed is done," Provine Sael waved a hand dismissively.

"So you expect the Emperor to free all the slaves?" I asked, rubbing my scalp. "That will ruin a lot of people." I was thinking of Master Horne in particular.

"The condition will be that he makes Rebigar's Emancipation the law of the land," Provine Sael explained. "Rebigar is a highly regarded legal scholar who penned a plan for the peaceful end of slavery. He summed it up in a simple plan, although the actual law runs into the dozens of pages. The plan is: when the law is passed no one may be made a slave for debts or crime, and five years to the day of the law's passage every slave is free. The trick is that during that five years, any slave owner may free his or her slave or slaves and have the value of those slaves deducted from his or her taxes."

"That way the businesses which are built upon slave labor have time to convert to a free work force," Hatcher pointed out. "There's lots of clauses and stuff, but that's the gist. No one goes bankrupt, no one loses their investment, everything is done peacefully and orderly."

"Fat chance of that," Hunter grunted.

Hatcher grinned. "Yeah, there will always be trouble with any new law, but it beats the Sagrit plan of civil war and revolution all rolled into one."

"True," Hunter admitted.

"Something has to give," Torl agreed. "The Empire is sorely beset, and the Sagrit don't care; they just want the old order pulled down without any thought to how a new order could be established, nor why the Dusmen would sit on their hands while the Empire tears itself apart from within."

"I wanted you and Burk to understand what the stakes are," Provine Sael.

I glanced at Burk. "I fight for you, my lady. Free or slave makes no difference to me."

She nodded sharply, looking sad for some reason. "I completed Burk's manumission paperwork already, and I will do yours tomorrow."

"Thank you." It should feel special, I suppose, but after all the trouble I had getting back to the group, I just wanted to return to following orders and leaving the thinking to others.

The next morning, after Provine Sael set off to do her research, Burk and I worked with buckets of water and other exercises, and then sparred for an hour, staying in the little cul de sac formed by the tents and booths nearby. All seemed to be living quarters because there was no casual foot traffic.

"That's a nice sword," Burk observed as I was sluicing off the sweat at the end of our session.

"Help yourself," I waved to where it was hanging from a tent pole. "I lost my dopplehander when I fell in the sinkhole."

"Light and quick, especially for its size," Burk replaced the blade in its scabbard.

"I like it. A stranger gave it to me for killing some bandits."

"Looks brand-new."

"Yeah. The fellow who gave it to me was really strange."

"So how was being your own master?"

"Hard: lots of thinking, lots of decisions. I'm glad to be back."

He nodded thoughtfully. "Things aren't like I imagined. We should stick to taking orders."

"That's how I see it."

"You really think she could get slavery done away with?"

"Who knows? It took everything I had to figure out a way to find her in the Concourse. Way I see it, she's smarter than both of us, so she does the thinking, we do the fighting, and everything ought to work out."

"Yeah. You see the people wandering around here? They dress like…I don't know what. It's no way to behave."

Burk and his Standards. "I think it has to do with this place, like the log statues and weird stuff they sell."

"It's just not how people should behave. And these Unicorns: that's no way to handle security. What's wrong with a well-swung length of hickory? You get the point across quick that way."

"You're not wrong. You just know that people who dress like they do here are going to be smoking flowers and running around with a cleaver before it's all over," I nodded as I slung my sword across my back. "You have to be ready for anything."

"How are the pits here?"

"Like going home," I poured us each of mug of ale. "Same smells, same sounds; they understand proper conduct, that's for certain. Trouble was, a brute staffer recognized me."

"Damn." He drained his mug and poured another. "I wouldn't mind a match before we leave, knock the rust off."

"Me either, but you know Provine Sael wouldn't hear of it."

"Do you suppose she's never seen a good match?"

"I think she doesn't like violence in general."

His brow furrowed as he considered the concept. "Why?"

"Dunno." I drew myself another mug and sat on a handy stool. "She's not afraid of it, you've seen that."

"That's just not right," Burk shook his head.

"What's not right?" Hatcher asked as she came up, trailed by Akel, who was leading a mule loaded with purchases.

"Provine Sael's attitude about fighting in the pits," Burk shrugged. "I wouldn't mind a match."

"She's a civilized person." Hatcher tossed me a horn document case, and gave each of us a heavy coin bag. "Your papers are now registered so you are free in every legal sense of the word, except that you still have to follow orders, so not much practical change."

"What's the money for?" I tucked both items into my belt pouch.

"Pay; you're free now, remember? Fifteen Marks in silver and copper, plus I got you another kettle hat, Grog."

"What does being civilized have to do with pit fights?" Burk wasn't distracted.

Hatcher grinned at him. "She doesn't believe thinking beings killing each other or beasts for entertainment is a reasonable thing."

"Huh." I could see Burk was far from convinced, but he wasn't going to push it. He weighed the little sack of coins. "What about *betting* on pit matches?"

She sighed. "C'mon, let us work on the basics of reading."

"Do you think the Emperor will accept her offer if we find the grave?" I asked as we sat down at the table with our slates and chalk.

"In theory he already has agreed," Hatcher shrugged. "He put the word out a couple years ago that if someone could get him the sword or helm, or both, he'll make Rebigar's Emancipation law. He's a good man; two years ago he made a couple laws that drastically reduced the conditions under which free men can be enslaved for debt or crime, and he put a tax on all slaves. It sent a message."

"What message?"

She rolled her eyes. "That the Emperor does not like slavery. Since then there's been a small but steady decline in the slave population. No one wants to risk having a lot of gold invested in slaves only to wake up one morning to a law freeing all slaves. It's not enough, but it is definitely a start. Rebigar's Emancipation protects slave-owners from bankruptcy, especially since it affords the opportunity to rook the Empire out of extra taxes by claiming inflated values of freed slaves."

"So why didn't Rebigar see that?" Burk asked.

"He did that on purpose: if you threaten to take away a person's property, they will be inclined to resist, even rise up and fight. Civil war has always been the threat slave-owners have used against efforts to end slavery. But Rebigar left loopholes in his law, and slave owners who see an opportunity to turn a profit by freeing their slaves are not going to rise up in arms. In fact, it gives slave owners an incentive to support the Empire. However, it means five years of lean tax years for the Empire and a lot of social and economic change, so the Emperor has been slow to embrace it. But getting the symbols of the first Emperor's power is worth a lot more than five years of poor tax revenues, and at the end of the five years he's rid of a divisive institution. But it all depends on us finding the items, and getting them to the capitol." She frowned. "And assuming that the Emperor will honor the promise he made unofficially."

"The Sagrit will try to stop Provine Sael from finding them," Burk frowned, clearly thinking hard. "Or seizing them if she does find them."

"Exactly. She's hardly the first to try, and several who did came to bad ends."

"So why doesn't the Emperor send Legion troops to secure them?" I asked.

"Because people have been looking for the first Emperor's grave for generations. Provine Sael stumbled upon a clue which has led her to this point, but over the years a lot of people, including past Emperors, have spent a lot of gold on people who thought they had the right clue. Nobody is going to believe her until she has the items in hand. There's even a chance we'll find the grave and learn it's empty, robbed by someone years ago."

"Makes you wonder why anyone would try," Burk noted.

"Because she wants slavery to end," Hatcher shook her head. "You would not believe how hard it was for her to buy you two and subject you to the risks of this endeavor. I thought she was going to explode on the spot when Grog walked into the ring at the Fist."

"I've had tougher matches," I shrugged.

"But not on her behalf. Anyway, let's get started; it's best to keep busy and out of sight."

After supper that evening Hatcher, Burk, and me were sitting outside looking at the stars and finishing the ale. "Is there any word on how Merrywine fared?" I asked.

"Yeah, a cohort arrived two days after we left, and the Dusmen took their toys and went home," Hatcher snatched a firefly out of the air, and then released it unharmed.

"That's good. So everyone went back to their strips of land."

"Yeah, pretty much."

"That was a good fight," Burk mused. "You really feel like you did something, after a fight like that."

"It was a good one," I agreed. "I liked killing that Ukar at the Fist, too. I haven't worked in close much since I got my last growth."

"You two are depressing to listen to," Hatcher tried to get a firefly to land on her finger.

"Why?"

"It gives an insight into how your childhood must have been."

"We had a good childhood," Burk noted stiffly. "Lots to eat, plenty of fresh air."

Hatcher chuckled. "I stand corrected. Sometimes I forget that there are different skills than traps and locks."

"The world is a lot more…mixed up than I expected," I observed. "I miss the barracks."

"Yeah," Burk sighed.

For three more days we laid low, exercised, and worked on sums and the business of building words from letters; Hatcher had picked up several primers intended for children, and we laboriously sussed out the undertakings of a small boy named Tam who picked flowers for his mother.

Hatcher had bought me a new kettle hat to replace the one I had lost in the water; she offered to get me another war hammer, but I declined, as I had gotten comfortable with the short axe I had taken from the bandits. I spent a lot of time working with my new sword, getting the feel of it down properly, and Akel sold one of the mules as it was developing a problem with one of its hooves.

Finally Provine Sael announced that she had completed her studies and we would be leaving on the morrow. "I'm afraid this final leg of our journey will be dangerous: the grave site is an area frequented by Tulg patrols, and the Sagrit will be looking for us."

"By now they'll have figured out what we did," Hunter agreed. "If it were me hunting you, my first choice would be the Concourse."

"I expect they'll send out more than one group," Torl nodded. "There are finite research options within a reasonable march."

"What I wish we knew is why the Sagrit group we ambushed had left our trail," Hatcher sighed. "I hate loose ends."

I had forgotten about all that. "You didn't find out?"

"They had dug into the karst and uncovered some plates etched with strange symbols. And by plates, I mean like you eat off of, made of thick green glass."

"Plates?"

"Yeah, thirty of them. Akel picked up some lumber and made a travel case for them after we got here, and Provine Sael arranged with a friend to ship them to Fellhome; maybe when all this is done we can find someone who knows what they are for, or about, or whatever."

"If you can eat off it, how important could they be?"

"They might not be for eating, but for display or something like that. Who knows?"

We slipped out of the Concourse just before dawn and headed west, pushing hard for half a day to put some distance between us and anyone who might be trailing us.

After the mid-day meal Hatcher walked with Hunter, deep in a debate about gambling or similar undertaking; I couldn't really follow the conversation. I drifted back and walked with Burk and Akel, and after a while I told them about Burya and Willen.

"They had no loyalty to their house?" Burk scowled. "Becoming free is a noble pursuit, but..." he shrugged.

"You two, if you're pardon my metaphor, are two race horses talking about a pit pony," Akel grinned.

"What's a pit pony?" Burk asked. In the past Akel had spent a considerable time explaining the nuances of a metaphor.

"A pony they use in mines to pull loads of ore-bearing rock to the surface."

"Racing isn't easy," I pointed out. "I've seen horse races: they have to run really fast."

"Race horses are specially selected, and fed and tended well," Akel explained. "They are carefully trained, housed well, and cared for. Yes, they have to work hard on a race, which lasts a few minutes, but they spend far more time training and idling than races. But pit ponies work six days a week, and nearly always underground."

"Huh." Burk shrugged.

"What I am trying to say is that you pair are not ordinary slaves. You were trained from childhood to fight in the pits, which is a considerable investment. When you were young, say ten years old, where did you sleep?"

We exchanged a glance. "Well, ten, you see...well, we always lived in the same barracks."

Akel nodded. "Did the roof leak?"

"Well, once, but the next sunny day it got fixed."

"Sleep on the floor?"

"No, we got cots."

"Straw mattress and a blanket?"

"Well, three blankets, but yeah."

"Get a dollop of mashed turnips or potatoes with a few bits of greens mixed in and a biscuit to start your day?"

"No, usually oatmeal, fried bread, and eggs for breakfast."

"Tomatoes when they were in season," Burk added.

"At a table, with plates?"

"Yeah."

"All you could eat?"

"Sure."

"Meat?"

"At mid-day and the evening meal. Sow belly at breakfast after we started the last phase of our core training."

"Anyone treat you inappropriately?"

We exchanged glances. "What do you mean?"

"Did any of the older boys or adult staff ever...well, *touch* you?"

"Oh. Well, a trainer got caught messing with one kid in the age block before us; the trainer was gone the next day."

"So you felt safe there?"

"Sure."

Akel grinned. "What I was describing is the life of an ordinary slave. Why would someone be loyal to a place that didn't feed them well, keep them safe, or bother with their well-being?"

"The Ebon Blades are a respected barracks of the old school!" Burk jabbed a finger at Akel.

"Of course," Akel held up his hands in a peace gesture. "But very few slaves experienced anything like the barracks of the Ebon Blades."

I thought about the slaves I had seen at Limerock. "I see your point."

Burk wasn't as convinced. "But if you have no loyalty, no pride, what good are you?"

"Slaves seldom have pride; it gets beaten out of them early," Akel noted. "To have hope you have to believe in something, and slaves with hope think about running."

"Huh." Burk thought about that.

"If they do away with slavery," I said slowly, thinking hard. "What will the slaves do? Willen and Burya were pretty useless."

"That is a problem," Akel nodded. "I'm afraid most will end up doing the same sort labor they did as slaves, and for a low wage. But their children will have chance for something better."

"So that's what Provine Sael is giving up so much for? That maybe the next generation will have things better?"

Akel shrugged. "I don't speak for her."

I pondered this as we walked. "We're lucky we learned a skill," I observed after considerable thought.

"Are you?" Akel asked.

"We are," Burk snapped, and I nodded. "We can earn good money in the pits as freedmen."

"Or join a mercenary company, or do escort work," I pointed out. "Hatcher says she needs muscle for some jobs, and Provine Sael will need bodyguards. There's plenty of work."

"Wouldn't you rather do something other than kill?"

"It's honest work," Burk shrugged.

Chapter Fourteen

As I trudged west with Hatcher on my shoulders talking about this or that, I pondered what Akel had said, and what I had seen.

Growing up in the barracks, the pit was at the end of the road we all were on, and the only fears we had was being sent away for not being good enough. We weren't sure where those who were Sent Away went, but they definitely went away, and none came back. Our age block didn't have anyone fail, but other age blocks did.

From the time we were big enough to walk and run there was training, first just building muscle, balance, endurance, and discipline, then the training in fighting, both armed and unarmed. Plenty of food, because you needed plenty to get the size and muscle the pit demanded; some barracks trained for speed and deftness, but the Ebon Blades tended to fight in the heavy classes. It occurred to me that Master Horne must have chosen us for our potential size when he bought us, and he must have a good eye for it, because even the shortest among us had good bones.

When we got older they brought in girls periodically; I wasn't sure if they had been slaves or free, but they knew what they were doing, which was good, because we didn't.

But training led to blood fights, or in my case, pugilism, and then into the pit itself, where death waited. In the barracks the number of empty cots increased as our comrades met their destiny, while others of us returned from the pits time and time again. That number dwindled steadily, and then stabilized as we became the Ebon Blades' fighting line.

Unlike most barracks, we had marched in full gear from our barracks (or our quarters in the rare occasions we stayed elsewhere) to the pit; Master Horne had had us pounding across the parade field until we could march like the Legions. He said it sent a message; I wasn't sure what that message was, but the Ebon Blades' reputation never faltered. We might not have been the top barracks in Fellhome, but we were always in the top three; Master Horne said that worrying about where in the top three we were was wasted time and blood; the only thing that mattered was who came out of the pit at the end of the match.

Looking at my life, and then thinking about those slaves at Limerock, I saw Akel's point: we had been fortunate to have as good a master as Master Horne.

"What are you thinking about?" Hatcher asked, three days into the trip. "You've been staring at the road like you lost something and are retracing your steps."

"About slavery. I saw some things while I was getting back to you, and me and Burk talked about it with Akel."

"What about slavery in particular?"

"That it is bad," I said slowly. "That I was lucky to have had Master Horne as a master, and that not too many slaves get that lucky."

Hatcher drummed her fingers on my head for a bit. "I guess you're right," she finally said, but her heart wasn't in it.

"You think that because he sent me into the pit, he was bad."

"How many of your age block are still alive?"

"I saw a place where they dug out limestone and burned it to make quicklime. I bet those slaves die a lot, and they certainly weren't getting fed much."

"Point."

"And if I wasn't a High Rate, you wouldn't have bought me. I have skills."

"Another point."

"Free men fight in the pits, too. Lots of free men have hard lives." I was thinking about the red-haired shoemaker who had changed his marker in Fellhome. "In fact, those men I killed for you in Fellhome were free."

"I can't argue with that."

"Slavery is bad, but not all slave-owners are bad."

"I'll concede the point."

"So, I have decided that I am against slavery being the law, but not against everyone who owns slaves."

"Not an unreasonable position. But let me ask you this: how did you feel about slavery before you came to this conclusion?"

"I didn't really think about it. I was born a slave, and even if I won my freedom, I didn't expect to leave the Ebon Blades, so it wouldn't really make any difference."

"And now you are free."

"I'm free, sort of."

"How do you mean, 'sort of'?"

"When I was on my own, I didn't enjoy it. In fact, I didn't like it at all. I had to deal with disagreeable people, make all sorts of decisions, and worry about money. If I hadn't found you, I was planning on going back to Master Horne and fight for the Ebon Blades."

"Some people like being part of an organization," Hatcher agreed. "The Legions and better mercenary companies are built around that concept. It is comfortable having other people deal with the day-to-day issues."

"It is."

"But choosing to be part of that organization, that is what makes you free. If you went back to the Ebon Blades, you would do so because *you* decided that that was going to be your fate. When you sign on with a group, you give up some of your freedom, but it is a choice. Freedom is about getting to have a choice; sometimes it is only a choice between burning limestone or starving, but it is a choice."

"It doesn't seem like much, really."

"Sometimes it isn't. Freedom is also the freedom to be cold, hungry, and alone."

We continued on in silence for a while. "I don't like having to think all the time," I observed after a while. "Ever since Provine Sael bought me I've done nothing but think and learn, and it makes my head hurt."

"Are you sorry she got you involved?"

"No. I miss the barracks, though. And there's not enough fighting."

Hatcher laughed. "Grog, you are a wonder."

"What will happen when we get the Emperor's things?"

"Well, I'll need muscle, so you and Burk are welcome to travel with me. Provine Sael will have the Sagrit seeking revenge upon her for the next couple years, so I'm hoping we can rope her into throwing in with us. I've got a lot of ideas for a group with these skills. Torl will go his own way; he doesn't like being with people too long. Hunter, well, it's hard to say; if there's money in it, he might stick around, or he might get a wild hair and go off on business of his own. I have no idea what Akel's plans are; an educated man working as a muleskinner can't be guessed."

"Akel seems like…I dunno, sad?"

"Yeah, I think he's lost something big, and is just adrift. You see people like that in our business."

"What is our business?"

"Getting things done," Hatcher drummed on my head. "Finding things. There's a lot of work for people who can get things done or can find things."

"Huh." I thought about that. "What will Torl do?"

"Prowl the frontier, hunt down Tulg scouts, snipe off Ukar leaders. It's what he does. He's a lot like you, in fact, if you substitute hunting the enemy for the pit. The Dusman have a price on his head."

"Why does he like to prowl the frontier?"

"Why do you like to fight?"

"Oh."

"You poke around the wild areas, you find wild men. Torl is like you: blood doesn't weigh hard on his mind."

"You've killed."

She sighed. "Yeah, I know. But I prefer not to, although I've gotten callous over the years."

Torl led us west, but not in anything like a straight line; we cut across meadows and fields, took country lanes and over-grown tracks, followed streams, and generally wove our way across the map like a drunk staggering home on a dark night. Hatcher let me and Burk look at the map every day, which is how I came up with that description.

"Why can't we just travel in a straight line?" I asked as we trudged down a rutted track into a tiny village that looked like any one of a half-dozen we had passed in the ten days since leaving the Concourse: a huddle of huts and outbuildings with goats, pigs, and kids wandering about. This one had a palisade of logs, so I supposed that meant we were getting close to wild lands again.

"Believe it or not, we are, mostly," Hatcher explained. "You go quicker if you follow the easier path rather than a straight line. And most importantly, Torl is taking us on the route with the fewest eyes; there's no way the Sagrit will have people this far out. They can only cover so many routes, even assuming they know we were at the Concourse."

"These people look like they've never seen a brute before, or a Nisker," I pointed out as we walked through the gate-less gap in the palisade that the track led us to. Women were dragging kids into the huts, casting concerned looks at us as they did so.

"They'll be talking about us until spring," Burk agreed, fingering his morning star.

"To each other, sure," Hatcher shrugged, banging her heels against my armored chest. "But only to each other. Not a lot of traffic in these parts, and the locals tend to be closed-mouthed about strangers for fear of getting caught up in someone else's problems. There's not a lot of law out here."

We halted in front of the largest structure the village boasted, which was a trading post; we waited outside while Hunter and Akel went inside and purchased supplies. Three old men sat on a bench in front of the trading post and stared at us, while a few dirty kids came creeping down the muddy lane, moving from cover to cover.

"They're picking up rocks," Hatcher flipped off my shoulders to land cat-like. "I'll show them..." she bent to pick up a stone.

"Hatcher," Provine Sael hardly raised her voice.

Hatcher sighed and stood.

Burk ducked a rock, while I got a slow thrower and managed to catch the one chucked at me. I held the stone up so the kid could see, and then tossed it underhand back to him.

His eyes as big as saucers, he turned and fled.

"If this were a Nisker village, would children throw stones at us?" Burk asked.

"If it were off the beaten track as far as this one is, yeah," Hatcher admitted. "You notice this stuff doesn't happen in cities."

That was the last village we entered, and two days later we stopped seeing villages at all. We travelled across increasingly rugged and stony hills, and in the far distance the horizon haze had vague shapes in it.

"What is that?" I pointed to the horizon the first time I noticed the shapes.

Hatcher squinted. "Mountains."

"Huh."

"On the other side of the mountains is the ocean."

"You mean like the sea?"

"Yup."

"Are we going there?"

"Nope. We won't even reach the mountains."

"So we're getting close?"

"I hope so. Keep in mind those mountains are quite a few days' march away."

"I thought you said this area was known for Tulgs?"

"It is," Hatcher eyed the surrounding hills. "I'm surprised that we haven't had a fight by now. Torl hasn't even seen any scouts."

The next night Torl came into camp as we were setting up, a freshly-killed and gutted deer across his shoulders. "We are close," he announced, dumping his kill onto the grass. "But there's a complication."

"What is it?" Provine Sael asked as Burk and I hung the deer from a nearby tree and began skinning it.

"I found a Tulg encampment," Torl sat on a handy rock and began to scrub the blade of his hunting knife with a fistful of grass. "It had been abandoned a while ago, at least ten days."

"Good news for us," Hunter observed from where he lounged against a log. "Tulg move around a lot, especially those who live close to the Empire's borders; otherwise the Legion pays them a surprise visit."

"True, but before they left these Tulg killed a dozen of their old folk and a few youngsters, and burned a lot of household gear."

Hatcher turned from where she had been watching Burk and me work. "That doesn't sound good."

"It isn't," the scout carefully examined his knife blade, and then sheathed it. "They do that when they are moving far or fast; they lighten their loads and ensure that the old or sickly don't slow them down."

"Lovely creatures," Provine Sael noted. "But it still sounds like a stroke of luck for us."

"It is," Torl agreed. "But it bodes ill."

"Everything bodes ill," Hatcher turned back to where Burk and I were getting the last of the hide free.

After our evening meal Burk and I read for at least an hour, and then I practiced with my sword. We had completed the adventures of picking flowers and a couple other simple primers, and were now bogged down in '*A Young Person's Abbreviated Guide to the Provinces*'.

It was not a really interesting book, but we had to admit that it was moving us forward by leaps and bounds in the business of reading.

Two days later we stopped an hour or two early and Torl, Hunter, and Provine Sael went into a little ravine while the rest of us set up camp. "I think we're here," Hatcher observed, her contribution to the camp-setting-up being sitting on a rock scratching a mule between the ears.

"It doesn't look like much around here," Burk ventured as he dumped a pile of dead wood.

"If it were notable, perhaps the Emperor's grave would have been found earlier," Akel pointed out. "This area has been contested by the Empire for generations." He pointed to a heap of crudely-worked stone on a ridgeline a half-mile away. "There's the remains of a watchtower that was burned or pulled down long ago, and there are old Legion camps scattered all through the area, if you know what to watch for."

"Why hasn't the Empire just taken it over?" I asked.

"It has secured parts of the region in the past, but it is poor land, and the garrisons got pulled out to deal with crises in more important places. This area marks the high tide of Imperial might."

I wasn't clear on what tides' purposes were; I did know it had something to do with water, so I really didn't understand Akel's point, but I was tired of learning things so I just kept digging the fire pit.

The trio came back after the camp was set. "We're here," Hunter said without ceremony, digging a bottle of brandy out of his pack and sitting on a rock.

"Don't sound so enthused," Hatcher grinned.

"The news is not good," Provine Sail sighed. "Something is going on inside the tomb."

"Dusmen?" Akel asked.

"No. The arcane nature of the place should tell anyone within a hundred yards to '*look here*'."

"What does that mean?" Hatcher patted the mule.

"It means that it won't just be a bit of chanting and looking," Hunter answered. "Power is loose down there, and it will be drawing trouble."

"What sort of trouble?" Hatcher persisted.

"That, we don't know," Hunter took a long swig of brandy. "But we can be sure that no one beat us here."

"Or if they did, they didn't survive," Torl noted.

"This is a fairly new development," Provine Sael was rubbing one of her horn-nubs. "A year, probably much less."

"What caused it, whatever it is?" Hatcher threw up her hands. "The three of you talk, but no one *says* anything."

"We don't know." Provide Sael noticed that I was watching her and dropped her hand into her lap. "Let us eat."

After our meal we cut saplings and made torches. Thinking about going underground brought up dark memories of my time under the karst, but I reminded myself that I wouldn't be alone, and that I would also mark our path so no matter what, I could find my way out; I had Hatcher pick me up thick sticks of chalk before we left the Concourse.

"In a forest, you said to follow water if you are lost," I reminded Hatcher as she watched me and Burk chop saplings and strip off the branches.

"I did."

"What about underground?"

"Ah. That's more tricky, but as a general rule, follow water upstream. The best thing when underground is to follow air flow, because there's no wind generated underground, so if something is pushing the smoke of your torch, head upwind. And upslope, of course."

"Good to know." I hacked a stripped sapling trunk into the proper lengths. "Pass me that twine, please."

The next morning Akel stayed with the mules while Hunter led us to a cluster of ruins in the lee of a ridge, just the stubs of crude walls of field stone surrounded by drifts of fallen stone and rotting wood beams. We had passed countless similar ruins in our travels.

"Looks like three rather small huts were here at one time," Hatcher noted, flipping off my shoulders to land catlike on her feet. "How old are they?" She absently rubbed her belly.

"Not that old." Hunter was checking the contents of his many little pouches.

"So why didn't they find the Emperor's remains?"

"Because it's not like they built over a doorway." Finished checking his pouches, Hunter pulled a larger scroll from a case he drew from inside his shirt and looked over at Provine Sael. "Ready?"

She had been leaning on her short staff as if it were a cane, her eyes closed. At his question she opened her eyes and tapped the end of her staff against the heel of her boot to dislodge any dirt. "Yes."

They walked through the remains of a hut to the stone ridge-face as I held a torch out and Burk struck flint and steel. Hunter began reading out loud from the scroll in a strange language while Provine Sael tapped the rock hers and there with her staff. After the sixth or seventh tap I saw a network of greenish lines crossing the face, converging where she tapped, but it wasn't as if she was making the lines, but rather, she was simply pointing out where they always had been. Which sounded stupid even as I thought it.

When Hunter stopped speaking the lines of light flickered and were gone, along with the stone they had overlaid, leaving an opening about five feet high and three wide going deep into the ridge.

"Well, we're in the right place," Hatcher noted, lighting a torch off mine. "Get ready, boys."

"What could still be in there after all this time?" Burk asked.

"Something that came in by another route." Hatcher suggested.

"There won't be anything in there," Provine Sael chided the Nisker. "There is more than concealment involved warding this place." She looked happy again. "Picks, prybars, and erosion couldn't breach these chambers."

"So how come that powerful of magic didn't get found quicker?" Hatcher loosened her knives in their sheaths and belched.

"Because the man who did this was a far better spell-master than the ones who came after," Hunter noted, brushing away the dust that was all that remained of the scroll he had used. "Magic ebbs and flows with the passage of time; he lived in a period where magic was legendary. He had no idea how far the flows of power would ebb in the generations to come."

"I still have a bad feeling about this," Hatcher was unmoved.

Provine Sael shrugged. "Then Burk and Grog shall accompany us. Better safe than sorry."

"I'll rove out here," Torl noted. "I've seen enough caves to suit me."

"As you wish. Hatcher, you lead," Provine Sael must have realized she was smiling because she struggled to set her face into its usual stoic lines.

The opening in the stone was a smooth-sided shaft running in and down for twenty paces before intersecting with a broad, rough-walled passage with an arced ceiling; I drew my sword and tried to touch the ceiling with it, but the point was several inches short.

"Nothing's too good for an Emperor," Hatcher observed.

"This was a concealed supply depot," Provine Sael noted. "It was intended to allow Legions to respond quickly and operate freely in the area. Later, as the tide turned, they used it to bury the Legion dead, free of disturbance by the enemy. It was natural to lay the Emperor to rest amongst his fallen troops." She looked both ways. "We go left."

I had expected to be more nervous after my time in the karst, but the worked tunnels were nothing like the natural passages where I had been lost, and the presence of the others were a great comfort. But I still was careful to mark the walls with chalk arrows, and I had a half-dozen spare torches on my back and three extra flints in my pouch.

Hatcher led the way, her battered flat-topped, short-billed leather cap pulled squarely over her hair, giving her a business-like look. Although she cast about intently, she wasn't finding any traps.

"I don't expect to encounter any mechanical traps," Provine Sael noted from the rear of the group. "The man who set this up was confident in his magical prowess."

"Not to mention sixty feet of featureless stone," Hunter added.

"Any yet, here we are," Hatcher muttered.

"Why didn't they come back for him?" I asked.

"He was an unsentimental man," Provine Sael noted. "Surrounded by like-minded comrades. They were building an empire with steel and blood, and frequently it was a desperate business. Mankind was in poor shape back then; the flame of civilization was flickering low before they stood and raged against the dark. The Emperor had fallen, but the work wasn't done, and they continued to carry out his plan, falling one by one in the course of their duty."

I fingered my sword hilt and thought about what Provine Sael had said as Hatcher led us into a side tunnel not much smaller than the one we had first encountered. They had died one by one carrying out the Emperor's plan, even after he was dead. The Ebon Blades were something like that: we fought for the honor of our barracks, and we were part of something larger than ourselves. That was what Akel had meant, back after that first fight: to be part of something bigger than yourself. To have a cause to fight for.

Burk and I have kept our charges safe; we freed slaves, helped defend a town, fought bad men. We had accomplished something in these last weeks. Even on my own I had slain road-murderers, and helped two escaped slaves. That last part had been grudgingly done, I admitted, but I had gotten them further than they had gotten on their own.

That brought to mind Fall and his small coffin, but I had no answers for that encounter. Why he wanted the coffin buried, why he didn't do it himself, how he had found me...too many questions. One thing I did know was that he hadn't liked the Sagrit, so he wasn't a bad man.

This smaller hall had niches dug into the walls, each about six feet long, two deep, and about one and a half high, usually in threes stacked together.

Hatcher stopped the examine the lowest. "What were these?"

"Originally, shelving space for supplies that were packaged for transport on pack saddles; later they were used to as the final resting places for Legion dead."

"Huh. So why are they all empty?"

"The Legions didn't lose that many men, I suppose, before the Emperor died and this place was sealed up."

Hatcher leaned to the side and copiously broke wind

"Feel better?" Hunter asked drily.

"I do," she nodded. "I think the last of that flask of bekker sauce has gone off; my stomach has been bothering me all morning.

"Can we move?" Provine Sael shook her head. "There is little air circulation in here, and now a great deal of methane."

Hatcher grinned and moved on, resuming her checking for traps.

"Mist?" Burk wondered out loud as we approached an intersection.

"Can't be," Hatcher slowed and moved her torch from side to side. "There's not enough air flow…"

But there was a fine mist hanging in the air before us, not much more than waist-high on me, and not very dense.

Provine Sael gasped as we reached the edge of the mist. "Necromancy!"

I had heard the term before, and I knew it was something bad, but not in what particular, at least until a half-dozen figures came from the right and left of the intersection.

They were constructs of bones, at least part from Human bones, but they had too many ribs and there were no ligaments or tendons holding them together, and some of the bones were jet black and glossy, while others were age-pitted remnants of once-living things. They were armed with spiked clubs and crude wooden shields, and their eyes sockets were pits of greenish fire.

"Get behind us, Hatcher." I tossed my torch to the side and brought my sword up to a high inside guard.

"This is so...wrong," Provine Sael protested as Hatcher scampered back and Hunter muttered something which caused colored balls of light to explode soundlessly against the advancing Undead, damaging two.

Burk was to my left, his shield up and morning star ready. "Push?" he suggested, twitching his 'star's short wooden handle so the spiked ball swung in a slow circle.

"Good idea." I stepped to my right to give us room and then we advanced to meet the oncoming bone-things.

A spiked club flashed over my head as I abruptly dropped to a knee, the sound of its passing suggesting a terrible strength for a creature with no muscles or connective tissue. Master Horne had us learn about the body from healers, because to understand its workings made for more efficient killing.

Even as I dropped I was swinging, a flat, harsh cleave that sheared off both legs just above the knees, and I was back upright even as the thing was collapsing to the floor. Another was boring in, leading with its shield, its head tucked behind the barrier and its club held ready. That suggested that these weren't just mindless *things*, but had some cunning and weapon-lore.

But I was a High Rate of the Ebon Blades, a barracks of the old school, and some cunning wasn't what it took to survive in the pits for match after match. I spun my sword, gripping it blade-downward, and reverse-thrust, going over the shield; my height, arm-length, blade-length, and the reversed blade letting me angle over the hastily-raised shield to transfix the blackened, horn-sprouting skull.

The fire in its eye sockets vanished as I ripped the blade free and flipped my hilt to a proper grip, the thing dropping to the floor, lifeless and inert.

Two were on me before I could look around, and I gave ground, parrying, as I got their measure. Still muttering, Provine Sael walked past us, looking like a ghost in the half-light of guttering torches lying on the floor.

One of my opponents sidestepped towards her, but she twitched her staff with a roll of her wrist and the thing collapsed into a short shower of individual bones.

I caught the other one's spiked club with my blade and twisted to kick the thing back. As it staggered I tried for a skull-thrust, but only sheared off its jaw. It clouted me on the ribs, failing to penetrate my armor, but I could feel my left-side ribs flex from the impact; I lost a lot of wind from the hit, but riposted, lopping off its right (club-wielding) arm at the elbow.

It hopped back, discarding its shield and catching up an abandoned club, and I let it go, staying put in order to catch my breath. As it cautiously moved forward more colored balls hit it, and it collapsed into loose bones.

Checking around, I saw Hatcher, knives in hand, covering Hunter, and Burk, bleeding from a gash on his cheek, checking the front of his shield for damage. Provine Sale was a distance ahead of us, at the center of the intersection, a torch in hand, looking around and talking to herself. The Undead were just scattered bones, including the one whose legs I had cut off.

"Mistress, would you please stay put?" I asked as I grabbed up my torch (my ribs giving me a nasty twinge as I did so) and moved to join her, Burk at my side. "It is very hard to guard someone who moves around unnecessarily."

If she heard me, she gave no sign, turning to peer down the other hallways, each in turn.

"Don't over-think it," Hunter drawled, strolling up carrying a black skull by a projecting horn, Hatcher close behind.

"This is *impossible*," Provine Sael exclaimed angrily. "This place is *sealed*."

"It is a curiosity," Hunter admitted, examining the skull. "There shouldn't so much as a cockroach in here."

"So a necromancer has gotten in?" Hatcher asked. "Are we too late?" She ripped off a fart.

"This place is *sealed*!" Provine Sael repeated.

"Are you sure all of it is?" Hatcher persisted, fanning behind her with her cap.

"Yes," Hunter headed off an angry outburst from Provine Sael. "I won't bore you with the details, but it is much like an egg: an all-or-nothing defense. We could never had gotten in if we hadn't had the key."

"So, you're telling me we had to walk across most of the Empire to find out where it *is*, but we had the key from the start?" Hatcher shook her head.

"More akin to that we had a ring of keys, and when we figured out where the door was, that told us which key to employ."

"Sound like a pretty poor job of hiding this place," Hatcher shrugged.

"Not so much. I am massively simplifying the arcane nature of the situation."

"To put it another way, we obtained copies of the key before we started looking for the door," Provine Sael pointed out, finally returning to the matter at hand. "The ring of keys was given to us, in fact. Before we leave, I will destroy the keys, and this place will reseal itself at dawn."

Hatcher shook her head. "This is why I could never be a spell-slinger. So now what?"

Hunter shrugged. "This is a complication."

"If the mistress can destroy these things…" Burk began, but she saw he was holding a bandage to his face, and immediately went to treat his wound.

"My use of that ability is not unlimited," she noted as she worked on his injury.

"So, are we the first to find this place?" Hatcher persisted, rubbing her stomach.

"Yes," Provine Sael had Burk tilt his head back as she worked. "In all modesty, no one had considered the ballad's original form before I undertook the task. Countless other approaches were tried and failed over the years. But before you ask, the nature of the wards are such that we could have detected if anyone else had entered this place since it was initially sealed."

"So maybe the Undead are guards left by the master of arts who sealed this place?" Hatcher suggested.

"No," Hunter shook his head. "Necromancy is a wholly separate field, and in any case none of the original Red Guard would have considered it. Additionally, these Undead were certainly not that old." He raised the skull he was holding. "The longer these creatures are active, the stronger they get; this is demonstrated by the 'bone' turning black and glossy." He tossed the skull aside and wiped his hand on his leg. "These are a fairly recent addition."

"None of this makes any sense," Hatcher took off her cap, scratched her head, and pulled the cap back on.

"It does not." Finished with Burk's injury, Provine Sael stowed the tools of her trade. "But that changes nothing. We press on."

Chapter Fifteen

"We are close," Provine Sael advised, keeping her voice down. "Just down that corridor and to the right."

"No point in being quiet," Hunter sighed. "They can see our light."

"It hasn't been all that far," Hatcher noted. "But no more Undead."

"They will be preparing to guard their master," Provine Sael noted grimly. "As Hunter noted, they are not well-aged, and I expect not numerous."

"Why not?" I asked. "This place is full of bones." The wall-niches in this corridor were all filled with coffins.

"Necromancy isn't just raising corpses," Hunter shrugged. "That's the bards talking. Bones are the smaller portion of what is needed."

"Oh."

I suppose I should feel special or excited as we approached the entrance to the side corridor because this was about to be the culmination of Provine Sael's dedicated efforts and all the changes in my life, but the fact was that I had only really known what was going on for the last few days.

So what it amounted to was walking down an underground corridor by torch light, my sword in hand and my ribs hurting, while a half-dozen feet behind me Hatcher was breaking wind and snickering.

Provine Sael must have been thinking along the same line, because she sighed. "I had hoped for a bit more dignity to the culmination of so many hopes."

"I can't help it!" Hatcher exclaimed, and tooted off another one. And snickered.

The humor stopped when we turned right and found ourselves standing on a platform in a chamber whose floor was fifty feet below us and the ceiling another fifty above; a bridge of iron-bound timbers ran from our platform to another platform on the far side, two hundred feet away; evenly spaced on either side of the span were three cranes.

"Bulk storage warehouse," Hunter noted somberly, sending a small ball of light sweeping across the chamber.

"And the Emperor's resting place," Provine Sael nodded to a niche the size of an inn's common room which had been hacked into the far wall at the rear of the platform.

What attracted my attention, as the ball of lights made its way around the chamber, was the stack of crates blocking the far end of the bridge, and the line of skeletal warriors behind it.

"Well, we can't starve them out," Hatcher observed, rubbing her belly.

Hunter shot her a look before rubbing his scalp. "There's no way to flank them. I can't see anything other than a head-on charge to certain doom."

"They have no missile weapons," Provine Sael noted, frowning at the barricade, her fingers on the nub of one of her horns. "Of course, other than Hatcher's axes, neither do we. Grog, how would we fare in melee?"

I had been thinking about that while they had been discussing the issue. "If these are no tougher than the ones we already faced, fair to poorly in a straight up fight."

"What if your weapons were enchanted so that a single strike would slay them, insofar as they can be 'slain'?"

I glanced at Burk, who was studying the foe; after a moment he gave a slight nod. "With luck, we could take them."

Provine Sael sighed. "Hunter, how much damage can you do to the foe?"

"Thanks to the wards, modest amounts. But I can hamper their ability to move."

"That will have to do. You shall do what you can while the rest of us assault the barricade."

"Mistress, you cannot go with us," Burk blurted, and I nodded.

She lifted her chin. "I will not send you into battle, I will lead."

"You have no armor, and a short blade," I pointed out. "Hatcher is small and deceptively quick, but even she needs to stay on the edge of the fight."

"Taking cheap shots," Hatcher agreed. "Provine, who is going to patch us up afterwards if you catch a blade? Not to mention make the trade with the Imperial Court? Without you, Hunter will just sell the items to the highest bidder."

"Not impossible," Hunter agreed.

"I…," Provine Sael struggled for words, then turned away for a long moment; finally she shook her head and faced us again. "Very well. I will do what I can in support."

She went to each of us, touching our weapons and whispering under her breath. When she came to me she stopped halfway through the process. "Grog…is this the sword we bought in Fellhome?"

"No, mistress, I lost that one in the sinkhole. I was given this one by the man who showed me the way out. Why?"

She fingered the blade. "It is an alloy…Hunter, look at this sword."

He came over and ran his fingers over the blade. "Death blade," he nodded. "A high content, higher than I've seen before, but I'm not an expert, either."

"What does that mean?" I asked.

"That it is a very good blade. A man gave it to you?"

"Yes, the man who led me out of the underground. I buried a coffin for him, afterwards."

"There's a story for another time," Hunter shook his head. "Don't lose it."

"You don't need my incantation," Provine Sael stepped over and did Hatcher's blades, then her own short sword. "Just in case," she advised me and Burt.

"So, do we shout something as we charge?" Hatcher asked as we stepped out onto the bridge. "I haven't done much of this sort of '*hey-diddle-diddle, right up the middle*' work before."

"We don't charge," Burk worked his shoulders, loosening up. "They don't have missile weapons, so we just walk over and kill them."

"Don't waste breath yelling," I added, running my sword through the basic manual of arms in order to loosen up. "You'll need it for the fight."

"I thought pit fighters did all sorts of dramatic stuff to get the crowd fired up," Hatcher leaned and broke wind. "What kind of gladiators were you?"

"The sort who survived every match," I noted.

"Two enter the pit; one or none exit," Burke nodded.

Hatcher sighed. "I forget who you two are, sometimes. Don't die, guys, I don't think I could bear it."

"We don't," Burk glanced at me. "Ready?"

"Might as well. Hatcher, lag behind a few steps; we'll get things started."

We walked across the bridge, and it was much like walking through the dark, cool tunnel leading into the pit. The walk always seemed to take forever, and yet you arrived at the entrance to the pit so quickly, your eyes a little dazzled by the sudden light, and your ears filling to overflowing with the noises of the crowd. Half-blind, you moved to your mark and waited while the herald finished the proclamation of origins and records of those fighting, followed by a few choice comments by the master of ceremonies. This let the crowd get a good look at you and make their final wagers, and to let the combatant's eyes adjust to the light.

Then the horn would blow, and nothing else existed but the fight. Non-lethal events took place elsewhere; when you entered the pit, death was always there. I had always come back out, and came back alone. Master Horne said that the pit was a good example of life: when all the drama and posturing ended, it all came down to yourself.

Master Horne was very wise, and I missed him greatly. I was glad that Burk and I had gotten a letter off to him at the Concourse; if I died here today, at least he would know that we were still true to the Ebon Blades.

The skeletal warriors stood behind their barricade like a row of statues and watched us approach. "See you afterward," I advised Burk.

"Count on it."

I lept to the top of the barricade, and the empty crates collapsed beneath my weight in a cloud of must, dust, and the sour odor of dry rot. As I fell I heard Burk crashing through the age-weakened boxes to my left.

A club swung at me as I fell, catching the edge of my kettle hat, the chin strap parting and the headgear spinning away.

It was a good trick: we should have realized these crates were too old to serve as any sort of barricade. But I had grown up training on every sort of footing, even sparring while standing on posts, because Master Horne always said that if you can fight under terrible conditions, you will never be caught completely off guard.

Staggering, only half in control of my own progress, I lurched forward through the rotted crates, parrying one club-swing and catching another on my uninjured ribs. Then I was through their line and skidding to a stop, still on my feet. I spun and parried two club-swings as Burk crashed into the end of the skeleton line; like me, he hadn't completely lost his footing.

We should have been dead, despite our trained reactions, but the Undead were armed with improvised clubs, half of which shattered against our armor. The Legions had interred their dead here, but they had taken the fallen warriors' arms and armor when they left.

So long as I avoided taking a strike to my unprotected head, the numbers didn't weigh too heavily against me; Burk and I managed to get back-to-back, and I focused on parrying while Burk took a toll.

Hatcher was a low blur in the background, chopping at legs on the move, doing only limited damage, but keeping half the enemy busy.

It was Hunter who really won the fight: he systematically picked off the skeletal warriors with bursts of colored sparks; the Undead were too focused on the three of us to turn to the two figures at the end of the bridge, and one by one they perished, if a construct animated by dark Arts could really be called alive.

"Well, that was a lot of work without much glory," Hatcher panted as the last foe collapsed into inert bone.

"These didn't have much black to them," Burk noted as he slung his battered shield. "I guess the first bunch were the best."

"I thought we were done for when the two of you went through the crates," Hatcher kicked a rotted board off the bridge. "That was a pretty cunning trick."

"This is the Emperor's resting place," Provine Sael, a ball of light hovering above her head, brushed past us. "Finally. After all these years…we are here. We have done it."

"Best find a seat," Hunter took a swing from a flask. "This part will take some time."

It took over an hour, measuring time by the consumption of torches, before Provine Sael and Hunter were done examining the area around the coffin, the coffin itself, and its contents. Both seemed excited and pleased with what they found.

She took time to heal our bruises (and my ribs), and then Burk and I each took the end of a simple wood coffin whose lid was covered with incised writing in a language I didn't know, and followed the others back across the bridge.

"You would think the Emperor would rate a better box," Hatcher observed as we went.

"That's ironwood," Hunter noted. "Lasts for centuries, and worth its weight in silver."

I frowned: the wood reminded me of something, but it wasn't coming to me.

"Good thing the skeletal warriors didn't use it to make their clubs."

"They couldn't," Provide Sael noted, holding a torch delicately to the side. "They couldn't even approach the coffin."

"So did you figure out where the Undead came from?" Hatcher rubbed her belly.

"They put a few of the Emperor's trophies in the niche with his coffin. One of the items was the staff of a necromancer; it was warded, but over time it overcame the wards and started raising Undead. That was what we detected before we entered."

"So, what, the staff was *alive*?"

"No, just...created with a strong purpose and commands. Hunter and I renewed the wards as best we could. It will break loose again in a few decades, but that will do no harm, sealed up as it is. They made powerful items in the old times."

"What about the sword and helm?" Hatcher hunched over for a second as she spoke.

"In the coffin." Provine Sael noted with satisfaction. "Our work is done."

"We need to pick up the pace," Hatcher said with sudden urgency. "I need to damage the local flora."

"What?"

"I need to drop a vile staff of my own. And *soon!*"

Hatcher scurried off into the brush the instant we reached sunlight, and we headed to camp. There was no sign of Torl.

"Should we wait for her?" Provine Sael frowned.

"She can catch up in her own time," Hunter grinned.

"I can't believe this is *done*," Provine Sael ran her hand across the coffin's lid, and I realized why the wood was familiar: the small box or coffin I had buried for Fall had been made of the same wood. I was dumb, taking so long to make the connection, but that is just how I am.

"Why did they use such expensive wood for a coffin?" Burk asked as we trudged back to camp.

"Because ironwood is very resistant to dry rot, insects, all sorts of long-term issues that plague wood," Hunter took a pull from his flask. "It's used for all sorts of storage devices."

"Not more than three hours to fulfill the dream of a lifetime," Provine Sael marveled, lost in her own world. Her hand was still on the coffin, fingers tracing the writing, which I realized must be the ballad.

"So, what will you do, now that you've saved the Empire?" Hunter grinned.

"What?" she dropped her hand from the coffin and moved away. "Oh, well...I'm sure suitable duties can be found. There are many things that need doing in this world."

"Going home not being one of them?"

"The Sagrit will make that impossible for now," she sighed as we trooped into camp. "But they are not eternal."

"But perhaps we will endure long enough," a stranger said, as if in response. "Keep your hands in plain view, please."

The speaker was a Dellian male in elaborate robes of light blue and gold, his horns long and swept back over his skull. His face was hard and angular, and although he was smiling, it did not reach his eyes. He was unarmed except for a short baton of gnarled horn or bone bound with rusty wire.

He didn't need to be armed, because two Men armed with expensive-looking crossbows were stepping out from around the mules, their weapons aimed at Provine Sael and Hunter, and a half-dozen heavily-armed brutes emerged from the bushes, three to either side.

What shocked me the most was that Akel was sitting on a stump, his spear across his knees, staring at the ground.

"Yinran Genges," Province Sael hissed the name. "How did *you* get here, you turncoat?"

The Dellian tilted his head to indicate the muleskinner. "Akel and I are old comrades."

I don't think Provine Sael had noticed the muleskinner before. She looked at Akel and sighed his name; the muleskinner flinched but did not look up.

"So, that is the coffin," Yinran nodded. "Set it down carefully and step back like good chaps."

Burk and I exchanged a glance, and then complied; it went against the grain to take orders from this intruder, but his command freed our hands, which was a useful thing.

"You're short two members of your party," Yinran continued. "Chabney Torl and a Nisker."

"Dead," Hunter advised, taking a swig from his flask. "The Imperial remains were guarded by constructs."

"Really?" Yinran cocked an eyebrow. "That doesn't seem likely."

"It caught us by surprise as well, which is how we lost two people," Hunter shrugged, took another swig, and stowed the flask.

Yinran eyed the blood across Burk's armor. "And where are their bodies?"

"Resting in a tomb considered fit for an Emperor," Provine Sael answered, still staring at Akel. "It seemed appropriate. Akel, how could you?"

"I serve the Cause," he said quietly.

"You fought alongside us, shared our food…have you no honor?"

"Honor is meaningless in a state where people are property." He looked up at her.

"But we are working to correct that! In five years' time there will not be a slave left in the Empire."

"And the slaveowners will still be rich, perhaps richer," he stood restlessly. "The overseers will simply become foremen, the auctioneers will sell other goods, the hunters of escaped slaves will find other duties. No one will pay for *generations* of suffering."

Provine Sael shook her head. "So you would rather see a society torn apart in blood and violence solely for *revenge*? Slave uprisings inevitably fail, and innocent people always get caught in the middle. No amount of blood will undo the past; it will just add bitterness to the line between free and former slave, assuming that slavery is even ended."

Akel just shook his head.

I was wondering where Torl was, and why he hadn't warned us when we emerged, but then it occurred to me that he had figured this was a confrontation, not an ambush.

"Well spoken, my dear," Yinran tucked his baton under his arm in order to clap. "Your passion is commendable."

"Mind your tongue, traitor," Provine Sael snarled. "Your honor was sold long ago. Whom do you call master now, Yinran? The Dusmen? Some tawdry conspiracy of indolent nobles?"

Yinran flushed. "You know nothing, youngling."

"I know you are a slave to gold. Whose errand-boy are you these days? Whose feet will you kneel before, hoping for praise when you proclaim your meager chore complete?"

He scowled at her, cut to the quick. "I am inclined to spare you, child, but do not presume to press your luck."

She spat on the ground between them. "I will die in the performance of my duty; if you precede me, my life will be doubly well-spent."

"Personally, I would like to be spared," Hunter pointed out. "I'm just the hired help."

"Hunter, you, Grog, and Burk can seat yourself to the side," Akel spoke as the two Dellians glared at each other. "We'll leave a couple warriors with you to ensure you stay in place for a couple days."

"All right," Hunter moved onto to the log the muleskinner had indicated and sat down.

Burk was in his Noble Ukar stance; I crossed my arms and stared at Akel.

"Sit down on the log; you're free now, free of all obligations and duties forced upon you," he said after a long moment.

"We are of the Ebon Blades, a proper barracks of the old school," I advised him. "When you engage the Ebon Blades, you get quality work, that is the rule."

"You're not of the Ebon Blades anymore, you're free…" the muleskinner began, but Burk cut him off.

"Who and what we are is not for you to say, turncoat. We know our place, and our duty."

Akel made a wordless gesture that took in the armed Men and brutes facing us, and Burk chuckled. "We are of the High Rate, fool. We don't fear steel or iron."

"The reputation of the Ebon Blades is built upon success," I added. "We will not abandon an escort job so easily."

Inside I was feeling both hollow and warm, just as I did when I was in the pit waiting for the horn to sound. This was where I was going to die, this little camp made under the broad branches of a thick-trunked tree. I had survived all the battles in the pit, the defense of the walls back at Merrywine, and my trek underground, only to find my end here. I was sorry that Master Horne wouldn't know we had stayed true to the honor of the barracks, but that was how it went. I had always known there was a bloody death waiting for me, and now I knew the where and the when. The knowledge was liberating, I found.

Akel shook his head and turned away.

"Enough, child," Yinran finally ended the glaring. "Order your minions to stand down, and drop your staff. You have done far better than anyone else who undertook this quest, but that is finished now. The bones will be destroyed, and the items delivered to other hands. You will learn that life takes us down many unexpected roads.'

"Life doesn't," Provine Sael snapped. "The choices we make determines our path."

Yinran shook his head. "This does not have to end in death, child."

"All roads end in death; it is what we choose along the way that matters. You chose to be a traitor, a renegade, and a murderer. Take *your* minions and walk away, Yinran. You can sell your services to another master."

"You really think I will simply walk away?" He managed a hard smile. "For your mother's sake I would spare you..."

"Do *not* mention my mother," Provine Sael snapped. "Her brother betraying his oaths, his people, and the

Empire broke her heart; it killed her just as surely as a dagger's blade, if not nearly so quick or merciful. For that alone I will stand against you." She glanced over her shoulder. "Burk, Grog: this is not your fight. You are free beings; join Hunter."

"I'm free, so I can choose my own course," Burk grinned evilly at the brutes to our left.

"It's a good day for a match," I nodded, shifting slightly to my right.

Provine faced Yinran. "So, uncle, will you add 'kinslayer' to the many epithets attached to your name? Or did you think I would offer you quarter? Do you think me that enlightened?"

Yinran started to say something, but there was a flicker of movement between the two Dellians and the left crossbowman had a longbow arrow transfixing his throat.

Both Burk and I had caught her use of 'quarter' (meaning it was time to attack) and moved; the brutes had been caught off-guard by the sudden drastic change in the situation, which was compounded by the other crossbowman's hair erupting into flames and a throwing axe flashing out to rebound off thin air a hands-breadth from Yinran's head.

The brutes were wearing good mail and conical helms, armed with short swords and goedendags: essentially a combination of club and spear. Each was a five-foot wooden staff with a diameter of roughly three inches, tapering to a bit wider at the business end, and sporting a sharp metal spike whose tang was gripped by two studded iron bands. It could thrust (and penetrate heavy armor) and deliver savage crushing blows. It was a cheap, handy weapon for unskilled militia, and a dangerous tool in the hands of a trained wielder.

I had faced goedendags in the pit, where they were popular with the crowds; they were one of the few weapons intended to be easy to both thrust and swing that actually worked as they were intended to. But Master Horne had scorned them, saying that a warrior trained to fight in a variety of styles and approaches with different weapons was far superior than someone who relied upon weapon designs.

I closed with the right-most brute with my sword at the high guard center position: held two-handed with the pommel about three inches above my head; it opened up my face and torso, and the brute immediately thrust, aiming for my face while keeping his weapon between us, a safe and predictable counter.

The trouble for him was that I was not just an expert with the sword, but with the goedendag as well: Master Horne might scorn their use, but he knew the best defense against a weapon was knowing how to use it. The goedendag's weakness is that it is best suited to military use, rather than duels between single skilled opponents; it required a thick shaft of hard wood to sustain its role as a bashing weapon. A thick shaft meant that the user did not have the speed and flexibility of a swordsman whose carefully-proportioned hilt (in the better-made swords) allowed for fast movement and quick changes in blade angle.

As he thrust I half-stepped to the right and dropped to my knee, bringing my sword around in a hard side stroke that caught him on the thigh a hands-breadth below the hem of his mail shirt and a foot below his hip socket. My blade sliced through his stout trousers leg, the thick thigh muscle, the heavy bone, and on into more muscle as the spike point of his goedendag skidded across the top of my scalp, too blunt to slice and not pointed enough to catch hold to the skull-curve. It hurt like blazes, but pain was an old companion to me, and it only drew a little blood.

I wrenched my blade free as I pushed up to my feet, both actions combined as one; the entire exchange had taken two or three heartbeats from start to finish. The brute wasn't fatally wounded, but he would not stand upright again without extensive healing, assuming he didn't bleed to death.

As the other two brutes closed I moved back a couple steps to ensure that I was out of the downed brute's reach, and to hopefully give the impression I was afraid: as Master Horne always says, a fight can be won on small things.

The brutes knew their business: they moved apart, but not so much that there was enough space for me to try to attack one before the other could react. I had no reason to stand my ground, so I retreated as I parried, focusing on maintaining our relative distances while watching for an opportunity. They were not in a hurry to press their advantage, because with good armor and favorable numbers, time was on their side.

I suppose I could hope for help from my comrades, but from quick impressions from my peripheral vision I could see that arcane lights and sparks of all colors were flashing, and I caught a glimpse of Hunter sprawled across the log he had been sitting on, dead or unconscious, so I didn't really hold much hope.

A half-dozen exchanges established that the two were too skilled for me to be able to turn the tables with a superior twist of skill; I had already picked up a couple small wounds, and the outcome was inevitable unless I could change the odds. And there was no safe way to change the odds.

When safe options are off the table, all that is left are the desperate and the dishonorable; I was a pit fighter, and my world was a small circular chamber filled with death; there was no surrender or retreat in the pit: you won or you died, and in some cases you died even as you won.

Death comes for us all, I grew up knowing that; for me the place was here, and the time was now. Leading with the point, I lunched into the attack against the left brute.

He was faster than I expected: the spike of his goedendag hit me in the chest, slipped up and to my left, and then caught and punched through the scales, leather cloth, and deep into my upper chest, even as I struck. My sword-point sliced apart ring mail, leather, underpadding, and drove into his sternum, splitting the bone and transfixing his heart.

The right-most brute's goedendag caught me just above my right knee even as blood burst from his comrade's mouth and nose. The impact pulped muscle and flexed bone; the leg folded and I crashed to the ground, releasing my sword as I fell. I would never stand on that leg again, but I wasn't beaten: I hit the ground and rolled into the brute's legs as the spike of his weapon punched into the dirt an inch from my head.

He crashed down on top of me, and we grappled like wild beasts, punching and clawing for purchase as we rolled across the ground. My world was a haze of pain and dirt, and I could feel my life ebbing as the blood ran from my wounds, but I was of the Ebon Blades, a barracks of the old school, and I would not quit while there was strength to fight.

I ended up atop the brute, my crippled leg stretched out behind me, staring down into a face very much like my own, at least until I brought my short axe down and transformed it into a red ruin.

Ripping the axe blade free of the sundered skull, I struggled erect, my right leg all but useless. Hatcher was staggering away from Burk's fight, bleeding from a wound to the belly even as Burk's star showered her with the contents of a brute's skull. A few feet away an unfamiliar Man whom I had never seen before was sprawled on his side, his armored torso transfixed by several arrows.

There was no time to see more, as Akel was approaching me, his spear in hand and his shield squared. "I'm sorry," he said.

My left arm was losing feeling, I discovered, no doubt from the wound in my chest, and the world was taking on the dreamlike quality that blood loss and heavy exertion brings. "I thought you were wise," I said after spitting out blood mixed with dirt.

"I hoped..."

What he hoped was lost to the world as I hopped forward, hooking the shaft of his spear with the down-swept beard of my axe and jerking it to the left, before slamming the head of my weapon into his face, which was momentarily unprotected as he had let his shield droop when I jerked on his spear.

I hooked his right leg out from beneath him with my axe, and then stove in his skull as he crashed to his knees. "A wise man doesn't face a High Rate," I muttered. "Especially a High Rate of the Ebon Blades."

Hatcher was back up, pale and gripping her wound with one hand, a bloody knife in the other; nearby Burk was painfully pulling the broken remains of his shield from his mauled left arm, dead brutes scattered at his feet.

The world was getting a little unsteady, so I dropped to my good knee, discarded my axe, and dragged a bandage from my belt pouch. Ripping away the wax paper with my teeth, I wadded the cloth through the rent in my armor (the goedendag's spike had ripped away two scales as it had exited) and into the wound, which hurt.

Yinran was on his knees, his robes torn, bloody, and dirty; his baton was nowhere to be seen and his left arm was just a blackened stump ending somewhere around his elbow. He was fumbling in his belt pouch with his remaining hand, but he never found what he was seeking, because a battered, dirty Provine Sael staggered over and planted her short sword into his chest, the blue gems in the silver-decorated hilt catching the sunlight as she released the blade and the tall Dellian slumped forward into the dirt.

"For..," she coughed, gagged, and spat. "For...," she started hacking again. "To blazes...with it." She spat and wiped her nose.

"Easy, Grog." Torl was kneeling beside me, a knife in his hands, and I felt my armor sag as he cut its bindings. "Let me get your belt." With limited help from me he got my armor off and cut away my shirt. "Is blood coming into your mouth?" he asked as he bound my chest wound.

"No. It must have missed my lung."

"That's good news."

"Who is that Man?" I asked, jerking my chin towards the dead stranger.

"Yinran left a couple guards with their mounts. They were bringing the horses up when the fight broke out. I got them both, but it kept me out of the rest of the fight."

"Is Hunter dead?"

He glanced in that direction as he eased me down to prone. "No. But he's not unwounded."

"Is Hatcher going to live?"

"Yeah, and so will you."

"My leg is ruined."

"Only for now; Province Sael has repaired worse."

"I've had worse. My left shoulder, a few years ago."

"How is he?" Provine Sael knelt by my side.

"Blood loss and a bum leg."

She laid a hand on my chest and stared at nothing. "You'll be fine, Grog. Tomorrow I'll have you good as new."

"Will Hatcher and Hunter live?" I had seen Burk standing, so I knew he would.

"Hunter is hardly injured, just battered and unconscious. He bested Yinran; I merely applied the coup de grace. Hatcher has a nasty gash, but she'll be fine."

"I killed Akel."

She sighed. "It had to be done."

"I thought he was a wise man. I listened to him."

"So did I, Grog. So did I." She stood and moved off.

"Are you sure there aren't any more?" I asked Torl, who was using dirt to scrub my blood from his hands.

"Yes."

"How did they find us? I mean…"

"Akel must have gotten word to them while we were in the Concourse, and marked our trail since. How, I don't know, but I am going to find out."

The world was getting fuzzy. "Why do you stay on the frontier, Torl?"

"What?"

"Hatcher said you stay on the border, hunting raiders."

He gave a rare grin. "There's no point in being the best if you aren't out proving it." He dragged over a brute's corpse and positioned my legs so my boots rested on the body. He tried to be careful, but moving my right leg wrung a groan from me.

Raising the feet sent more blood to your head and reduced shock; it was a familiar fact. We had had a lot of training in the difficulty of killing people; blood loss and shock were the big killers in any battle, with infection culling a lot afterwards, but none of those were all that useful in the pit. People are surprisingly tough.

I realized Hatcher, flushed, sweating, and filthy, was standing over me. "How are you doing, big'un?"

"You'll need another horse," I tried to grin. "But I think Yinran brought some."

She sat on the dead brute. "You'll be fine in a couple days. Once Provine Sael gets some rest she'll start healing everyone."

"How are you?"

She touched the bandage around her middle. "Fine. It hurts like hell, but it's not deep. I'm just glad I wasn't with the rest of you when the dance started; those brutes were killers."

"How is Burk?"

"If we didn't have Provine Sael we would have to amputate his arm above the elbow and hope for the best. Hunter's in the best shape after Torl. Provine Sael has some cracked ribs, and minor burns, but she's fine. Did you see the fireworks show?"

"No."

"It was something, Hunter against Yinran, with Provine Sael doing what she could. Yinran was winning, or at least it looked like it, until his baton suddenly caught fire and burned off most of his left arm. Hunter went down right after that, but Yinran was finished."

"I killed Akel."

"Yeah, I saw." She glanced at the muleskinner's corpse. "He was good; I never for a second suspected him, and I'm the one Provine Sael counts on to see through machinations like that."

I didn't know what 'machinations' meant, but I was hurting too bad to ask. "I'm glad you're all right."

"I'm glad you are, too." She grinned her old grin. "How's it feel to be a wanted man? The Sagrit will have plenty of gold on all our heads now; Yinran was high up in their organization."

"He should have had more bodyguards."

Hatcher chuckled. "I imagine this was a rushed job; they'll send more, next time. Now I'm going to have to be nice to Hunter so he'll stick around."

"You and Torl saved us."

"Torl, certainly; I hamstrung one brute and nearly got gutted for my efforts." She patted her bandage. "Torl killed four men, and although he couldn't get an arrow through Yinran's wards, I expect him trying was a distraction. You and Burk carried the day, really: six veteran brutes between you."

"We are of the Ebon Blades, a proper barracks of the old school; Master Horne trained us well."

"That he did, and if we succeed, much will be owed to him, although no one will ever know." She stood with a grimace of pain. "Rest. I'll go lend Torl a hand."

Chapter Sixteen

Torl and Hunter helped me get to a pallet under a raised tarp; Burk had the adjoining pallet. Provine Sael gave me and Burk a thick syrupy drink that tasted like berries in spoiled milk, and I slept.

The pain woke me up much later, in the depths of the night; my chest had been re-bandaged, and my leg was bound in a heavy splint. Burk was still snoring, so I laid in the dark and concentrated on not groaning. I tried to work out how long it had been since we left Fellhome, but I couldn't really sort the numbers; it was somewhere between two and three months, I guessed. It seemed like forever.

Looking into the darkness, I thought about Akel. He had always been friendly, and had had educated things to say. He had worked harder than anyone else, and hadn't ever complained; I could think of a dozen favors he had done me personally. He had been quick to help us learn new things, and he had seemed to genuinely happy to see that I had survived the sinkhole.

Yet the whole time he was helping the Sagrit find us. In the end, he had looked ashamed, and tried to get Burk and me not to fight, but I wasn't sure if that was to save us or just make things easier for his real comrades.

It was like I could still feel the back-shock the axe-stroke that had split his brain pan. I didn't know many people, and I had considered Akel a friend; friends were even a smaller group than people I knew.

But I had killed him, because I had been wrong: he was the enemy. He would have let Provine Sael die, and the Ebon Blades do not surrender an escort without a fight. Our reputation wasn't built by failing jobs.

Provine Sael was different; I still did not know what to think about her as an individual, but one thing I knew was that she was a good person undertaking good deeds. Even Hunter, who was a scoundrel, had stood by her, and us. When the steel came out, he had proven himself. Thinking on him, I realized that he usually did what was right more often than not, he just complained while doing it. I am not inclined to like complainers, but I decided that Hunter was an exception. Like Burk and his Standards, you had to accept the bad with the good.

My thoughts wandered back and forth; I thought about our age block, Burk's and mine, and how one by one they had all died. I hadn't liked all of them, but I hadn't been glad that any died; it was just the way things played out. We had grown up seeing the age blows ahead of us dwindle in numbers; some blocks lost all their members before anyone made High Rate. The Ebon Blades are a proper barracks of the old school, but we took losses earning our place among the other barracks. Some barracks went broke from losing too much.

After a bit Burk groaned a little and woke up. "*Umpnh*," he muttered.

"Pain back?"

"Yeah. You?'

"Yeah."

We lay in silence for a while. "I still can't understand Akel," Burk said slowly.

"Me, either."

"I'm glad I didn't have to kill him."

"It wasn't all that special, but I would have preferred to leave it to someone else. What I would really like to have done is ask him why."

"Who knows? He betrayed us from the very start. Was anything he did or said not a lie?"

"I don't know."

"I have to say, it…*hurts*, inside. I thought he was a friend."

"Me, too. This business of being free is nothing like I thought it would be like."

"Yeah. The pit was straightforward…honest. You went in and killed whoever or whatever they sent against you. Master Horne told you what he expected, and you did it. People out here are strange. The Sagrit especially."

"Hatcher says they'll be coming for all of us."

Burk snorted. "Let them try. I'll keep count of how many I kill."

"Those brutes weren't half-bad."

"In numbers, sure, but one-on-one they wouldn't have been that great. We each went through three, and you didn't need any help."

"You didn't either; I got lucky and killed one before they could team up. A sword is faster than a morning star."

"I think of changing now and then, but a star hits so *hard*. And I like a shield."

"I'm going to save up my money and buy a steel breast-and-back." I winced as my chest gave a particularly sharp stab of pain. "Scale has its points, but I think plate is the way to go, for me."

"That'll be expensive, but it is a thought. I think about half-plate, myself."

We talked of weapons, armor and tactics in low voices until the sky grayed and the others got up.

After some broth and warm flatbread Provine Sael Healed my chest wound and worked on Burk's left arm for a long time. She retired to her bedroll afterwards and Hatcher gave each of us another draught that killed the pain and put us to sleep.

It was noon when I woke up again; Torl had fashioned a crude crutch for me, and I was able to hop around a bit, enough at least to attended to my needs. Otherwise I sat on the stump Akel had been sitting on, and thought about the world.

Since leaving Fellhome the only time I had felt sort of comfortable had been in our service with the Barley Company, and at the pit in the Concourse. The world wasn't too great of a place, I decided, given the disorderly forests and all the hostile people. If this group lost a need for me, I would go home to the Ebon Blades. The company of warriors was where I belonged; Akel had said to leave something behind other than a trail of corpses, but now Akel was just a corpse in my wake. I needed to remember that I was a tusker, and that a brute has to prove his worth every single day he lives.

"You look like a man waiting for his own funeral to start," Hatcher observed, coming up on my left.

"My leg hurts and I'm not happy about Akel."

"Yeah, that sort of thing will shake your view of life."

"What have you been doing?"

"Torl and Hunter have hauled off the dead, and I have been sorting through their belongings for information and to determine what we will keep. They had quite a bit of money, and as you know, they had good equipment. We'll see a handsome profit from that fight, at least."

"That's something."

"It is. The big issue for us right now are their mounts; we acquired ten warhorses and a mule-drawn cart. Ten *good* horses, which should draw a pretty penny even without a bill of sale. The cart will be handy to transport the coffin, but it leaves us with a lot of animals and not a lot of hands to tend them. Torl is in favor of letting at least half the horses go, but me and Hunter are against that, for profit's sake. Torl also wants to dump the saddles and put you and Burk in the cart, but again, Hunter and me oppose that. We figure it is better to wait a couple days until you two get your strength back, and pile the saddles on top of the coffin. It would be better if we could simply ride out of here, but I'm too short to ride a war horse and Torl is an indifferent horseman at best."

"I've never ridden," I admitted. "Neither has Burk."

"We figured. A medium warhorse out in the wilds is not the way to go about learning the skills involved, either. Provine Sael can heal flesh and bone, but she can't replace blood, so you two aren't going to be at your fighting best for four or five days." She absently rubbed the bandage encircling her midriff."

"Could there be another Sagrit group following Yinran's?'

"I would expect so, and no one else disagrees. The solid gold question is how far behind they are."

I thought about that. "If we have a cart, our mules, and all those horses, we'll be easy to track, even if we take another route back."

"Yep, at least until we can reach a well-travelled road. And even then, a group such as ours will be noticed and remembered. So the points under debate are what to do with the animals, and how long do we wait before we leave here. As you can see, the two are connected."

"What does Provine Sael think?"

Hatcher sighed. "She's worn out from the fight and healing, and still rattled from having to face her uncle; I told you before, she's high-strung. And there's the taking of a life to contend with; I don't think she's ever killed a living creature before, much less someone she was related to."

That was hard to imagine, but obviously most people went through life without killing.

"So it will be Torl who carries the weight of the decision-making, at least for the next few days." Hatcher took off her scarf, ran a comb through her mop of hair, and re-tied the scarf.

"When will he decide?"

"Sometime tomorrow. From the condition of the horses, Yinran had been pushing hard for days, probably weeks, to catch up with us, so a follow-on group ought to be at least a week behind him, although it is risky making assumptions like that. I'm glad I don't have to make the final call."

I was glad I didn't even have to voice an opinion.

Just before dark Provine Sael finished Burk's arm and shoulder, then Healed Hatcher's belly. She looked worn before she even started.

Her powers spent, she examined my leg and then splinted it again. "No broken bones; there is a great deal of muscle damage and considerable harm to the connective tissue in the knee, but I will undo all of that as time permits."

"Thank you, mistress."

"You fought for me, Grog. I need to thank you."

"We all fought, mistress. We will fight again, as often as it takes."

She buckled the last strap on the splint, and patted my bound leg. "I wish I had your courage, Grog."

"I'm not brave, mistress, it's just that I know how my life will end."

She stared at me for a long moment. "Someday soon you, Burk, and I will talk about this in great depth. Until then, I want you two to concentrate on staying alive."

"Yes, mistress."

The next day Provine Sael fixed my leg, although it was still a bit stiff; I had had major wounds healed before, and knew that it would be a few days before things felt normal. The worst part was that she could not replace the blood we had lost, leaving Burk and me shaky and weak.

We broke camp at noon and headed due south, the coffin on the cart buried under saddles and the whole covered with a tarp. Provine Sael reclined across the canvas-covered load, while Hatcher drove the cart. Torl scouted, Hunter rode, and Burk and I led strings of horses, which turned out to be pretty easy. Our two pack mules brought up the rear of the horse strings; all together we made a lengthy caravan.

The first half-day's walk was hard for me and Burk, but after a pain-free night's sleep and a big breakfast we were able to put in a full day's march the next day. Provine Sael had recovered a bit from her exertions and rode the smallest of the horses.

The clouds were misting down upon us as we walked, which actually made it nice and cool, and we were making good time. Hunter had stopped his horse on a high point and was studying the terrain for a bit; as the group caught up he walked his horse down and rejoined us.

"See anything?" I asked, mainly to pass the time.

"No, although I'm no woodsman. Anything that can escape Torl's attention certainly would have no trouble fooling me," he admitted.

"How far behind us do you think the next Sagrit group is?"

"I don't think they'll be too close; their resources are finite, and we wiped out one group before we encountered Yinran. A lot of the Sagrit are just talkers and dreamers, inclined to mischief; to go after a group like us will require people with skill."

"In Fellhome they sent street thugs after us."

"I don't think that was a general plan; I suspect they had a man watching me, and he thought to grab some glory when he saw Provine Sael. That's an organization's weak point: there's always some overly-ambitious git who decides to act on his own initiative."

"Why were they watching you?"

"I expect they had people keeping an eye on every unaffiliated 'slinger in Fellhome, which wouldn't take up the fingers on one hand. If you reduced it to 'slingers whom Provine Sael knew personally, then the number drops to one."

"What is a 'slinger'?"

"Slang for my sort of practitioner of the Arts."

"How do you know Provine Sael?" Hunter had never seemed inclined to speak before, so I thought to keep him talking.

He grinned, and took a swig from his flask. "We crossed paths once before. She is a woman of very strong principles, and I have almost none, so it seems we are fated to encounter each other periodically."

"Instead of just watching you, it would have been smarter for the Sagrit to just have paid you not to get involved."

He nodded thoughtfully. "It would, but the Sagrit have been lurking in the shadows plotting and manipulating for so long that thinking in plain terms is difficult for them. Plus there's a good chance I would have taken their money and still hired on with Provine Sael," he admitted.

"Remember, they didn't know that one of their agents would get the idea to attack her."

"Huh." I thought about that. "But I thought you said that there wasn't much money in this job."

"Well, if we can get these horses and arms to Hatcher's contact, that won't be true. But yes, Provine Sael couldn't pay me much, although her influence cleared up a sticky situation for me."

"The Sagrat couldn't do that?"

"No." He took another swig. "Worried about motivations, Grog?"

"Yes. I had to kill Akel."

"Ah, Akel. He was clever; in retrospect, I should have sniffed him out, but Provine Sael has a tendency to gather such unlikely followers that he slipped past me."

"Unlikely?"

He grinned. "Hatcher is well-known in her circles, and Torl is the stuff of legend, a genuine folk hero along the north frontier. Torl also habitually works alone, yet Provine Sael brought him into a group. And two first-rate pit fighters; I didn't realize you two were Ebon Blades until after the fight at the Fist. And me, well, in the ranks of nere-do-well practitioners of Arts I tend to stand out. She has a way about her, does our lovely Provine Sael: she gets people to follow her when it is certainly not in their nature to do so, or even in their best interests."

"And now you have the Sagrit after you."

He laughed. "I've had a price on my head before. Are you worried about the Sagrit?"

"No. But I don't know much."

"Live long enough, Grog, and you'll discover than most people don't know much, and that even most of those who do know a great deal seldom make use of it. That's why one person in a hundred rules the others."

"You sound like Akel."

"He was an educated man, right up to the point where he got his skull split open." Hunter checked the horizon behind us. "You meet men like him on occasion, men driven by personal loss into wandering the world, either looking for answers or fleeing a truth. I suspect that under the lies, he was one of those."

"Why did he betray us?"

"He didn't: he joined us with a purpose, and he carried out that purpose; you can only betray a trust if it is honestly placed. What I wonder, is after being with us so long, he decided to go through with it. He was smart enough to see the measure of this group, and should not have been surprised at how things played out. Especially when Yinran decided he was going to get cute about the business; if I were in charge, I would have had an ambush in place and started the fight without any conversation. And I would have made damn sure where I knew where Chabney Torl was before I did anything at all."

I wanted to ask what he knew about Provine Sael's uncle, but I decided it was best not to pry.

"What are you talking about?" Provine Sael brought her horse alongside Hunter's.

"Grog was wondering why a blackguard such as myself is in the service of a righteous churchwoman," Hunter grinned.

"I ask myself that every single day," she sighed. "As a penance for my sins, I suspect."

"It is because she has the power to cause men to fall in love with her, Grog," Hunter winked.

Provine Sael flushed and half raised a hand to the knub of a horn before catching herself. "I am surrounded by fools." She urged her horse into a trot.

Hunter snickered. "She is many things, and young is one of them. In another decade she'll be a force to be reckoned with, if the Sagrit don't kill her first."

"Hatcher said she gave up a lot to undertake this task."

Hunter nodded, the humor fading. "She did." He took a pull from his flask. "That is a powerful thing," he said, half to himself. "A person who has tremendous potential for success and who throws it all away isn't as uncommon as you might think, but someone who does it for the greater good is very rare." He stowed his flask and turned his horse to canter up to another vantage point.

After heading south for a couple days, we swung east and crossed the frontier into the Empire, avoiding villages and the main roads, continuing east for three more days.

Running low on salt and flour, we turned down a trade road in the hopes of encountering a trader, finally making camp six miles from a modest town.

"Tomorrow Torl and Hunter will go into town with a pack mule and buy supplies," Provine Sael announced as we sat down to our dinner. "They are the least remarkable among us."

"All these animals are creating problems," Torl noted. "We can't go much further into the Empire without taking roads; cutting cross-country will draw unwanted attention."

"Then we will travel boldly on the main roads," Provine Sael forked up greens from her plate. "Hide in plain sight. The Sagrit will expect us to skulk and hide."

"That might help, Torl shrugged. "For a bit. It's a shame we don't know who to trust among Imperial officials."

"With every hour and every mile the danger of a Sagrit interception recedes," Hunter noted. "The real danger will be at the capitol: they know we're heading for the Emperor, so they'll have a force in place for a last-ditch try."

"That will not be a problem," Provine Sael took a sip of wine. "I have a secure means of communication within the Imperial Court. When we are close. I will send word ahead, and a detachment of the Red Guard will escort us the rest of the way."

"That's good."

"But first, we must get close."

We were just breaking camp when Torl trotted into the little glade. "Horses and armored men coming."

Provine Sael turned even paler. "How did they find us?"

"Well," Hunter looked at the mule-less cart. "Only one option, really."

Hunter climbed atop the wagon, Torl faded into the brush, while Burk, Hatcher, and me arranged ourselves in front of the cart. Provine Sael paced restlessly to one side, clearly agitated.

We heard the horses and the rattle of armor before the riders hove into view: a dozen Imperial cavalrymen and a tired-looking man in civilian clothing.

"Well, that was anti-climatic," Hatcher chuckled.

"Maybe not," Hunter noted as the officer at the head of the group saw us, and led his men off the road and into our camp, where they dismounted.

"Who owns these animals?" The officer, a Captain with blonde whiskers, demanded.

"I do," Hatcher stepped forward. "Shelly Winterbloom, horse trader and freight-mover. These others are fellow travelers going the same direction and banding together for safety."

"Captain Devons." He waved a hand, and a corporal started examining the horses. "Do you have bills of sale for them?"

"Not with me," Hatcher jerked a thumb at the corporal. "What is your business with my animals?"

Captain Devons produced a document. "By order of the Throne, etcetera, I am authorized to seize such suitable remounts as I encounter, paying a fixed value thereof."

"Remounts?" Hatcher rubbed her chin. "Since when does the Imperial Army need to *buy* remounts? You have your own horse farms."

"Where have you been?" Captain Devon looked surprised.

"To the west, across the border. I have connections with hill-folk."

"Bandits, more than likely," Captain Devon noted sourly.

"I don't inquire."

The Corporal came over and took the Captain aside for a moment.

"All right, I'm taking all ten," Captain Devon announced, gesturing at the civilian, who unstrapped a heavy box from behind his saddle. "I'll pay seventy-five Marks apiece."

"Ninety would be their fair market value," Hatcher protested.

"Seventy-five is what you get."

"Fine," Hatcher sounded disgusted, but she winked at me when the captain wasn't looking. "You want saddles?"

"No, but I will give sixty Marks for any of your mules, complete with pack saddle. And I'll be taking two."

"That's highway robbery! We're travelling in a group to *avoid* bandits!"

"I'm leaving you one to pull your cart."

"Gosh, thanks. How do you sleep at night?"

"They're remounts, not your children."

"Yeah, speaking of which, you didn't answer my question: why are you buying animals?"

Captain Devon was watching the civilian counting coins. "That's right, you hadn't heard. We're at war."

"So what else is new? The Legions haven't been on a peacetime footing in my lifetime."

"No, we're *really* at war: the Dusmen are massing to invade south. They're going to hit the north frontier like an avalanche of steel and iron."

"Seriously?"

"It's why we're buying remounts and dray animals. I'm one of about fifty officers across the central provinces buying animals, and others are buying fodder, grain, meat…everything. We're fully mobilizing."

"When did this happen?"

"The Emperor signed the declaration ten days ago; I'm coming back from delivering my second string of new purchases."

"Damn."

"Count yourself lucky: sooner or later we're going to start issuing promissory notes instead of hard coin. If you have more stock, sell it quick."

"I will. I'm gone two weeks and the whole country goes to hell. Anything else worth telling?"

252

"Hmmm? Oh, the Emperor is heading north to take command of the Army, and before he set out he made a law that will eliminate slavery in eight years. Someone's Emancipation."

"Rebigar's Emancipation?"

"Yeah, that's it. He said that we would need every hand to stop the Dusmen, and he's not wrong at all. The Legions have seized thousands of slaves as recruits and support personnel in order to get up to full strength; they'll be free after they serve an enlistment. If they survive. The owners got tax exemptions, and they weren't happy, but most understand that if we don't stop the Dusmen, it's all over. The tax collectors are going to have a rough few years until everything gets sorted out, though. Now, about those mules…"

Hatcher sold him the mule we had taken from the Sagrit, one of ours, and both pack saddles. When the money had been counted, the ledger signed, and the cavalry, with nearly all our animals, were jingling down the road heading south, Hatcher whistled and shook her head.

"Well, that just took care of a big problem for us: the Legion isn't going to question the legal origins of any animals they've already purchased, and the Sagrit won't be able to locate us by asking about a mixed bunch with a lot of horses. The price was pretty sweet for branded horses without papers, too."

"The Dusmen are invading," Hunter jumped down from the cart. "Don't let that bit of news escape you."

"We always knew they would," Hatcher shrugged. "I guess they finally decided to go for it."

"In mid-summer? They've lost half the campaign season."

Hatcher removed her scarf, re-folded it, and tied it in place. "I'm no general. Maybe they thought it would catch the Empire by surprise."

"Point," Hunter nodded. "I'm surprised, in any case."

"The Emperor enacted Rebigar's Emancipation," Provine Sael said, wonder in her voice. "Slavery is finished."

"Eventually," Hatcher nodded. "I'm sorry it worked out this way, I know you gave up a lot for this quest."

"What?" Provine Sael snapped out of her reverie. "No, don't be sorry. There was still a chance the Sagrit could have intercepted us before we reached the Emperor, or manufactured some reason to block the Emancipation. No, this is better: by the time the war is over the idea of the end of slavery will be the norm."

"If we win," Hunter observed as Torl came in from the brushes. "And there's a good chance slavery may have run its course before the war ends, even with Rebigar's plan being three years longer than expected."

"Well, I'm glad all this we've been through wasn't pointless," Hatcher shrugged. "Now, we still have the remains and the artifacts, and no altruistic goal to be achieved…"

"Stop." Provine Sael shook her head. "The Emperor will still need what the coffin contains. With the Emancipation already in effect, we can expect a small reward for our actions, no more."

"Define '*small*'."

Provine Sael sighed and rolled her eyes.

"You're really all right with how this played out?" Hatcher asked Provine Sael later that day. Hatcher was back to riding my shoulders, and Provine Sael was driving the cart.

"Completely. My hope was to see the end of slavery through peaceful means, and that has been accomplished. On a purely personal level, I solved a mystery that no one else could, and in the grand scheme of things, the first Emperor's trappings will help the current Emperor in this time of crisis. And on a selfish level, the Sagrit's desire for vengeance against me will be muted."

"But you gave up a great deal."

Provine Sael made a dismissive gesture. "What I gave up only had what value I placed upon it, and when I gave it up I had no idea if I would succeed in any particular. When we secured the coffin it was all made worthwhile. Hearing that emancipation is made real is a great weight off my shoulders; I have always feared court machinations more than any other risk. Emperors face many challenges and hurdles, and I feared that my success could be thwarted by courtiers. After all, legally, the contents of the coffin belong to the Emperor."

"All right."

"And what of you?" Provine Sael asked. "You had other paths before you; you could have risen far in your peoples' endeavors, but you chose the life of a wandering bravo; Hunter and Torl both could have taken more conventional paths as well."

Hatcher drummed her booted heels against my chest. "I did it for personal reasons."

"All reasons are personal. Do not think my choices to be more noble than yours; you were with me through all the risks."

"For money."

"Much less money than you could have earned otherwise."

"I guess. So, what are your plans now?"

"I would like to keep this group together, if possible. There must be some good we could do together; there's a war on, after all."

I felt Hatcher shrug. "Why not? The Sagrit will still want our heads, so we might as well stick together."

"And you, Grog?" Provine Sael asked. "Will you still guard me?"

"When you engage the Ebon Blades, you get quality work, that is the rule. I will guard you until you no longer need me."

"Now, as to the reward we will ask for...," Hatcher began, and Provine Sael sighed.

Later Hatcher took a nap atop the canvas-covered load on the cart, and Burk and I trailed behind. "I told Provine Sael I would guard her as long as she had need of guarding," I noted. "What are you thinking of doing?"

"The same. When you engage the Ebon Blades, you get quality work, that is the rule."

"You're free now."

"Free to choose to work for Provine Sael," he shrugged. "Freedom is different than I thought it would be. I thought it would be special, somehow. Turns out it's just following orders and obeying rules, same as the barracks. The only difference is you get to pick who gives the orders."

"I suppose we might get paid regularly now."

He shrugged. "Maybe. I don't really understand money, not the way people out here seem to look at it. If I had a cart full of money, I would still be a brute, and people would still call me a tusker."

"And they would try to steal the money," I nodded. "But when I was on my own, I had to think about money all the time, because I had to feed myself."

"That's a lot of worrying," Burk shrugged again. "Better to let someone else worry about food and where to sleep. Provine Sael has done all right by us: good equipment, plenty of food. The sleeping conditions could be better, but that's the way it goes. She's a first-rate healer, too, which you really can't do without in our trade."

"We do have a trade, don't we? More than one, in fact: the pit, escorting…we could even hire on as mercenaries if we needed to."

"This war will be good for fighting brutes like us," Burk nodded. "We should do all right."

"True." We walked in companionable silence for a while. "The world is a lot different than I expected it to be."

"It is," he nodded. "Not as well-organized as it should be, and a lot of improper behavior. Master Horne is a lot wiser than I had thought before we left Fellhome."

"He trained us well. After we get our reward we need to get a letter to him letting him know what we accomplished; that will do the reputation of the Ebon Blades no end of good."

"We could write it ourselves, probably. And maybe find a better book to read, something interesting. In the Concourse Hunter told me there are books written on weapon use and exotic fighting styles."

"I thought 'exotic' meant girls who dance without much clothes, if any."

"I believe it means fighting without armor, too."

"That makes sense."

"One thing money is useful for, is renting girls," Burk pointed out.

"That is a worthy use," I nodded. "And after all this, we deserve some time to rest and train."

Burk expounded upon his thoughts regarding the uses of down time, and I trudged along, grunting agreement where it seemed appropriate. I still didn't know what was special about my sword, or how much money I could hope to be paid, assuming we were to be paid regularly, or what my share would be from the animals, armor, and weapons taken from the Sagrit. They probably had had money, too, and I was sure if they did, Hatcher would not have missed it. Or what sort of reward Provine Sael would ask for us, and what my share, if any, would be.

But none of that really mattered; I would find out in due course, while new questions would rise up to take their place. What mattered was that I was a High Rate of the Ebon Blades, a proper barracks of the old school, and I was upholding its good name. I would serve Provine Sael, and continue to learn what I could manage to learn, and that was more than enough for me.

I am Grog, and Grog is all I wish to be.

****

If you enjoyed this book, please take the time to leave a favorable review. Reviews are hard to come by for indie writers.

About the Author

Born and raised in the icy wastelands of North Dakota, RW Krpoun joined the US Army, serving two enlistments before being honorably discharged at Fort Hood, Texas. Delighted to discover a land where snow was a novelty, he settled in Texas and took up a career in law enforcement, serving over thirty years before retiring. His service included a Sheriff's Office and two Municipal police agencies, as well as two enlistments in the Texas National Guard as a Criminal Investigator.

RW lives on lakeside acreage with his lovely and amazingly tolerant wife Ann, and a band of ill-mannered animals who are all highly photogenic. His hobbies include reading, history, various forms of shooting, collecting battle-ready examples of medieval weaponry, and learning to use such weapons.

Grog is his twenty-first published work; he has (as of early of 2020) twenty-one published novels.

Made in the USA
Middletown, DE
29 March 2022